# Saxon Dawn

## Book 1

## in the Wolf-Brethren series

## By

## Griff Hosker

D1510999

Published by Griff Hosker 2013
Copyright © Griff Hosker

SWORD BOOKS
HOME OF EPIC HISTORICAL FICTION

A CIP catalogue record for this title is available from the British Library.

# **Dedication**

This is dedicated to you, my readers. I am gratified that you continue to buy my books and, I hope, enjoy them. I will continue to write them, if only because I enjoy creating the stories and the characters and, I hope, bringing history to life. A special thanks to Rich and Alison who are always the first to get my books. I appreciate your support and your comments. I am also grateful to my wife, Eileen, for her much-needed proofreading.

# Chapter 1

### Hen Ogledd 570

I was seven years old before I ever heard of either the Angles or the Saxons but their coming changed my life forever. My name is Lann, and my people were the last of the Britons, the last of the people who lived alongside the Romans before the Angles, the Saxons and the Norse came and stole our land. Our life, before they came was simple and hard but bearable. We lived in the land which the Romans had called Britannia but they had left in the time before my grandfather. We had been told tales of their buildings and their warriors, but they were just a story, to be told at night when the wolves howled and we listened for the sound of raiders coming for slaves. They were told in the hope that one day they would come back and bring prosperity and security to this land once more. The wall, which the Romans had built, lay many days' travel to the north. We lived in a land called Hen Ogledd. We were the last of the Britons or so my parents had been told by the King and his warriors when they had once travelled through our land. I had seen neither him nor his warriors, but my mother and father assured me that he lived still and fought against the slavers and the invaders.

My family lived in an old hill fort which came from before the time, even of the Romans. It was called Stanwyck and it had many ditches to protect it and high ramparts. A stream ran through it and we were comfortable there. There were many families who lived within its defences but we were not a community; we had little to do with the others. Each family kept to themselves. In times of strife, the men and boys defended the walls but there was no leader and no clan. We kept a few animals and our diet was augmented by hunting and gathering. There were four in my family; my father was called Hogan. He was a quiet man but immensely strong. He had sired me when he was little more than a boy himself for he had been orphaned in a slave raid and had chanced upon my mother, Radha, who had also been left alone when the northerners raided. They were a well-matched couple. My mother was called Radha for her red hair and my father swore that she had some of the Hibernian in her; she had a fiery temper. She was also something of a shaman and healer. It was said that she could read dreams. Others said that she was a witch, although they always said that when well out of hearing distance of both of my parents. She had given birth to me when she was but fourteen. We lived in a harsh world in those days. By dint of my father's hard work he had served others and earned money enough to buy a few animals. He was also a powerful man with animals and could train them well.

So it was that as I grew I began to learn from the gentle man that was my father. He gave me a pup he trained so that I could look after the small flock of sheep we had gathered over the years. Many of the animals had been the ones who escaped the wild northerners and were without owners, others had been gained through trade and barter. When my brother Raibeart came along, three years after me, I was given the task of training him. We kept the sheep on the higher pastures in the summer which is where we spent most of our time. I learned, when guarding the flock, how to use a slingshot and hit the occasional rabbit. My father promised me that, when I was a little older and stronger, he would make me a bow and teach me how to use it. He was so powerful that he could pull back a yew bow which was almost as tall as he was. It meant we ate well for he was a good hunter. When we had a surplus, we traded it with the others who shared our hill fort or with the traders who still trudged up and down the old Roman Road which ran nearby. They were our only contact with the rest of the world and it was from them that we learned of the coming of the Angles and the Saxons. We were told that they came from across the sea and they were fierce warriors. The traders left us in no doubt that they would come to our quiet backwater of Britannia. It was only a case of when. I saw the looks my parents exchanged and it worried me. I saw the concern on their normally calm faces. If they were worried then the Angles were to be feared.

Raibeart and I had been out with the sheep and Wolf, my sheepdog. We drove them from the hills back to the willow pens my father and I had built. We had just put the last hurdle in place when Wolf put his ears down and began to bark; that meant only one thing, strangers. I took out my sling and looked towards the ramparts in the north. Others had emerged from their huts with sticks and farming tools. We were not violent people but I knew that we would defend ourselves if attacked.

I saw the adults relax as they saw the frail woman and the thin, emaciated child come through the entrance to the south. The rest of the people went back into their huts but my mother and father remained outside. They were both intelligent and thoughtful people. When visitors passed through, it was they who spent the longest time asking questions and they were both hospitable. Perhaps it was the fact that they had been left alone that made them so compassionate, I do not know. The woman and the thin, emaciated child made their way towards us.

"Welcome, I am Hogan and this is my wife, Radha. You look as though you have travelled far."

In answer, she collapsed to the ground and the child fell upon her crying and hugging her still form. "Take her inside. Lann, fetch some fresh water from the stream."

By the time I returned to the hut, with the pot filled with cool water, my parents had laid the woman on the furs by the fire. My father smiled as he took the water from me. "Look after the boy, eh, Lann? He looks terrified."

We always had a pot of thin soup on the fire; somehow it never seemed to run out and my mother put some in a beaker and held it to the woman's lips. I turned to the boy. "What is your name?" He stared at me in terror.

My father handed me a deer bone from a pot. There was a little meat still on it. "Give it to him. He, too, looks hungry and then pour him some water."

I handed the bone to him and he began to attack it as though he had not eaten in days. When I passed over the beaker he still retained hold of the bone. He reminded me of the dogs when they were given food and they protected it with their paws and growled at any who looked enviously at it.

"Come we will eat now. The woman is sleeping and the boy looks happier."

Our fare was the same as the woman and the boys. We also had soup which we ate from crude pot bowls my mother had made from local clay. She could have bought some from the pot maker who lived not far away but it was cheaper to barter some meat for the use of her oven. Thanks to my father's skill our diet was more varied than most.

We had finished when the woman stirred and the child raced to her side. "Thank you for your kindness. We have not eaten for some days."

"You are welcome. Have you travelled far?"

With the boy nestled in her arm, she told us her story. "I am Monca and this is my son, Aelle. I lived south of the old Roman fort with my husband and three sons. One day the Angles came and they killed my husband and my sons." Her voice was flat and without emotion as though she had cried all the feelings out of her. "They killed every man and boy. I was then taken." She looked at my brother and I and I saw the look exchanged between my parents. I did not know what it meant but they did for they drew closer together. She pulled her own child in tightly to her thin body. "This is the child I had with Scead." She gave a shudder. "He was a cruel man and he liked to beat me. The river fever took him in the spring and I left with my son before the other Angles discovered it for I would have been taken by another." She shuddered. "Were it not for Aelle, I would have killed myself. We heard that some of the older people lived near to the wall and we have walked all this way seeking people of my own kind and not the invader. You are the first that have shown kindness." She hesitated, "Are you Christian?"

"No, we worship the older gods and you?"

"No, I also worship the gods of this land but Christians are said to show kindness to strangers." She struggled to rise. "Thank you for your help."

"Where will you go?"

The blank look on her face told them that she had no idea; she was just doing what she had done since fleeing the Angles. She was getting as far away as she could from the pain and the torture of regular beatings. Mother looked at father who nodded. "No, you shall stay with us. You will be safe here."

Her eyes showed her gratitude as she burst into tears. My father was embarrassed by it all and he bustled about. "Lann, get the spare skins and lay them over there."

And so our family was extended; we had two more mouths to feed. In the long run, it saved my life and my brother's as well as Aelle's and we did get along. Monca was a hardworking woman and not without skills. She could make fine pots and my father made her a small oven which gave us more goods to trade, apart from the woollen garments my mother made and the dried meat hunted by my father.

We learned to understand the language the boy spoke and he learned ours. Monca was grateful to be speaking her own language again but she knew that the Angles would come again and she wanted us prepared. If we could speak their language then it just might help. Aelle was younger than me and older than Raibeart and he soon fitted in with us. With three of us looking after the flock he was an asset and the following winter my father made me the promised bow. "You will be able to leave your brothers watching the flock and you too can hunt as I do." Aelle had become my brother as much as Monca had become my father's second wife. Both women were with child at the same time and neither seemed to resent the other. I think it was my father's nature that made it work. My mother and Monca seemed to get on really well and it was good to hear them laughing and giggling as they worked together.

In the long winter nights, as I worked on my bow and was shown how to make and fletch arrows, Monca told us more stories of the

Angles. It appeared they had left their land when the gods of the sea reclaimed it and that there were many other tribes who lived in similar lands in the same position; all of them were looking for a new home. It was a depressing thought that these people were the first but not the last of the people who would invade us. She told us that many had mail shirts and helmets. They used shields and axes. Her description terrified me as I pictured giants who would kill us and then eat us. We wondered if the gods of the land had deserted us but my father told us that one day the Romans would return, as had been foretold by his grandfather, and they would right the wrongs of the Angles. Certainly, we knew that the Romans had been powerful and their work could still be clearly seen across the land. If it was built of stone then it was Roman.

My father took me to one side, as spring began to peer from beneath the snow. "You and I must learn to become warriors, Lann, or these Angles will kill us and take your mother as they did with Monca." He held the bow and the arrows in his huge hand. "These can kill men as well as animals. I do not want to fight these people but I will defend what we have."

"Don't we have a king?"

He shook his head. "There was one but we have not heard of him for some time. There are many chiefs who have warriors around them but none bother themselves with us. After the Romans left they took over the forts the Romans built and rule the land around them." He pointed beyond the wattle and daub walls of our hut. "We live here because we can defend it but not against the warriors Monca describes."

I thought of the Roman stone and I remembered somewhere close to the river. "When we went across the Roman bridge near to the Dunum, did we not see a Roman building?"

He smiled and ruffled my already unruly hair, "You remember well for we only visited there once. Aye, there is a fort there but much of the stone was taken by men to build their own homes north of the river."

"Did the Romans not leave weapons behind?" My father's grandfather had served with the last Romans and I had heard tales of their weapons and armour. It sounded to me as though that might defeat the Angles when they came.

He gave me a strange look. I think he was telling me an untruth when he spoke. "I think not. My grandfather had a sword but he used it to chop wood." He scratched his beard. "He may have had a helmet somewhere and some mail but they were lost to the family when the slavers killed my father."

The rest of the winter I spent making my arrows as straight as I could with feathers taken from our noisy geese. If I did not have a helmet, sword nor armour, I would, at least, have the best bow I could and I would stop the Angles from killing my father and stealing my mother. When I took the two boys out on the fells that summer I became a harsh taskmaster; I taught them how to use their slings well. I practised with my bow until I thought my arms would fall off. We killed many rabbits and squirrels. Our parents were pleased for it filled the pot but I had an ulterior motive, we would become the defenders of our family when the Angles came.

That summer we found more refugees fleeing west. These were families who knew that the invaders were close and wished to avoid the consequences. They did not stop but headed towards the Roman fortress in the west, where, it was rumoured, there was a king who offered protection. It had a magical name, Civitas Carvetiorum, and was reputed to be the most magnificent palace in the whole of Britannia. The King was supposed to ride around on a white horse righting wrongs. My father was not convinced, "What would we do there? Would we have land as we do here? Better what we know than the unknown. I think they dream still of Artorius, the last Roman."

My two sisters were born in the autumn. Their mothers and my father cooed and awed at them but to me and my brothers, they were just noisy and irritating. The early morning screaming just drove me and my brothers out earlier. As we headed for the pastures I deviated from our normal route. Raibeart saw this but Aelle was still finding his way around the land. "This is not the route to the pastures?"

"No, brother. It is the route to the river and there the grass is juicier at this time of year. We will fatten them up and it is a shorter journey for us to take."

He grudgingly agreed for it meant more time for our practice. Wolf could easily control the flock and the three of us knew that we had a very easy time of it. When we reached the river I left the two boys with strict orders to stay put. Aelle always acceded to my demands but Raibeart was flexing his muscles a little and questioning his older brother. He gave me a defiant look and was about to open his mouth when I slapped him across the side of the head. "That is before you even think of arguing!" Tears welled up in his eyes but he bit his lip and stormed off with Aelle in tow. "Mind what I said! Do not leave this place." Confident that they would obey me I crossed the Roman Bridge. I could see from the weeds and grass growing on its surface that it had seen little traffic. I could see, on the other side, stood the stones and remains of the old Roman fort. I was disappointed for it looked as though they had demolished most of it before it was abandoned but I was determined to search anyway. I could see that they had destroyed anything in the fort which had been useful but I also saw places where the soil was in mounds, as though something had been buried. I found a charred piece of wood which had a pointed end and I began to dig away at the nearest pile. Once I got through the grass and weeds it became quite easy and I felt a thrill as my wood struck something solid. I was encouraged to dig harder. The wood was no longer helping me and so I took to using my hands to clear away the dirt. I found a wooden box. The top had started to rot but it was still quite solid. I made a hole down the side of the box and reached down. I found a leather handle and I pulled. I strained as hard as I could and I was about to give up when, suddenly, it sprang up and out at one end. I dragged it clear. There was no lock and I pulled at the top to open it. I have to admit that I was excited. What treasure would I find within? When the lid finally popped open I was disappointed. After I removed the sacks covering the contents I saw that it was filled with nails and shoes the Romans had used. My father had said they were called caligae and the Roman soldiers had used them.

I was about to turn away in disgust when I suddenly thought that the nails and shoes might be useful. We wore shoes made of leather and fur but they were not very serviceable and needed repairing frequently. I took a selection of shoes and nails, enough for the family and put them in the sack. I saw that there were still six mounds. I would return. This was just the start. I hid in the woods and watched my brothers who were still using their slings. I found a hollow beneath an oak tree and covered the sack with a pile of loose leaves. It sounds silly now, after all the intervening events, but I did not want to take back some shoes and nails and claim it was treasure. I wanted to come back triumphantly, with weapons and arms.

When we returned to the settlement the men were gathered around my father's fire. I was going to join them but a quick shake of my father's head told me that I was not welcome. Ruefully I realised that I was not yet a man. When I had a beard then I would be able to join them. The two mothers were busy with the babies and so I took my bow and went to practise. I had three arrows I used for practice. They were my first attempts at fletching and they were not the best. I reasoned that, if I could loose these effectively then the better arrows would be even more accurate when I used them. I used the stump of a lightning struck tree as my target. It was about man size and I had worked myself progressively further away to improve my accuracy. I was so accurate now that I could imagine that this tree was a man and

I chose where to hit him. He was an Angle; the enemy. Nine times out of ten I hit where I aimed; even at sixty paces; smack between the eyes. Further away than that and it was luck which took over. I knew, from my father, that I needed a longer bow and greater strength to make my arrows go further. But I knew that day would come. I had been marking, with a piece of charcoal, my height on the doorway to the hut and I had grown by two hand spans in the last year. I was almost as tall as my father but his broad shoulders and muscled arms made me look like a girl, however, I was becoming bigger and stronger each day.

While we ate my mother asked my father what had been discussed. "It seems we have a king, or at least we did have, for Cynfarch Oer, has died, or been killed by the Angles and his son Urien Rheged is now king."

My mother cooed at my sister and asked, "Well, what has that to do with us?"

"It seems he wants us to be prepared to fight the Angles. He is visiting his lands to find out how many warriors he has."

Mother snorted, "His lands! I do not see him guarding the flocks or repairing the hut or tending the fields. His land indeed!"

Monca had learned my mother's ways and she and my father smiled at her outburst. "It seems to me that it matters not who claims the land so long as we are left in peace and, if this Urien wishes to defend this land then I can at least help him." Mother did not look convinced. "What is the alternative? Do as the people of Monca's settlement did and wait for them to come and kill us?" My mother had no answer to this so she ignored the question and carried on feeding my sister who seemed to make more noise than our pig when he ate. "We are going to try to make some weapons. Spears probably."

My ears pricked up. This was more my kind of talk. "Who will make them?"

The three adults all flashed me a look. We normally sat in silence at meal times and listened. I almost regretted my outburst until I saw my father smile and reach over to ruffle my hair. "Arden has some skill with iron. We are going to build a fire to melt the iron." He pointed to the hills to the west. "There is iron in those hills. We have the winter to make them." He shrugged at the snort from my mother. "We have time enough in the winter and working the forge will keep us warm, eh, lads?"

I was delighted to be included. Last winter I had made a bow and arrows; this winter looked to be even more interesting with the prospect of making real weapons. Of course, I would still try to reach the other weapons, which I knew must be in the fort and I would return a conquering hero.

I had my next chance when we took our flock for the last time before winter set in and the conditions became too harsh. I left the two boys with the flock and Wolf; they were more than capable of protecting them. Raibeart was suspicious but I told him I would be hunting and my glare threatened another blow about the ears. He was quickly cowed and I left for the fort. Vindonnus was with me that day for he brought me a young doe as soon as I started hunting; I knew he had brought her for she had an injured leg and would not survive the winter. She was an easy kill and I took my stone knife out to remove her entrails and to take a bite out of her still warm heart. I felt her strength go into my body and I left the rest of the heart for Vindonnus. I hung the beast in a tree; I would reclaim her on the way back. I took the liver with me to placate Icaunus, the river god. Perhaps when I had crossed the bridge the last time without making an offering I had displeased the god and had been punished with such a paltry haul. I would remedy the situation this time. I dropped the liver into the water and said a short prayer of thanks to the god for allowing me across the bridge.

I did not know if the offering worked but I felt much happier as I crossed the bridge to find the fort still deserted. Perhaps I had done the right thing; I looked at the mounds and one called to me. It was the smallest of the mounds but I dug anyway. This time I knew what to expect and I retrieved the chest much more quickly. This time, however, the box broke as it cleared the soil and the contents spilled out. I could not believe my fortune and I held my breath as I saw the glint of metal in the soil. I reverently cleared away the dirt. The metal I had found was a sword. It was as long as my arm and had come free from the oiled cloth in which it had lain. There were a couple of spots of rust but otherwise, it looked as though it had just been placed there. I put it to one side and took out the other wrapped parcels. There were four swords and eight daggers. It was a mighty haul. I wrapped them up again in their cloth. I was about to carry them across the river when I saw another bundle in the soil. It had obviously fallen from the bottom of the chest. It felt heavier than any of the swords and I wondered what it could be. As I unwrapped it, I said a silent prayer to Icaunus for it was a shirt of mail. There were a couple of links missing and it had more rust than the swords but it was a mail shirt. I quickly wrapped it and fled back across the bridge, peering fearfully over my shoulder in case I had been seen. I buried it with the caligae and then went back for the swords and daggers. They were too heavy to take back to our home and I chose a sword and three daggers. They would make a suitable present and then I would reveal the others to my father. I would be a hero!

The doe and the weapons were heavier than I had thought but I made it to the flock before dark. Aelle and Raibeart were impressed by the doe but when I showed them the weapons they almost soiled themselves with joy.

"Where did you get them?"

"Can I have one?"

"Never mind where I found them and father will decide who has them. Now you two, carry the doe and we will return home. Say nothing about the weapons. That is my honour!" The boys were quite happy to do as I instructed and Wolf happily chivvied the sheep along.

When we reached the hut my father was outside the hut with the forge they were building. I could see that they had almost finished building it and, when the clay was dry it would be ready for its first firing. My father had said that the iron we could produce here would not be of a high standard but at least we could make crude weapons with which to defend ourselves. He left the forge and strode over to meet us. "What is that you have in your hands, Lann?"

I was so proud as I opened the cloth and displayed the weapons. I was disappointed with my father's reaction. His face darkened. "What is wrong, father?"

"Where did you get these?"

I could see that he was angry for he was normally peaceful and it was my mother who chastised us. The look on his face did not bode well. I did something I had never done before. I lied. "I found them in the woods when I was hunting the deer." I pointed to the dead animal being carried by my brothers.

He seemed relieved. "Good, I thought that you had stolen them, or even worse, taken them from the Roman fort."

My heart sank down to my feet. Now I could not tell the truth, my father would think badly of me and I could not bear that. "What is wrong with the Roman fort?"

"There are weapons buried there but they are cursed by the Romans who buried them. My grandfather told me that. They were to lie there until the Romans needed them again."

"But the Romans are gone. They may not return. You told me so. And we need the weapons."

He shook his head. "It does not matter the curse is there forever." Then he smiled. "But it matters not for these were from the woods and the curse will be on the one who took them." As he examined the sword I furtively clutched at the stone charm I wore around my neck. It had been my grandmother's and I had been told it protected me from evil. Now I needed that protection.

My father swung the sword. "This is a fine sword. It has good balance. It is too big for you just yet so I will use it if you are in agreement with that?"

I forced a smile and mumbled, "Of course."

The boys had deposited the doe outside the hut and now stood expectantly looking at the daggers. "And now I wonder who shall have these?" They were all the same design, I later found out that they were pugeo, a Roman military dagger, but one had no sign of rust at all and my father handed that to me. "As the finder, the best goes to you, my son. And you two can have these but you must make them as shiny as Lann's." After he had handed them to the boys he put his huge arms around them. "And tomorrow we shall sharpen them but tonight we have the meal provided by Lann to prepare."

The normal pride I would have had at the praise was dissipated by the knowledge that I was cursed. The weapons I had cached would have to stay hidden. I dared not bring them forth. My dreams of glory were reduced to ashes. I had a dagger with which to fight the Angles. What kind of hero would I be?

# Chapter 2

### Hen Ogledd 577

I had wondered for the last couple of years if I was cursed. Nothing bad had happened to me in the intervening years. I did not sprout another leg nor did my face break out in some plague. I was not whisked away by a wight and the Angles did not come. But I still worried; I knew that *Wyrd* had a long memory. For the last year, I had regularly visited my cache of weapons. I had tried on the mail and found that it almost fitted me. Thanks to the forge I now understood metals a little better and I had fashioned a couple of crude rings to replace the damaged ones. I was desperate to sharpen the swords and daggers I had hidden but knew that I daren't. My secret seemed to grow larger each time I visited my secret dell. The boys loved their daggers and it seemed to make me more of a hero in their eyes. Father too practised with his sword each day although he had no one with whom to practise. I still exercised with my bow each morning and evening and I now had a longer, man-sized bow. I had learned to make my own arrows and I had secretly melted down some of the nails I had found to make better arrows than the ones I had. No-one seemed to notice and I hoped that my arrows were not cursed too.

It was just before the time we took the flocks out to the pasture again when the King came. Of course, we knew not who the king was then but we were soon informed of the fact. One of the other boys was watching from the ramparts and he raced down shouting to us. "Horsemen! Horsemen appear!"

Although we did not think it was Angles, for they fought on foot, it did not pay to be careless and the men armed themselves with their crude weapons. My father had his sword and a spear while other men had spears and axes. I stood next to my father with my bow strung. The ten horsemen rode through the gate from the west. They all wore mail and I noticed that it looked identical to my mail shirt. Their helmets looked like metal caps with two cheek pieces and a guard at the rear. They each held a spear and carried a shield. The second man carried a standard which flowed in the wind and made a strange howling noise which caused my sisters to hide behind their mothers, I later found out it was a standard from the times of the Romans and warriors who had fought on the wall called Sarmatians.

The leader reined in his mount and dismounted, he handed his helmet which had a long red crest upon the top to one of his warriors and approached the men with a smile on his face and his hand held out palm uppermost. It was a sign of peace. "I am Urien Rheged and some people call me King of this land." This was the first time I met him and I fell under his spell immediately. He looked to be older than my father had been but something about him made him appear younger; it is hard to explain but the King seemed magical even on that first visit. He had a fine red beard and moustache but it was his eyes which you noticed; they were a green which seemed to sparkle and shine. You felt as though he was looking only at you and you were the most important person in the room. "I am visiting those parts of the kingdom which are, as yet, free from attack."

My father stepped forwards. No one else had had the temerity to grasp the proffered hand but my father did. "I am Hogan of Stanwyck and this is my family."

He waved to include us and we bobbed, bowed or just gave an awkward smile according to whatever thoughts ran through our minds. How do you address a king?

"Are these your entire people, headman?"

The King obviously thought my father was a chief but he shook his head vehemently in denial. "No, we merely share this old hill fort for protection. We are our own men."

"Good. It is what I have heard. And what will you do when the Angles come?"

"We will fight."

He looked at the weapons as did his men. I noticed looks of derision and pity from some of his men but not the King who merely nodded. "They are a start but you will need more." He gestured behind him. "Bladud, bring me your shield."

Bladud rested his standard next to his horse and brought over his shield. Bladud was even bigger than my father and his feet had almost touched the ground when on his horse. He handed the shield to the king. "If you are to fight the Angles then you need to make these." He turned it over so that the men, who had all gathered around, could see. "There is a handle here and a hollow for your hand." He turned it over. "Your hand is protected by this piece of metal and you can use it to hit your enemy with. The shield is made of thin boards glued together and covered in leather. If you make them and learn to use them well then you have more chance of surviving when the Saxons do come."

The man called Bladud, who carried the dragon, gave a snort and my mother stepped forwards her eyes angry, almost protruding from her face. "We will defend ourselves, do not worry!"

Bladud looked bemused as he took the shield and went back to his horse. The King smiled. "I would arm your women, Hogan, for they are like she-bears."

My father pointed to Monca. "She has suffered at the hands of the Angles once before but my sons and I will see that none suffer again."

"This is what I wished to hear. When I have gathered more men I will return for I need warriors like you and your sons to fight in my army." He looked suddenly serious. "The Saxons are coming. Aella, their king has reached the Dunum. When he has settled those lands he will head west and he will be here."

My father looked beyond the King to the east. "When?"

"If you have another winter of peace then the White Christ will be smiling upon us. You have a good place to defend and I will return with my warriors next year for we could make a good fight here. Take care, Hogan of Stanwyck, for there will be dark times ahead but we shall prevail." He turned to ride away and then halted, looking at the four entrances to the hill stronghold. "If I lived here I would block up all but one entrance and put a gate in the last one. If you bar it at night you will sleep easier and you might save yourselves from a surprise attack."

They rode off and, surprisingly, I felt better. The men in the fort looked depressed but I had seen my first warrior and I wanted to be just like him. I determined to practise with my weapons all that I could. I took to spending time in the woods with my sword. I had chosen the best one I could and taken a sharpening stone into the forest to hone it. My new-found strength from the bow and my increased stature made it seem easy to wield. Although as I had never fought an opponent it was hard to determine how I would fare against an Angle. My father and I worked on his shield first. Alone, out of the men, he had heeded the king's advice. It was not easy to cut the wood and to glue it. We found that mixing beer with vinegar and making a paste which, if applied when still wet, appeared to hold the wood together well. While we waited for it to dry my father said, "It is a shame the Romans are not still here. They made fine nails. They would have made the shield both stronger and able to withstand sword blows."

I saw a chance to bring some of the cache to the hill fort. "I could look in the river near to the Roman Bridge. You never know some may have fallen in."

He looked doubtful but finally nodded. "Do not waste too much time. We have other work we must do."

Leaving my shield to dry I raced to the cache and, taking two handfuls, ran to the river. I dropped them in and picked them up again with river sand. I put them in my leather pouch and walked slowly back. "I found some, not many but they may serve."

I felt really guilty when his face lit into a smile as wide as a sunset. "What a fine son I have raised. These will be perfect. Here, we will share them out equally." He counted them into two piles and then hammered them around the edge of the leather-bound shield. I noticed that the skin he used was the doe I had killed a couple of years earlier. *Wyrd*! He was a careful worker and he was methodical. He placed them evenly around before hammering them in. He retained eight long ones for the metal boss which we had yet to make. When mine was completed I couldn't wait to try it out but my father shook his head. "There is no boss yet and the glue needs to harden fully. There are no enemies to fight yet, eh, son?"

Raibeart and Aelle were envious of my weaponry and now looked at their Roman daggers with disdain. I had a shield which made me look like a warrior. Many of the men in the hill fort now had spears and I wondered if we could hold off a determined band of Angles.

As winter began to bite my father suggested that we heed the words of the King and improve our defences. At first, the others were reluctant; late autumn and winter was a time to do the tasks within the warm huts, not labouring in the cold. Our hut was close to one gate and my father shrugged his shoulders, "Well boys. We will have to make our own gate, eh? At least we shall have some warning. What they do with their entrances is their own business."

We went into the forest with his huge axe and my small one and the two of us began to fell trees. He chopped them down and I removed the side branches. My two brothers took the small branches back for firewood. We were soon warm and I wondered at the indolence of the other men. It was about that time that I began to discern differences in men. Until then they had all been grown-ups and I was a boy but, as the first wispy hairs sprouted on my chin and upper lip, I began to see differences. Men like my father and King Urien made the world a better place by working hard. Others, like the men in the stronghold, just existed and accepted what life brought them. I suppose that is why I am the last of the Britons for the Angles and the Saxons were also men who shaped the world to suit them.

When we had enough long logs we hauled them back to our hut. Although my smaller axe was not as powerful as my father's the two of us were able to work together to make the logs the same length. Two of them were kept long for they would be the gate posts. By the end of the day we were exhausted but Radha and Monca, who had watched us work while casting evil glances at the other men who sat around their fires observing us, had made a stew with an old sheep which would not see out the winter. All day long it had bubbled and boiled; cooked with the autumn berries and wild herbs. After a hard day's work, we were all ready for the fine feast they had prepared; the food tasted much better because of our efforts.

That night I fell asleep quickly but when I awoke I ached all over and my muscles seemed to scream as I tried to move. My father laughed. "Now you are becoming a man. Those pains will go and then you too will have arms like this." He flexed his muscles and they rose like mountains. I went out feeling no pain for when I was as strong as my father then no Angle would dare to face us.

The next morning brought a damp day which suited us for the ground was soft and we were able to dig the two post holes easily. It took all of us, except for my sisters, to raise them and seat them while their base was packed with stones. We stood back and admired our work. Now it looked formidable, even without the gate between it. With my brothers' help, my father and I soon made the two gates and we used the leather hinges mother and Monca had made. The final part, the bar and the locking mechanism, took the longest time and it was dark before we finished. I was even more tired than the day before but I felt a sense of achievement. My only regret, as I slipped away to sleep, was that I had not had the chance to practise with my bow but I now knew that I would have time.

When we viewed the gate in daylight we were even more proud of our achievement. The other men came to admire it too. Perhaps they thought that building one gate was all that was needed for they praised us and then went back to drinking their beer and telling tales. My father shook his head. "We have done our part. Now it is up to them. Come, boys, we will hunt." With the sheep penned we had the opportunity to increase our food stock for the winter. We would kill more than we needed and dry the rest. When the long dark days of winter came we would still eat, the meat would be chewy but it would help us survive until spring brought new life.

We only managed to hunt for one day before a sudden cold snap descended upon us. The snows came early and fell for a week. The whole of the land was locked in ice and even the wild animals struggled. It was one night when it was so cold that even the furs we had did not seem to keep us warm that the wolves came. The pack must have been starving in the forests and came to the hill fort for easier pickings. They came silently and, as we had a gate, entered at the far side, over fifteen hundred paces from ours. We heard nothing but the family who lived by the open gate did. It was a new, young family who had just built a hut there. Aed was a little older than me and his wife the same age. They had a young baby and the first we heard was the screams of the young couple as the pack broke through their flimsily constructed door. Thinking it was the Angles my father and I grabbed our weapons and raced out. He shouted to my brothers. "You two, guard the women!"

With my bow notched we ran to the noise. Others had left their huts and were hurtling towards the howling, screaming cacophony. The snow was being whipped by the wind and it was difficult to see where the commotion originated but we went unerringly towards the gate. As soon as my father saw the first wolf he yelled, "Lann! Loose!"

While he ran towards the hut I loosed an arrow which buried itself in the flank of a wolf. Next, to me I heard growling and saw my dog, Wolf, with teeth bared. It reassured me but I did not want him to take on these half-starved beasts. "Stay!" I commanded.

My father was hacking his way through the wolves aided by two of the men who had had the wit to bring spears. I saw the leader crouch and prepare to launch himself at my father's unprotected back. I pulled back the bow and the arrow caught him in mid-flight, crushing through his skull to kill him instantly. My father turned and saw the wolf and waved his free hand at me. The death of the leader made the others flee. I loosed two more precious arrows but I heard no yelp and I assumed that I had missed. My father stood at the entrance of the hut with his head bowed. Before he could stop me I peered in. The baby was not there but the two dismembered bodies of the couple were. The man had fought bravely and a dead wolf testified to his heroism but the missing limbs told us that the wolves would have food in the cold winter.

The men of the fort buried the bodies before the night was over. None of them wanted the women and children to see the devastation which had been wrought. I, for one, would be having many sleepless nights with the mutilated, mangled bodies haunting my dreams. It was backbreaking work to dig in the frozen ground but we owed it to the couple to bury them deeply and we placed a layer of stones to prevent the wolves returning to dig up their decaying corpses.

After we had said the words of the dead my father gave an accusing look at the shamefaced men who surrounded us. "Now do you see why I asked you to work on the entrances? There are three lives which have been lost because you were too idle to build a barrier!" He pointed through the darkness to the gate we had built. Although it could barely be seen against the snow it was visible. "See what my sons and I did in two days. All you need to do is block a hole! Think about that!"

When we returned to the hut the two women watched us as we wiped the blood from our hands. We had dragged the two wolves I had killed and laid them next to the hut. We would make use of them later. My mother and Monca said not a word but my mother put her arm around me and said, "You may have no beard, my son, but tonight you became a warrior; you became a man and I am proud of you."

As I lay down to try to sleep I thought on her words. I had not been afraid when I had faced the wolves and yet I had seen what they could do. I had killed when I had to. The question at the back of my mind was, would I be able to do so with a man?

Erecura, the earth goddess, must have decided we had been punished enough for when we woke the next day the snow had ceased and was already melting. When we emerged from the hut we saw that the men were already filling the gateway where the wolves had entered with trees and earth. My father shook his head. "A day too late. And now, son, we will skin these beasts you slew. A wolf skin makes a fine cloak and will keep out the rain and the cold."

The Roman daggers we had were of far better quality than any other blade and their sharp blades made short work of the skin of the wolf. Once we had them skinned and pegged out we butchered the wolf. The meat was not the best but it would augment the mutton and venison we used. Wolf and the pigs would eat well. By the time we had finished the men were moving on to the second entrance. "Come, boys, we will go and help them." He grinned, "And we will show them how to do it properly, eh?"

The three of us were proud of my father. I supposed all boys felt that way about the man who had sired them but to Aelle, my father was a stepfather and he still felt the same as we did. He now spoke our language well but we had learned enough of his to help us should we ever meet the enemies of my people.

After the work was finished I hunted down my arrows from the previous night. They were too precious to lose. Only three were damaged beyond repair but I managed to salvage the heads. The shafts were the easy part to make. We spent the rest of the winter making smaller shields for my brothers and fashioning the wolf skins into cloaks for me and my father. My mother had skilful hands and she managed to retain the head so that it fitted above mine. My father smiled when he saw it. "My grandfather told me of the Romans who used wolf skins and wore them much as you do. They had a helmet underneath."

"I wish I had a helmet."

"If we can get some more iron we could fabricate some but it would require more metal than we have here. Perhaps in the spring, eh, son?"

When spring came it was as though I had suddenly spurted for I was not only as tall as my father but a little taller. When I stood at my measuring post next to the hut I saw that I was higher than the door. I seemed to tower over my siblings and, best of all, I had begun a beard. I could see that my parents were both proud of the man I had become. For my mother's part, she looked forward to me taking a woman and siring her grandchildren. For my father, it meant that we now had two men to protect the family. I had no intention of taking a woman. The prettiest had been taken by Aed and she had died with him in the winter. I was more concerned with improving my skills as a warrior.

"I will go and hunt a deer to celebrate my beard!"

My father nodded, "Yes, for Raibeart and Aelle are now the sheep herders." I looked sadly at Wolf. "Yes, son, it means Wolf passes to Aelle now." Growing up was not all good.

I took my bow and arrows and my leather satchel. I had worked the leather from the cow which had been slaughtered in the autumn and made, not only a satchel but a belt and baldric for my sword. I had done it in secret. I had wanted to make a scabbard too but, for that, I needed the sword and I dared not risk the sword in the hut. I had also made, from the deerskin, some new boots but they were, as yet, unfinished for I had a plan. I would combine them with the caligae and make a much sturdier piece of footwear. I hoped that I could hide them from my father but, now that I was a man, perhaps I could face him with the truth.

My cache was still where I had left it. I had used a sheepskin to keep them dry and I examined them for rust. There was none. I slid the sword into the loop on my belt and it hung well supported by the baldric across my shoulder. I was pleased that it felt balanced. I practised taking it out and using it. I reluctantly returned it to the sheepskin and fixed the caligae to the deerskin. As I tried a few tentative steps I felt more confident about moving. They were heavy but my feet did not slip, even on the slimy leaves left from autumn. I left my hiding place and sought some game.

The harsh early winter had decimated much of the herds and it took me some time to make a kill. In the end, it was the god Vindonnus who came to my aid as I stumbled across a sow. She looked as though she had been injured and could not move swiftly. It took three arrows to finish her and I had to climb a tree to await her death but it was worth it. It was a measure of my new strength that I was able to haul her on my shoulders and carry her home. Once again I felt the pride which comes with praise as I was lauded, not only by my family but the other men, for a boar kill, managed alone, was rare. I knew that I had been lucky and I made a sacrifice of the heart to Vindonnus.

The spring leading to the summer was the best and the happiest of my life. I was becoming the most accomplished archer in the stronghold and my younger brothers looked up to me as a sort of leader. They say that pride comes before a fall and so it was with me. I felt that life could not get any better and I suppose that I was right for it suddenly got much worse.

It was a day in late summer and the boys had taken the flock to the hills early and I was helping my father to make a new axe head. He had become more proficient using the communal forge and the disasters we had suffered only served to hone his skill. Radha came out with our midday meal. "Those boys were so keen to get out this morning that they forgot their meal and Wolf's."

I laughed. "I would make them suffer but Wolf is a different matter. Here give it to me and I will take it to them." I slung my bow for I knew not what game I might come across and waved goodbye to my family. I ran through the woodland trails to the meadows. I was feeling good and it was joyous just to run. I knew the pastures they would use and I tried each of them in turn. I found them in the second one.

"What a pair you two are. It is bad enough forgetting your own food but to forget Wolf's? Unforgivable!" Wolf began to attack his food with his glare directed at my brothers.

Neither seemed worried about the lack of food. "We came out early to practise." Raibeart went to the tree which stood alone at the side of the valley. He brought out my old bow which I had used a couple of years earlier. "We found this in the roof of the hut a few weeks ago and we have been using it. Watch!"

Raibeart was the younger but the bigger and the stronger of the two boys. Perhaps it was Aelle's father who had been small, I do not know but Raibeart took the bow and carefully selected an arrow. I smiled to myself. It could have been me when I was first learning. I felt suddenly guilty that neither my father nor myself had taught the boys as I had been taught. I would remedy that soon. "See the wood pigeon!" I could see, on the branch of a tree some eighty paces away, a wood pigeon sunning itself. I nodded. It would be a magnificent hit to strike the bird at this distance but I said nothing." I will hit it!"

He pulled the bow back and held his breath, slowly he released the bow and the arrow flew. He had chosen his arrow well and it struck the tree where the bird had been until it flew off. He looked disappointed. "That was well done Raibeart. Had you aimed slightly ahead of him you would have struck him. And Aelle, what can you do?"

"I can hit the tree."

It was a modest claim but he struck it square in the middle. Had it been a man he would have hit him in the chest. "You have both done well. Now if you will take some advice from me…"

The afternoon sped by as I showed them what I had learned. When I saw the sun beginning to dip below the western skyline I knew that we were late. "Come boys or your mothers will be cursing me for keeping you out." We were a boisterous trio as we headed east to the hill fort. Wolf gave us the first warning that something was amiss; his ears went flat and he began to growl.

I trusted him implicitly. "Get your weapons ready." I strung my bow as did Raibeart. Aelle took out his sling. "Wolf, guard the sheep!"

The sheepdog went down on all fours and watched the small flock. I raced forwards, towards the fort with my two brothers close behind. We could hear screams and the clash of weapons. There could be but one explanation; the Angles had come and, they were attacking our homes. I crouched as I crested the rise before the northern ditches. I could just see over the top and then I saw mail shirts. It was the Angles and they had breached the wall. The wolves were once again in my home.

# Chapter 3

I turned to my brothers. "Our home is being attacked and we must save our family." It says much for them that they just nodded, biting back on their lips but gripping their weapons with determination. "We must be careful. We will climb to the top of the north wall. Aelle, you will stay at the bottom." He looked ready to argue. I held up my hand. "They will come for us when we attack them and I want you and your slingshot ready to strike every warrior who appears on the wall behind us." He nodded. That was the first time I had led warriors into a fray and the skills appeared to come instinctively to me. If a warrior knows why he is doing something then he will fight better. So it was with my brothers. "I do not know what we will see, Raibeart, but you must be ready to loose and keep on loosing until I tell you to run back to Aelle."

"I will not let you down, Lann."

"I never thought you would. Now let us go!"

We climbed the steep wall. I had steeled myself for anything but what I saw almost made me cry in anger. The Angles had killed many of those inside already. Their bodies lay in untidy heaps throughout the settlement. I could see a knot of people with my parents and some three other men fighting twenty Angles and it was clear that the Angles were winning. Monca and my mother had the shields the boys had used and were striking with our small axes while my father fought manfully against two mailed warriors. I could see that it would only be a matter of time before all was lost. "We must get closer. Aelle, stay there!"

We slid down the slope. When we were a hundred paces away I notched an arrow. "Raibeart, wait until we are closer." I paused and loosed an arrow. It struck a warrior in the back and he fell. The rest stopped for a moment and we were suddenly twenty paces closer. I loosed again as did Raibeart and three more times we loosed; the arrows were coming as though we were not doing anything. It was hard to see whom we struck for over half of them raced towards us. There were eight of them but I had seen that they only had swords and axes. We could still outrange them. "Run like the wind, Raibeart!" We laboured up the mound but I knew that the Angles would be slower. "Turn and loose one more." We both turned and loosed. We could not miss our targets for they were but twenty paces from us and two warriors fell with arrows sticking from their foreheads. We slid down the bank to land at the bottom of the ditch. As we scrambled to the other side the six warriors stood on the top. Aelle was accurate and his stone struck one firmly on the forehead. We reached the top of the other bank and turned. My breath was coming in short spurts but I had to concentrate. Aelle struck a second warrior and then Raibeart and I loosed two more arrows and two more warriors fell this time struck in the legs. When Aelle hit his third warrior there was but one left and he was at the bottom of the ditch. Our two arrows struck home and he fell dead.

"Come brothers. We will help our parents." I paused to grab the dead warrior's sword. As we climbed the bank two of the wounded warriors tried to crawl towards us. Raibeart loosed at less than four paces and the arrow went through his throat to embed itself in the earth bank and I thrust my newly acquired sword through the groin of the second.

When we reached the top of the bank I saw that my father was fighting two men and there was a ring of bodies around him. I screamed, "No!" and raced towards him; I could see that he was wounded already. I heard the panting breath of my brothers as I raced the last fifty paces. We had no arrows left but Aelle and my brother took out their slings and one of the warriors was hit twice by their stones. We were too late for my father for the huge warrior he was fighting stabbed him in the side when he slipped on the blood-soaked grass. The warrior had started to turn to face me but my arm was already swinging the long sword behind me and the blade sliced through his neck with such force that his head flew into the air, a surprised expression fixed forever on his face.

I knelt down next to my father. He was barely breathing. He opened his eyes and smiled at me. "Thank you, my sons. I can go to my ancestors knowing that you truly are warriors."

"Do not talk, father, we will heal you."

He pulled his arm away from his stomach to reveal that the sword had sliced him open. His entrails were clearly visible. He gave a wry smile, "I am dying and you, Lann, son of Hogan, must protect your brothers and fight on against these pirates and murderers. Swear it."

"I so swear!"

He closed his eyes and I thought that he was dead. His voice was thin and raspy as he said. "Bury me with my wives and then leave this place. You must hide. Find the hidden house on the way to the fort." I looked perplexed and he gave me the familiar smile I knew so well. "It was your grandfather's home and your mother and I hid there from the slavers. It is safe and you can find a sanctuary. It is my last gift…"
With a sigh, he died.

I turned and saw the tear-filled faces of my brothers. "We have no time for tears, we have a job to do."

I went into the hut and brought out the spades. We dug three holes each one as deep as my legs. When they were done we reverently picked up the body of my father and laid him in the middle one. I placed his sword on his chest with his hands folded about it and then placed his shield upon his face. We placed my mother and my sister on his right. We put her dagger across her chest and Raibeart's shield upon her face. We did the same with Monca and her daughter. Then we covered their bodies with the soil and found stones to cover them.

We stood together, bound by love and grief. "Sucellos, take these people and watch over them until our time to join them is nigh. We swear that we will not rest until they have been avenged. We so swear." My brothers repeated the oath and we stood in silence.

Our next task was even more grisly. We owed it to our neighbours to dispose of their bodies too. It would not do to let the animals despoil their resting place. We could not bury them all so we put them into the largest hut; placing families together and then we piled all their belongings with them and set fire to them. The flames rose high into the evening sky. I suddenly worried that there might be other Angles nearby and they would see it but I was beyond caring. If they came they would find three angry, vengeful warriors.

My two brothers suddenly found the emotion too much for them and I saw quivering lips. They had managed to perform the grisly tasks easily enough but now they were left alone and my promise to my father suddenly became a burden I could not avoid. "The Angles we slew may be part of a larger band; we cannot stay here and Wolf and the flock will need us." I saw the relief on their faces that a decision had been made. I glanced around the stronghold which had been my home for fourteen years. We would never see it again. "Take whatever you need from our hut and then I will burn it. We will then burn all the huts." My last decision was made out of spite. I knew the Angles would come and I did not want them to benefit from our work. Then I had another idea. My spirit hardened with resolve.

I went into the hut and retrieved my wolf skin. I found father's and brought it out. I picked up my shield from where it had fallen. "There is father's wolf skin cloak if you want it." I held it to the two of them.

Aelle nodded kindly. "He was your father, Raibeart, and it will fit you better." I was gratified that my two brothers got on so well without any arguments.

"If you wish anything from the Angles then take it." They looked shocked. "They are well armed and armoured. Much as I hate to take what is theirs it is better than what we have." I shrugged. "It is up to you."

I had my sword, and although my brothers knew it not, I also had a mail shirt but I had no helmet. I went to all the bodies and searched until I found one which fitted. I noticed that the owner had a leather cap beneath and I took that. I saw that Aelle and Raibeart had taken a shield apiece and Raibeart was struggling to remove a mail shirt from an already stiffening body. I helped him to remove it and he donned it. It was slightly too big but he would grow into it. I found a short sword which I gave to Aelle and, while I did so, Raibeart found his own. "Put all the other weapons into our hut and then fire it and the others."

"What will you do, brother?"

"I will leave a message for the Angles."

My brothers raced away and I performed my grisly task. The hardest one was the first but I was helped when I remembered what they had taken from me, my family. By the time I had finished I was cold and numb. There were no feelings left. I sought the spears which both sides had used and had placed them in a circle in the middle when the last hut was fired.

I had just finished leaving my message when Aelle let out a gasp of horror. He looked at the twenty heads arrayed on spears in a circle; I had just found the nearest twenty warriors and it seemed an appropriate number. The others I left where they lay as a reminder to our enemies that there were still Britons ready to fight them. My two brothers looked at me, I suspect seeing a different person from the one who had taught them the bow. "They will now know that someone survived and that they were defeated. Today we do as father had wished, we go to war with the Angles.

I had taken food before we left the hut and, when we reached the flock and Wolf, we just collapsed on the ground and ate. Wolf sensed something was amiss and nuzzled into me licking my hand gently. Raibeart and Aelle slept beneath father's cloak and I drifted through the nightmares of dead Roman soldiers and decapitated Angles.

When I woke, I was resolved. Wolf wandered over and licked my face and I looked at my two brothers who were still sleeping. They were, now, whether they wished it or not men and warriors. They had killed their first men and those Angles would not be their last. We could no longer be farmers and so we would become hunters; hunters of the invaders. I would trade the sheep; we could not tend to them and we would barter them for something useful. There was a village south of us called Aelfere close to the Roman road. Men there did trade with those who used the road. I knew that it was perilously close to the

Roman fort which I knew to be held by the Angles but I hoped that we would be able to discover news of where the enemy warriors were.

"Come on lazy bones. We have many miles to walk."

As we trudged down the road, with Wolf herding the sheep, Raibeart quizzed me about our future. I reminded him of father's last words. "We will find the hidden house of father's grandfather after we have traded the sheep and then we will become warriors and fight the enemy."

Raibeart looked doubtfully at his brother and me. "Three swords against the Angles? Have you taken leave of your senses, Lann?"

"Yesterday we bested twenty warriors with a sling and two bows." I cocked my head to one side. "What do you think?"

He suddenly grinned and punched Aelle playfully on the arm. "Yes, we will become warriors; and the Angles will come to fear us!"

We saw the village nestled close to a river. I picked out four of the better sheep and said to Aelle, "You and Wolf guard these and our belongings. Raibeart, take off your mail and shield. Give them to your brother. We will return soon." I pointed to a small wood. "Take the sheep there and wait for us."

He looked seriously at me, "I shall brother and I will not let anything happen to our flock!" He might not have been of our blood but he was as close to the two of us as if we had shared the same womb.

Aelfere was a prosperous place and there were many Angles there but they appeared not to be warriors but traders and farmers. On the outskirts, about half a mile from the village was a farm with a wall and fences. The farm dog yapped a warning to us and we halted as the farmer approached. He looked admiringly at the sheep. They were a healthy flock for we had tended to them well and looked after them. He assumed we were Angles for he spoke to us in their language. Thanks to Aelle and Monca I could speak the cursed words.

"A fine flock. Where are you taking them?"

"To Aelfere to trade."

A cunning look appeared in his eye and he shook his head. "There are many thieves in the town you would not get a good price."

I knew his game and I played along with it. Whatever we could get for the sheep would be better than abandoning them to the wolves. "Would you have something to trade for them?"

"I might. Bring them into my enclosure and we will talk." He opened the gate and Raibeart drove the sheep in. "What do you wish to trade them for?"

I looked around the farm which looked prosperous and was made of stone. From the looks of the stonework, the farm had been built from old Roman stones stolen from one of their forts. I heard a neigh and knew he had horses. "You have horses?"

"I have horses. Come and see."

There was a fenced area and six horses of various sizes pranced around. They were not in good shape and some of them were little more than hill ponies. I suspected they were bound for the pot. "They are of poor quality but I will take four of them in exchange for the flock."

He snorted in derision. "I will trade you two and those of my choice."

"Four or nothing."

"I tell you what I will do I will give you three."

"Of my choice?"

"Of your choice and that sword." He pointed at my sword.

Raibeart burst out, "No, not the sword."

I held up my hand. I had a much better sword and others of better quality hidden by the river. "And the tackle to ride them?"

"I have reins but not the saddles. I had a saddle but it is broken."

I held out my hand, and offered the sword with the other, "Then I will take three, the reins and the broken saddle."

He clasped my arm but asked, "We have a deal but why the broken saddle?"

"So that we can make more of the same design." He nodded, it now made sense to him and I saw him regretting not getting a better price. "Come, brother, let us go and make our selection while our friend here brings the reins." The farmer strode off to bring the reins and the girths.

"Lann, why did you let him have your sword? It was a fine weapon."

"Because, little brother, I know where to get more." I tapped the side of my nose and said, "Ssh!"

There was one horse which looked tall enough for me but the other taller horses were old and thin. I chose to accompany my horse the two smaller ponies who looked sturdier than the nags who would probably die within a day. I knew I had made a good choice when I saw the sour look on the farmer's face. I did not want him to know that we knew nothing about horses so I said, "You can put the reins on them for they know you. We will get to know them on our journey south."

He saw nothing untoward about this and he fitted the reins. Raibeart and I paid close attention. "You go south then?"

"Too many raiders from the north around here for our liking. We seek our fortune south." I did not distrust him but if any Angle saw the sword he would ask questions and I wanted a false trail for any Angles who chose to seek us.

He brought out the saddle and I could see the crack in the middle which rendered it useless as anything but a template. He put it apologetically on the back of my mount. "I thank you, sir."

"Will you not be riding them?"

"No, we will walk them awhile and let them become accustomed to our smell." I did not want him to see that we were novices and so we led the three horses south. As soon as we had cleared the farm and were hidden from view we left the track and headed down a small vale where we could mount our new horses. I took the saddle from the horse I would ride. "Raibeart, which would you like?"

The decision was made for him as the black pony nuzzled his head. He grinned, "This one."

I put the saddle on the other pony. It was a golden colour and it reminded me of Aelle's colouring. This was *Wyrd*. There was no getting around it; I had to mount my horse. I was the eldest and it was my duty. "Hold the other two." Taking the reins in one hand and a hunk of mane in the other I threw my leg over the back of the horse. It did not look elegant, in fact, it was downright clumsy, but I was on the back of the horse with a stupid grin on my face before I knew it. I saw Raibeart smiling too. "Give me the spare pony and you mount." His beast was smaller and he did it much more easily. I remembered when the King had come the men had clicked their tongues and the horses had moved. I did so and nothing happened save that the horse looked round at me as though I was stupid. I wondered if they had ever been ridden. Raibeart stifled a laugh and I reddened. This was annoying. Would we have to walk back with them in our hands? In frustration, I said, "Come on! Move!" and kicked hard in his side. To my surprise, he moved forwards and I was nearly unbalanced. I jerked the reins around and headed him north again. "Come on, Raibeart, let us find Aelle." The movement of my horse meant that my brother's pony just needed a click and a slight kick and he followed.

We had gone barely a mile when I found out why men do not ride bareback. Every time he landed it felt as though someone was kicking me in the balls! I was in agony but I dared not speak of it. I was the head of the family now and I would have to bear it although I doubted that, after this ride, I would have any family of my own anyway.

Wolf barked at our approach. The smell of the horses masked ours. Aelle's mouth fell open as we rode into the clearing and Wolf cocked his head to one side. I slid, gratefully from the back of the horse and I was pleased that Raibeart, too, looked pleased to be on the ground. I handed the reins of Aelle's pony to him. "Here, brother. This is yours. We will walk a while. Put your cloaks and bags on the backs of the horses. Raibeart, our mail can go on the backs as well."

"Where are we going, Lann?"

"To the hidden house father mentioned. Come, we have far to go. Wolf!" I threw my hand down and Wolf herded the four sheep.

We had gone but forty paces when Raibeart asked, "But how will we find the hidden house?"

"Father said it was between our home and the Roman Bridge but not on the road. There are woods and forests to the west of the road so we will look for somewhere which could have been a trail."

It was not the best of plans but my brothers accepted it for it was, at least, a plan. "Why the horses, brother? We are no horsemen."

I could almost hear the pain in his voice and I suppressed a smile. I knew the pain he was suffering. "The mail and our weapons will tire us out and we may need to move swiftly. "Besides," I shrugged, "we could not keep the sheep. Regard them as a gift from the gods."

"And why keep four then, Lann?"

"Because, Aelle, we will have food should hunting prove difficult and I have a fancy that the sheepskin will make a more comfortable ride."

"Why, does riding hurt?"

Raibeart and I looked at each other and gave a rueful smile. "Oh yes, and we will definitely need to make saddles."

We avoided the stronghold for many reasons and headed up the Roman road. As the sun began to dip we left the road, for we were now north of our old home and headed west. It would be too late to find the hidden house that day and I sought a quiet place with grass and water for the sheep and shelter for us. The animals found all three for us. My horse, which I had yet to name, began to tug for the left. At first, I tried to keep him on my line but then wondered why? His choice of direction would be as good as mine. He brought us to a small stream. There was some cleared ground with scrubby grass and the remains of what looked to be a woodman's hut. All three of us knew that we had found our bed for the night. I did not want the horses to wander off and so I tied them together although they seemed happy enough to be with us. As the animals ate I took out the last of our dried food and we ravenously ate our first food since the morning.

As we lay under the tree, the animals contentedly grazing and Wolf watching from half-lidded eyes, we looked up at the moon rising over the trees. "Do you think father and mother are watching us?"

"They may be but, more importantly," I tapped my chest, "they are always in here," then I tapped my head, "and in here. We are part of them as they are part of us." I smiled at the two of them. "When I look at you two I can see your mothers, from their eyes to their hair."

Raibeart nodded. "When I awoke this morning and saw you standing over us I thought that it was our father I saw. You are his double." If my brother had wished to pay me a bigger compliment he could not have done so.

"When I close my eyes I can see our parents and this may sound ridiculous but I hear their voices in my head and it is comforting." We fell asleep with happy thoughts and memories and my night was free from headless Angles and wolves in the night.

We led our mounts the next day, partly because it was easier and also because Raibeart and I still had thighs red raw from riding the previous day. As soon as we found a stream I followed it west. From what I knew of the land the hidden house was neither to the east nor to the north as I had traversed them many times when heading for the bridge. I had hunted in the woods and I knew that there was a stream but I could not remember a building or a trail. Of course, I had not been looking for one then. Every time we came across part of the wood which did not have trees growing we explored but found nothing. It was, of course, Wolf who did eventually find the trail. His ears pricked and he looked up at me; despite the time he had spent with my brothers I had raised him from a pup and I was still his master. "Find, Wolf!"

He trotted off leaving the sheep and horses with us. He came trotting back with his tail high and, as soon as he reached me, he turned again. "Let us follow him and see what he has found." As we made our way through the brambles and elder bushes I wondered at the route. This was a tangled mess and no one had come here for years and then it struck me, the last people to visit here, if this was the sanctuary we sought, had been my parents and that had been sixteen years ago. The vegetation would have grown vigorously since then. I heard the stream before I saw it as it bubbled down the shallow valley. I then noticed that the tree cover was becoming lighter and then we found it. It was overgrown but it was, unmistakably, a substantial building. I could see two ditches running around a mound and the remnants of a palisade at the top. There had been gates but they looked to have been burned at some time and had fallen away. "Take out your swords. Wolf!" I pointed at the sheep and the dog dropped to all fours. I strung my bow and notched an arrow. It looked deserted but it did not pay to take chances. I entered first and I could see that there had been a cobbled yard but it was now overgrown. The tiled roof looked to have been damaged by fire and violence as had the doors which gaped open on broken hinges. I slowly entered the doorway and saw that the wind had filled it with seeds and weeds; it was definitely deserted. A long corridor led off the first room and we found many rooms some of which still had a roof over them. There were remnants of furniture, some of it usable. At the rear, I found what had obviously been the kitchen. There were damaged pots and crocks littering the floor but there was an oven. I now knew why my mother had dreamed of an oven. In a wooden hut, it was impossible but in this stone house, with a chimney to take away the smoke, it was a reality.

"Come, we will check the outbuildings but I have no doubt that this is the haven my father told us of. This was his last gift to his sons." We found some stables, obvious because of the stalls and we found that it had a roof. Even better was the discovery, in the loft space, of two saddles. They looked different to the one the farmer had bartered, having four pieces of wood sticking out but they were saddles and they were covered in leather. We would be more comfortable the next time we rode.

"I will fetch the horses."

"And I, the sheep and Wolf."

While my two brothers went to bring in the animals I wandered to the door. This had been where my father had been safe and his grandfather before him. I assumed that this had been in his family before that. It was substantial. As I looked out of the door I could see the wall and mound which would have deterred any attacker. We, of course, with a bare three of us, could not hope to defend this place but I felt sure that we would be safe. I decided that I would find other entrances. It would not do to wear a path and make it easy for others to find us.

I turned to look at the work we would need to do in the stables and idly kicked some old decayed hay to one side when I did so I stubbed my toe on something hard. I knelt down and was clearing away the detritus of years when my brothers returned with the animals. Wolf nuzzled me and looked curiously at me and when the horses and sheep were in the stalls Raibeart and Aelle joined me.

"What is it, Lann?"

I looked at Raibeart. "I did not tell you and father that when I found the daggers and the sword I found them buried at the old Roman fort." I took out my dagger and rapped the floor with the handle. "See it is wooden. There is something buried here too and grandfather was a Roman soldier."

Raibeart's eyes lit up. "You mean there may be weapons here too?"

"Don't get your hopes up but there is something buried and I cannot see someone burying rubbish, eh? Give me a hand."

With three of us working and Wolf scrabbling too we soon cleared the edge of the box. This one, unlike the ones at the fort, had a handle and I pulled it open. "It is just sacks!"

I smiled at my brother's disappointment. I lifted the sacks carefully already knowing what would be beneath. I saw more sacks but this time they were wrapped around objects. The first one was long and I almost held my breath as I peeled back the oiled rags. The pommel told me that it was a sword and the fine jewels told me that it was not the sword of a common man. It was the sword of a mighty warrior, a lord or a king. As I unwrapped the blade I heard the gasps from my brothers. The scabbard was leather with strange runes and markings upon it. Holding the scabbard in my left hand I withdrew the blade with my right. The light from the setting sun in the west caught the silvery blade and it seemed to shine. "Thank you, father, and thank you, Belatu-Cadros. You have delivered me a weapon with which to fight our enemies."

I saw the looks of rapture on my brothers' faces and I handed over the sword to them. The next treasures were almost as good. There was a fine helmet with a red crest and cheek guards. The armour which lay within was not mail but looked to be overlapping pieces of metal. I took it out and held it; it felt lighter than the mail I had found in the fort. Beneath it lay a padded undergarment, a bow, quiver and a dagger.

Raibeart looked at the prize which was spread across the stable floor. "I think that father's grandfather was a great warrior." I nodded, unable to speak. "Do you think father knew it was here?"

I shook my head, "Had he known that he would have used this. No, I think that he and mother stayed in the main building. They would not have had animals and would not have come in here. I stumbled across it, literally, perhaps it was meant to be."

Aelle nodded in awe, "*Wyrd*!"

"Aye, brother. *Wyrd*."

# Chapter 4

We spent the night looking at the weapons and marvelling at the skill which had made them. "Our great grandfather must have been a great warrior to own such a magnificent sword and such fine armour."

"But why, Raibeart, did he leave it here? Why did he not die using it?" Aelle was confused as we all were. Had we had these weapons we would not have buried them.

I confess I could not work that out. Warriors died with their swords in their hands. My father had not been a warrior but he had died as a warrior. "Perhaps he became old..." Wondering what happened in the past would not help us now, "we have the sword and we must use it well." While my brothers cleaned the blade, not that it needed cleaning, I examined the helmet. The red horsehair crest looked magnificent but I could not see how it would aid you in battle. I discovered that it could be removed by taking out a small plug at the bottom. and, when I had done so, it looked more like the helmets of the Angles. "Tomorrow I will ride and bring back the other swords, shoes and daggers. Then we must make this house our home."

Aelle looked up; he had been quieter since his mother had been killed and it struck me that he was now totally alone, all his blood kin were dead. "When do we fight the Angles!" There was a quiet determination in his voice and I knew what was in his heart, he wanted revenge.

Raibeart also looked up in anticipation as I sombrely answered them both. "When we are prepared then will we fight back. We were lucky the first time we fought. We caught them by surprise and our father killed many of them. We need to be able to fight with swords as well as bows and slings. That will take time." I smiled, we were alone and yet we were still together. The three of us were more powerful as a group than we would ever be as individuals and I took comfort from that. Perhaps my father was looking down and approving of my actions.

While my brothers fixed the roof and made the house more habitable, I took Raibeart's horse and the horse I had named Blackie for his jet black coat and headed for my buried treasure. In the short time, I had left it the metal had begun to deteriorate and I saw how lucky I had been to find it in such pristine condition. I slung the bags on the pommels of the two saddles and saw how efficient they were compared with the broken saddle given by the farmer. I approached the hidden house from a westerly direction. I discovered another overgrown path and a second damaged gate through which I entered.

For the time being, we had two ways in and out should anyone stumble upon us. I was just grateful that the Angles had not, so far, pursued us and, as I saw the storm clouds fill the sky, I knew any trail we had left would soon be washed out by the imminent rain. We would slaughter a sheep and stay within the walls for a few days and then I would scout the old stronghold and see if the Angles had returned.

My brothers stopped working when I clattered on to the cobbles. I think they were eager to see what I had with me. I handed the mail shirt to Aelle. It was slightly too big at the moment but he was growing all the time. I think he had been mistreated and malnourished by his father as well as the other Angles and my mother's food had already started to put muscle on him. "Here are Roman shoes. Find some that fit." I showed them my footwear which was a mixture of leather and caligae. "You could make yours like this if you wished." As I unsaddled the two horses they examined the contents of the sacks.

"We will need arrowheads, Lann."

"I know." Despite having collected the arrows we had used against the Angles we still only had thirty shafts between us. Now we had no goose feathers we would struggle to replace the ones we already had.

"There is a forge, Lann."

Raibeart and I stared at Aelle. "Are you sure?"

"Aye. I found it well away from the house close to the north wall. There is no roof and the bellows need repair but it is there."

"Well done, Aelle. We will leave that for another day but, with the Roman nails, we have enough metal to make many arrowheads and we can use the existing arrows for a template. Raibeart, choose a sheep. We will slaughter one. It means we will not need to leave here for a while and, if the Angles are seeking us, they will not stumble upon us."

When we had skinned the sheep Aelle scraped all the oils and fat from the hide. It would be useful as a lotion for our thighs after the horse riding and it helped to preserve the sheepskin. I butchered the mutton and we put all the bones in the one surviving cooking pot we found and covered them with stream water. When we had eaten the sheep we would still have stock for soup. I now reprimanded myself for not bringing salt from our home. Had we had some then we would have been able to preserve the meat. We would have to use the other method my mother used, cook the meat in animal fat and let the fat protect the meat. It would make the meat last another eight or ten days. Now we needed to husband and watch our scant resources; we had no Radha and Monca to organise our lives. The three of us would have to provide everything that we consumed. We would have to learn quickly!

Over the next few days, we used two of the short Roman swords to learn how to fight. I also regretted not bringing one of the shields as I was loath to use our good ones. We soon discovered that both Raibeart and Aelle needed to build up their strength. My work with the longer bow meant that my right arm was powerful and I wondered how I would fare against a warrior who knew how to use a blade.

"Tomorrow we leave before dawn. We will travel to our old home and see who is there. If there are no Angles yet then we can travel further afield and see just how far they have come."

"Will the King not return? He said he would."

"The problem is, Raibeart, that the King may have other enemies closer to home and he may think that all is well here in this part of the land."

"Should we join him then?"

"I do not know, Aelle. Why would he want three such inexperienced warriors such as us?" It had been on the tip of my tongue to say boys but my brothers deserved better. They had fought; they had killed; they were warriors.

We had still to make a saddle for Aelle but, by using the girths and the sheepskin, he was able to ride and, after we had negotiated the copse and were riding south, he remarked how comfortable it was. It set me to thinking that, when the other sheep were slaughtered, we could use their skins to make riding a little easier. We rode mailed and armed. The horse and ponies could rest while we scouted; they were transport and that was all.

The closer we came to the old hill fort, the more familiar became the scenery. We had spent most of our lives within a few miles of the ramparts and ditches; Raibeart and I could almost navigate without the use of our eyes. We knew of a copse a mile or so from the north gate. We tied the horses there and left them under the watchful glare of Wolf. We had travelled less than two hundred paces when we smelled them. It was a mixture of fire and different men. We could have turned around then for I knew the answer to the quest. The Angles had occupied the fort. Dawn was still just a faint lessening of the dark and I gestured us forwards. The gate, we knew was blocked, but the rain would have washed away some of the earth used to pack the trees and make an impassable barrier. Had we still occupied the site then some of us would have been given the task of putting more soil and turf there but the Angles had not had time yet and we climbed the wooden ties which were like steps cut into the ramparts.

As I edged slowly towards the top I took off my helm and slowly eased my head up above the top log. I could see a handful of fires burning and tendrils of smoke seeping from the shelters erected by the invader. The burning of the huts which had seemed petty at the time now seemed justified as the Angles suffered on the sodden turf beneath branches and pine. I could see that they had taken down the twenty heads; they had received my message. Aelle grabbed my arm and pointed to the west; there was a solitary guard on top of the mound some forty paces from us. Luckily, he was peering in the opposite direction but he would inevitably turn, and when he did so he would see us. I notched an arrow and half raised myself. Perhaps the slight movement alerted him but, whatever the cause, he turned. He made it an easier strike as my arrow took him in the throat and he was pitched from the wall, landing with a dull thump in the bottom of the ditch. There was no time to see if the others had heard and we fled back to the horses. We quickly mounted and I led us towards the road in the east. They would easily see our tracks in the mud but, once on the road, it would become more difficult to track us. Dawn broke as we approached the bridge of the fort. I did not turn towards home but carried on across the bridge.

"Why cross the bridge, brother?"

"Because, Raibeart, I do not know how good they are at tracking and they may be able to follow us on the road. We will just make sure." I grinned, "We may get a little wet but we will disappear, trust me."

Once across the bridge I turned west through the bushes and headed down to the river. There was a shingle bank and after we had negotiated it, I led us into the water and headed upstream. Our father had told me that horses were good swimmers and this seemed the opportunity to try out his theory. The water was flowing quickly but it only came up to the haunches of my horse and he kept his feet all the way across. The other two were only swimming for a few paces and then they, too, were walking again. I watched for the shingle and stone I knew were ahead and took us out of the river about a mile upstream from the bridge. It would take a skilful tracker to follow us there.

Raibeart appeared a little downcast as we stabled and fed our mounts. "Is that it then, Lann? One Angle killed and we flee with our tails between our legs."

Part of me wanted to do as I had when he was a boy and cuff him about the ears but he was a warrior now and he needed to know my mind. "We went there to find out if they had returned and they have. Now we can plan to hurt them, knowing that they are there. We know that it would be impossible for three of us to attack them there." He stared at me, veiled anger and frustration in his eyes, "Agreed? Or do you have a death wish about you?"

"Lann is right, Raibeart. We cannot attack the fort." It was unusual for Aelle not to support Raibeart and it took my brother aback.

"We need to hit them when they are not in the hill fort. What do you think they will do there?"

He shrugged. "I don't know. Raise animals, hunt."

I could see his mind working as he reached the same conclusion I did. "All of which means that they will be outside the hill fort and in the lands which we know far better than they do." I tapped my armour. "We will not need shields or swords or armour. We can ambush them and trap them in ground of our choosing. We can hit and run. When we are all stronger," I tapped my chest, "me included, then we will try to find the King and join him."

Raibeart grinned as he saw the sense in my words and Aelle looked pleased that we were not arguing. "We had better get the forge going then and make the arrows."

I shook my head. We wait for a day when the wind is blowing from the south for that." He looked puzzled. "It will blow the smoke away from the Angles. We do not want them curious about our presence, besides, we have a saddle to make for Aelle and nails to put into our shields. The more nails we use the stronger they will become."

Eight days later and we had completed our preparations. We now had thirty arrows each and our shields were far stronger than they had been. It would be easier to hit a nail than the wood. We had eaten a second sheep and I knew that soon we would need to hunt but first, we would hunt Angles.

As we were not mounted we used the south gate and I made the other two walk in my footsteps. We left early and, this time took Wolf with us; he would make an excellent sentry. We had spent the evenings discussing what the Angles might do. If they wished to hunt then they would head to the forests and woods to the west. If they were seeking meadows for their animals then they would go south and west. By heading south we hoped to cut across their trail. We each had a sword strapped to our belts. I had left the magnificent sword in our home. I needed more practice with it and I had the shorter Roman sword which I found easier to use. All three blades were wickedly sharp and their points honed to perfection.

Once again it was Wolf who saved us from disaster. We had been making our way along a trail which led through woods and scrubby bushes. Wolf suddenly dropped on all fours and gave a low growl, his ears back. The three of us dropped like stones and lay beneath the elder bushes and rowan trees. I began to wonder what he had smelled and then I caught a glimpse of them. They were hunters; there were six of them. Two looked to be younger than Raibeart while the other four were older than me. They halted and sniffed the air. I was not worried for the wind was coming from the east and helped neither party. Satisfied that there was nothing amiss they headed west. I waited until they were out of sight. "We know that they must return by this trail for the woods and the undergrowth are too thick further south. We will make a trap for them."

I left Wolf up the trail as a sentry and the three of us made some deadfalls using the springy young trees and lengths of leather binding. "We take out the four men first. They have swords as well as spears. From what I saw the boys only had bows." I sent Aelle up a tree, partly to act as a lookout and partly to give us the advantage of height. When the attack started the men would not look up and that might just make the difference. I took the point with Raibeart ten paces behind me. I found this much harder than either previous encounter for we had to wait and that filled my head with doubts. What if I had made a mistake and they did not return this way? What if other Angles came up the trail? I found myself breathing hard and reddening and I forced myself to stop. If they did not come back then at some time the traps would work and we would hurt them.

Suddenly Wolf was close to me and I knew that they were coming. I waved him next to me and notched an arrow. I signalled my brothers who acknowledge the sign. Then I placed two more arrows between my teeth. It would be short range but quick work once it started. I could see down the trail and, by remaining motionless, I was invisible. I saw that they had been successful and they had a wild boar which two of the men carried. I also saw that the lead warrior had blood from a wounded arm; the boar had not died easily. He stumbled into the deadfall and was plucked into the air. I heard a sickening crunch as his skull smashed into the bole of a tree. The others dropped their kill and began to spread out. At thirty paces I could not miss and my arrow struck the first warrior in his chest. I could hear the sound of his chest cracking. As Raibeart's arrow took out a second warrior one of the boys found a deadfall. They could now work out the direction of the danger and they hurtled towards us. I notched and loosed an arrow but it just stuck the warrior on the left arm. Aelle hit the last boy with a stone and he fell backwards as though poleaxed. The wounded warrior was upon me roaring a curse. I dropped my bow and drew my sword. I saw that it was shorter than his; I feared I would lose. He pulled his arm back to slice at my head but the tip of it caught on a branch. I had no such problems with my shorter sword and I stabbed upwards into his chest. He was advancing so fast that he drove himself onto the blade and he looked at me in surprise as the point emerged from his neck.

I quickly looked around for the last warrior and saw him clutching the arrow in his chest. Before I could run over to finish him Raibeart had drawn his sword and sliced it across the Angle's neck. Aelle climbed down from the tree and stood grinning at the two of us with our bloodstained swords.

Suddenly we heard a groan. The boy who had been trapped by the deadfall still lay dazed. Aelle drew his sword and said, "I, too, will be blooded today." The boy, who was of the same age as Raibeart, cried out for mercy. Aelle stood over him, "My mother begged for mercy as did my father and they received none." He sliced the blade so hard across the neck that the head was almost severed.

"That was well done. Now, let us leave."

Raibeart grabbed one end of the spear which held the boar. "Let us at least save ourselves the task of hunting. We will eat well for a while."

Laughing I took up the other end. "Aelle, collect the arrows, theirs and ours, and their daggers. They will make fine arrowheads."

We did eat well but I knew that they would come looking for us at some point. Our first visit and the death of one sentry could have been overlooked but the death of a complete hunting party was something else. They would seek us out. We had returned by another circuitous route to our hidden home but, if they were determined, then they would find us. We never discussed our first close killings but I know that it affected all of us in different ways. We were quieter for a while and then when we did speak again, we were gentler with each other as though we were afraid to upset minds already in turmoil. I admired Aelle more than anyone for what he had done took real courage and it had been necessary. Had the boy survived then they would already be at the door and hammering to get at us.

It was when we had just finished the boar that Raibeart voiced the fears of us all. We had deliberately gorged on the meat as we could not preserve it. "We need supplies for the winter, Lann." The summer days were waning and when autumn and winter came then food would be scarce. Two sheep would not keep us going all winter and we would need salt as well as storage jars. There was a bounty to be had in the autumn with wild fruits and berries, nuts as well as animals but they needed keeping over the winter and we were ill-prepared despite the security our new home provided.

"You are right. Today we will travel west. There are small settlements there and we may be able to trade."

"Suppose the Angles have already moved there and captured them?"

I shook my head, "Unlikely, Aelle. Remember how long it took them to reach us and we have bloodied their nose. They will need to regroup but we will travel armed as for war. We will take no chances."

"And the sheep?"

Although there were but two left they represented food for the winter. "If we bar the gate when we have gone then they can forage around the farm. There is a stone trough filled with water," I looked up at the cloud filled sky, "the one thing we do know is that it will rain and keep it filled. But we should only be away for ten days at the most." I know I sounded confident but I was not. The furthest I had travelled before was north to the Roman Bridge and I had no idea what settlements and towns lay west. My father had told me that the King lived in an old Roman fort which had a Latin name still, Civitas Carvetiorum. I only knew that it was to the west and close to the Roman Wall which marked the end of the old Roman Empire. I was guessing at the length of time it would take to reach it.

As we trotted through the gate we looked like warriors. As Raibeart climbed back over the wall, having closed and barred our gate again I could see how far we had come in a short space of time. Aelle now had a saddle which we had repaired and modified to make it look like ours. Our shields hung from the left pommel and our bow and quiver from the right. The two rear ones contained our sleeping blankets. I wore my wolf cloak over my helmet as did Raibeart. My long sword hung from my baldric and my brothers had fashioned their own scabbards which they had decorated with beads taken from the dead Angles. We looked martial enough and, having fought the Angles three times, we felt that we could face any who came upon us.

I was still aware of security and, when we reached the stream, I headed east along it. It would be difficult to backtrack. Once we emerged from the woods I led us up the slope for I was sure there was an old road which headed west. Wolf ranged ahead of us, turning to ensure we were still following every few hundred paces. Suddenly he growled and lay down. Danger! "There are enemies."

We all scanned the horizon and then Aelle said, "Angles behind us!"

I turned and saw a line of twenty warriors in a line heading for us. They had obviously been searching for us and my carelessness at riding on the skyline might prove to be a disaster. I was about to tell my brothers to ride west when I realised that Wolf was not looking east but west. Then I saw them. There were another thirty warriors spread out in a circle ahead of us. We were surrounded! I contemplated riding back and taking on the men behind us but we would be going uphill and our mounts would struggle. The others were ahead of us and downhill. There was a chance we might break through. "Take out your swords and follow me closely. Raibeart, take the rear, we will break through them."

I was not confident to use my shield and ride, besides which, it protected my left leg anyway so I left it attached to my saddle pommel. With the reins in my left hand and my sword in the right, I kicked hard and drove directly at a knot of four warriors in the middle of their line. They were taken by surprise, expecting us to head towards the men behind us and that allowed us to close with them before they began to head in from the sides. The warrior ahead of me had a spear held pointing upwards at me. I swung my sword back as he stabbed at my chest. The tip of the spear caught on one of the plates and jarred him. I continued the swing with my blade and it sliced him from the crotch to the neck. At the same time, the warrior on my left hacked at me with his sword but the blade bounced off the nail-encrusted leather of my shield. I heard his scream as Raibeart took his head. A third warrior ran next to me with an axe; with a backswing, I hacked at the haft and felt the blade bite deep. It must have jarred him for he stumbled. As he recovered Aelle smashed his sword into the back of his neck.

Suddenly the ground before me was devoid of enemies. I glanced around just in time to see an Angle hurl his spear at Aelle. It missed my brother but struck his pony in the haunches. The brave little beast did not fall but it slowed to a halt and the Angles some of whom were less than forty paces away lurched towards us. "Raibeart!"

We both wheeled our horses around as Aelle dismounted and grabbed his shield. "Run to us! Wolf! Kill!" Wolf turned and raced at the Angles who were now less than thirty paces from Aelle who was running quickly towards us. Although there were only five warriors who were close the rest were not far behind. I wondered how far my horse would get with a double load. That is if we managed to kill the nearest warriors.

Wolf took a mighty leap and plunged his teeth into the throat of the nearest warrior. Before his comrades could aid him I had charged my labouring horse into one warrior while stabbing down at a second. Raibeart despatched a third and Aelle returned to stab the fourth in the back. With our five nearest pursuers disabled, I shouted, "Aelle, get on the back of mine. Raibeart, bow!" Aelle hesitated. "Get on this fucking horse now!" I put my arm down and pulled him up. I heard my horse groan. It would not carry us far. I heard Raibeart's arrows as they left his bow and I glanced down the valley. Far ahead there were trees where we might lose them.

I kicked on and heard Raibeart join me. "I hit one and my second slowed them up but they are following." He began to pull ahead as my brave horse struggled to carry two armoured men and then I heard a strange noise; I heard the sound of howling, as though a ghost was flying over the land. I saw that Wolf's ears were pricked and he was looking north and then I saw them. At the top of the ridge was the dragon standard of King Urien and he was leading forty warriors! The whole line plunged down to the Angles who were spread out on the valley side, helpless targets for the King and his warriors. As I watched, the Angles fled back towards the south but the spears and swords of the King and his men slew them with disdain.

I reined in my weary horse and Aelle and I dismounted. We led our two mounts back up the slope to the pony which stood forlornly with the spear in its flank. Aelle had always been the one who knew animals well and he stroked his pony's nuzzle. "Do you want me to put him out of his pain?"

Aelle's eyes flashed angrily. "He will not die. I will save him." He tore a piece of cloth from one of the dead Angles. "Raibeart, hold his head." When the pony's head was secured Aelle took the cloth and held it to the wound. With his other hand, he gently pulled the spear from its side. Even I could see that the spear had only penetrated three fingers deep. Perhaps Aelle was right and we would save the beast. "Lann, light a fire."

I obeyed because of the certainty and authority in his voice. I owed my little brother that much at least. By the time the King and his men appeared over the skyline again the fire was going. "Raibeart, hold this cloth over the wound and Lann, take his head."

I watched the column of men approaching us as Aelle blew on the flames to make them hotter. The dagger in the fire began to glow. Aelle spoke quietly to his pony as he took the knife and, nodding to the two of us, he put the hot blade onto the wound. He had made sure that he was to the side and when the pony kicked back, he kicked fresh air. Aelle looked gratefully at the two of us. "Thank you. I could not bear to kill such a brave beast."

"Well, you did well." I looked up to see the King of Rheged and Bladud, his standard bearer, looking down at us curiously. I realised that I still had my helmet on and I removed it. He recognised me. "You are the son of the man at the fort." He saw my shield on my horse. "I see you took my advice but I am curious as to where you got the Roman armour and the magnificent sword."

"They were from my father's grandfather."

He looked around. "And where are your father and the other men?"

I shook my head. "They are dead; they are all dead. We are the only survivors from the hill fort of Stanwyck."

King Urien looked first at Bladud and then back at us. "We came east because we heard there were warriors killing Angles and we came to enlist their aid."

"We are those warriors."

Bladud snorted, "You three! Do not make me laugh. The Angles would kill you in a moment and piss in your empty skulls."

I felt Raibeart go for his sword. "Peace, brother. I have yet to see this blowhard do anything but wave a standard and laugh at those who fight the Angles. Perhaps he was kicked in the head by a horse and his wits are addled."

"Why you little piece of shit!" He began to dismount and I drew my sword.

"Any time you wish, I am ready for you!"

"Put your weapons up. I command it!" Bladud sheathed his sword but I kept mine in my hand. "Did you not hear me? Sheathe your sword."

I turned to look the King in the eye. "And why should I obey you? My family is dead and it is no thanks to you. We have killed twenty Angles with no help from you. As far as I can see you are king of nothing."

"Let me kill him, majesty."

King Urien had a curious look on his face. "No, Bladud. The boy may be correct and," he waved his arm at the corpses of the men we had slain, "they appear to be warriors. What is your name?"

"Lann, son of Hogan. And these are my brothers Raibeart and Aelle."

The King seemed to see Aelle for the first time. "Aelle is an Angle name is it not?"

"My father took my mother and he was an Angle."

Bladud's hand went to his sword again. "Touch my brother and I will gut you like a fish." My voice was filled with anger at this man who insulted us.

"And I will kill any who touches Lann."

The three of us stood in a half circle surrounded by the forty warriors of the king. He laughed, "I think I would like these warriors with me, Bladud, rather than against me. If they are willing to fight

forty of my warriors then perhaps we can give them a little respect."
He suddenly became serious. "Will you three join us and become
warriors of my household?" He saw our hesitation. "With three such
as you, who knows, we may be able to throw these Angles back from
whence they came."

I looked at my brothers who both nodded. "Then we will serve you
and swear loyalty to you." We all dropped to our knees and we
became the King's oathsworn.

# Chapter 5

One of Urien's warriors had died when he had been pitched from his horse and broken his neck with a hard landing. The King offered the rider's mount to Aelle, much to Bladud's disgust, but Aelle, instead, gave it to his brother Raibeart. "You are the larger warrior and one day I will ride Heart again." He was the most affectionate of the three of us and I suppose it was because he had had no affection from his father but beatings and hardship. It was his way of making up for that lack of paternal affection and he transferred that love to all that was dear to him and that included animals.

Raibeart took me to one side as we prepared to leave the scene of battle. We had stripped the bodies of anything valuable and the King had given to the three of us some of the amulets and swords we had taken from those we had killed. "You know you will have to fight Bladud sometime?"

I nodded. "He took exception to father and that has passed on to me."

"He looks to be a dangerous man."

"Do not worry, brother, we are all dangerous in our own ways and I will not face him before I am ready. I do not think the King would countenance it."

The King waved to us all. "Now we ride west."

Aelle looked at me. "What of the sheep?"

The King looked perplexed and so I added. "We left some sheep penned, ready for our return."

The other warriors laughed but the King said to Aelle, "And what would you do?"

"If they are to die then it should not be because we neglect them. I will collect them and then we can slaughter them and eat them. They deserve it."

The King nodded. "I can see that you have honour. We cannot wait for you."

"If you head west then I will find you."

"Head for the Roman Wall north west of us. We will camp there. You will find us if you take the road west."

He looked at me. "Can I have Wolf?"

"Of course. Should one of us stay with you?"

"No, brother. I must do this." He looked at me apologetically. "I do not understand it but it is here." He tapped his chest.

"If you have not found us within a day I will return for you." He nodded and left riding Raibeart's old mount and leading the injured pony with Wolf in his wake. I wondered would I ever see him again. Had I betrayed my father's trust? And then I knew that father would have wanted Aelle to follow his own destiny; just as we were following King Urien Rheged.

There seemed to be stations of rank within the warriors and we rode at the rear. That suited both of us for it meant we could talk. The meeting and the events had been so unexpected that we had not had time to plan for them. I had thought that we would, soon, return to our hidden house and continue our war. I now saw that that had been doomed to failure from the outset. The enemy had been looking for us and it would only have been a matter to time before they would have found us and killed us. Someone or something was watching out for us. *Wyrd*!

"You know, of course, brother, that we are no longer masters of our own destiny. We ride and serve another. Would our father have approved?"

I honestly did not know. I had not wanted to be given the responsibility of my brothers' lives but it had happened anyway. "I know not, Raibeart, and this meeting may prove ill but had we not stumbled upon the King then we would now have been dead. But our father did urge us to continue the fight and this seems the best way."

"I know but this seems so strange to be serving a king; until a short time ago we did not even know that we had a king."

I leaned over to Raibeart, "I suspect that king is a grand title. He may just be a lord of part of the land but at least he is of our people."

We rode in silence and I was able to examine the men who rode a few paces ahead of us. They had taken off their helmets when we rode away from the battlefield. They all had long plaited hair; some of them had pieces of bones and jewels woven into them. They all had a cloak of the same faded red colour. Their armour was the mail armour which Raibeart and Aelle wore and I suspected that it had originally been Roman. Their helmets certainly looked Roman. Their swords were as long as mine and they all carried spears. Their shields were not round as ours were but oval and painted the same red colour as their cloaks. In the middle of each one was painted a crude dragon much like the standard carried by Bladud. It was their horses which marked them as true warriors for they all rode tall horses. Even my horse seemed smaller by comparison and I looked enviously at Raibeart's borrowed mount.

It was heading towards dusk when we rode along the old Roman road and into the deserted fort which stood next to the stone marker which showed the end of the Roman world. It seemed they used this frequently for part of it had been repaired and made secure; much as we had done with our home. We were largely ignored as the warriors dismounted and took off the saddles. They all seemed to know what to do. We too dismounted and I watched the men as they led their mounts to a building which had a crude roof on it. We followed and left our horses and saddles in the same stable. We tethered them to a long pole which was attached to the wall and then gave them water from the buckets the others had used. The warriors left before we did as we were just copying them. "What about food for them?"

I looked around and saw a bier containing the last of the summer hay. I took two large armfuls and dropped them in front of the horses and they gratefully ate it.

By the time we had left the stables, the warriors had a fire going and were busy preparing the evening meal. I felt helpless. I normally did not rely on others to provide food. Then I remembered that we had brought food with us and it was in our saddlebags. "Let us take food. We would not be seen to be beggars, eh, brother?"

Raibeart grinned. "Especially not in front of Bladud."

We still had the two hind legs of the boar and we each took one to the pot. The warriors were busily stirring a cauldron filled with water and what looked like some cabbages and onions. I winked at Raibeart as I said, "Could we share our food with you? Perhaps this might enhance the taste of the cabbage soup."

Bladud threw us a look of pure hatred but the rest smiled and then welcomed us. The best way to ingratiate yourself with a warrior is to give him food, preferably meat. A rotund warrior took a large butcher's knife from his belt and strode over to us. "I am Tadgh and, as you can see, I enjoy my food and so they let me cook. If you would hand over your bounty I will make sure it goes as far as the feast of Christ did when he fed the five thousand." He took one of the legs and began to skillfully slice it into long slices which he dropped into the soup. When the bone was bare he dropped that in too and then proceeded to do the same with the other.

As he wiped his knife clean Raibeart asked, "Who is Christ and what is his feast?"

Tadgh seemed to see us for the first time. "You are pagans then?" We both looked at him blankly, we did not understand the term. "You do not worship the White Christ?"

We shook our heads at the same time. "We have many gods we worship."

"We worship the one God and when he walked the earth he fed many people with a few fish and some bread. That is the Christ feast. There are other stories about him but that is the one I like the best."

Before we could talk further, Urien wandered over to speak with us. "My men appreciate your gift. Come and sit with me for I have many questions. He led us to a log by the fire and the warriors there vacated it as we approached. "We had heard stories of how the Saxons had been attacked by warriors; how did you do it?"

I was confused. "We fought the Angles."

The King laughed, "They are the same people and they speak the same language. They are the Angles and the Saxons but we call them Saxons. How did you defeat them?"

"We used bows and slings and ambush."

"Ah. That is good. Did you fight from the backs of your horses?"

I shook my head. "We are not horsemen. We used the horse and ponies to escape." I looked at the King and saw that he had leather boots which would have protected his legs when riding. "You fight from horses?"

"Aye. It gives us an advantage over our enemies. Our ancestors who lived here in the times of the Romans fought on horses and held back the barbarians." He gestured towards my sword. "May I see the fine blade you bear?"

"Of course, your majesty."

He took it and began to examine it. "My men only call me by my title when we are amongst others. This is an old blade. You say it is a family weapon?"

I shrugged, "Before my father died he told me to go to the house of his grandfather and we found this buried with the armour. If it was my grandsire's house I assumed it was his."

"Then he was a mighty warrior. What was his name?"

"I know not." I suddenly thought how little I did know. There were many questions I would have asked my father now, were he still alive, but those questions would have to remain unanswered now; for my brother and I were the last of the line.

He handed me back the sword. "The armour is old but it will protect you well." He gestured at Raibeart's, "Our men wear much as you do but it is newer. Still, that should suffice for a while; it is well made and will protect you. Yours is good armour, Lann, son of Hogan. If that was your grandsire's then he was a leader of men. It is a good sign."

Raibeart chewed his lip, a sure sign that he had a question on his mind. "Will we have to fight on horses then?"

He smiled. "No, only my bodyguard fight on horses. I am going to raise an army and we are going to war in the spring. We will drive the Saxons from the northern part of the land." I must have shown my disappointment for he patted my arm. "I have allies north of the Dunum, King Morcant Bulc and King Rhydderch Hael who will go to war with me and we can recover the gains from north of the Dunum. When I have built up my army and defeated those enemies who live north of the Dunum then we will drive them from your lands."

"The Dunum?"

"It is the Latin name of the river which runs by the fort not far from where you live." Icaunus had repaid me for my sacrifice of the deer heart and brought this king to our aid. We just called it the river but it was good to know it had an old name, a name my ancestors might have used. It connected me and made me feel more secure.

"Food is ready!" Tadgh's voice boomed out and we wandered over.

I could see that each man had his own bowl. "Let us get our bowls from the stables."

"I am glad that we do not have to fight on horses. I prefer the ground beneath my feet."

"As I do."

Tadgh had waited to serve us and he winked as he ladled the soup with plenty of meat into our wooden bowls. "I made sure the providers of the meat should get their share." His face turned serious. "Do you hunt then?"

I smiled, "We are good hunters, all three of us." It was not a boast, it was the truth and father had always taught us to speak the truth.

The beaming smile and the huge hams on our shoulders confirmed his words, "Then I shall be your best friend and I will save some for your Saxon friend too."

We learned over the next months that Tadgh was a good cook and we had not eaten so well since our mother had been killed. We were just wiping the last of the juices with our fingers when we heard the clop of hooves and the baa of the sheep. Although the warriors looked over at the sound, the sheep told them there was no danger. We joined Aelle. "Any problems?"

"No, but as I headed away, I saw a warband scouring the woods. I fear our hidden home is no more."

"We are warriors now and we will not need our hidden home again. Come and we will take you to the food."

Tadgh was ready with his ladle. He nodded to the sheep. "They are for the pot?"

I smiled, "They are yours but the skins are ours."

"I can live with that trade." He fished out the bones and threw them to Wolf. "And as the watchdog hound, I will look after you too."

The sheep did not delay us as we headed for the King's stronghold. This too was a Roman fort and this one had been repaired and strengthened. The towers had guards upon them and there was a drawbridge over a ditch. It stood out on a hill as we approached. It was faced with white stone and seemed to gleam. The towers were manned and there were standards fluttering from their tops. This made a statement to the enemies of Rheged. The Saxons would struggle to overcome this bastion!

The King waited for us as we entered. "I will leave you with my son Ywain. He is the commander of my forces." A tall young man, almost the double of his father, walked over. "These are three brave warriors who have killed many Saxons. They are joining our army. They are archers and they can handle swords too."

Like his father, he had the most engaging of smiles. "Archers! Then you are welcome for we have few skilled with that weapon."

Aelle suddenly looked shamefaced. "I use a sling, my lord."

The King clapped him about the shoulders, "Aye, but you are the one who can speak the Saxon and as such you are more valuable than ten archers."

Ywain nodded his agreement and Aelle's face lit up. Urien had a way of making all men wish to follow him. He was a leader men knew would lead them well and, when we fought under his banner, we were never bested. Ywain led us to a long building. "This is the barrack block for those not in my father's guard. As yet it is largely empty but we have the winter to bring more men to our banner."

I saw the dragon standard flying from the top of the tower. "I have never seen this before."

"It was the sign of the Roman Sarmatae who rode beneath it. My family is descended from their leader, Arteros, and it brings fear to Saxon hearts." When we entered we could see wooden slatted beds. It looked as though half were occupied for they had belongings upon them. "Choose any that are unoccupied and when you have stowed away your belongings and stabled your mounts then you can meet me in the Principia." He saw our confusion. "The big building in the middle. Today we begin your training."

We left Wolf in the barracks and approached the imposing stone building in the middle. There were two guards outside and they crossed their spears when we approached. "We were told to report here," I added lamely, "we are new."

They both looked stern and then grinned. "Fresh meat!" The taller one nodded to the door and said, "In you go!"

Once inside we were greeted by an old man who had a shaven head and a brown shapeless tunic. His fingers were blackened and he held a quill. He did not look up but asked, "Name?"

"Er Lann, son of Hogan."

He scraped away. "Yours?"

"Raibeart, son of Hogan."

"Next! Come along now we have not got all day."

"Aelle, son of," Aelle's face filled with confusion.

"Son of Hogan," I added and Aelle and Raibeart smiled gratefully at me.

The old man looked up for the first time. "Strange that someone does not know their father? Still, I can see that you are brothers even if you had not the same mother." We looked at each other in shock. Was this a witch who could discern such things? "I am Brother Osric and I keep the records of the King. As king's men, you will be fed and you will share in any booty you capture. We have a smith should you need your armour repairing."

"Have you a fletcher?"

He leaned back. "I see the King has begun to recruit warriors who can think unlike the lumps like Bladud." Already I liked this old man if only for the fact that we shared a dislike of the standard bearer. "No, we do not but I assume you can make arrows?" I nodded. "Good, then tell me what you need and I will acquire them for you."

"Goose feather or duck for the flights, but goose is best. Straight wood and iron barbs for the arrows."

He scribbled away. "I will let you know when I have them. There will be payment for the ones you make." He saw our excitement, "I should warn you that so far we have yet to gather any booty to share and to pay smiths and fletchers. But the good lord will find us some I am sure. You are now to go out of the north gate and you will find Lord Ywain there with his warriors." His head dropped and we were dismissed.

It was easier getting out of the gate than getting into the Principia. If I thought Lord Ywain would have a huge army I was in for a disappointment. There were forty warriors on the grassy plain. I could see a couple of targets with archers loosing arrows and the rest were using wooden swords and shields. Lord Ywain saw us and said something to one of his men and then strode over to join us. He was an astute man and none of us were adept at hiding our feelings. "It is not much of an army I know but it is a start. Until last month we had just my father's bodyguards." He looked at Aelle. "We have some slingers." He pointed to a knot of boys somewhat younger than Aelle. "I know that the King has plans to use your talents as a Saxon speaker but I would be grateful if you would command them and give them some sort of discipline. My father said you have fought and killed Saxons which gives you more experience than any here, including me!" I think Aelle was even more surprised than any. Ywain thought the confusion was over command and so he continued. "We use the old Roman system of command. We have a warrior in command of ten and ten tens are commanded by a captain of a hundred." He waved a self-deprecating hand across himself. "I am the only captain of a hundred. There are twelve slingers so you would be a leader of ten."

"I would be honoured."

"Good, then you can take command." He leaned over to say confidentially, "I know you have killed in battle. These have slain squirrels and wild cats. Be firm with them." As he walked over I wished I could be there to help him and then I saw that that would do him little good. If he was their leader then he had to command. "And let us see what kind of archers you two are. Although, to be honest, we have so few that anyone who has a bow is welcome." He looked at mine. "Yours is longer than the ones we use and the one your brother has."

"My father was a fine archer and he taught me from an early age. You need greater strength to pull a longer bow such as this."

We had reached the others and they stood in silence watching us. "These are two new archers, Lann and his brother Raibeart." He pointed to a young man about my age, the one he had spoken to before meeting us. "That is my cousin Gildas. He commands ten swordsmen and we are the only two commanders as yet. The field is yours."

I walked up to the targets and removed the arrows from two of them, placing the spent arrows on the ground. Then I paced out a hundred and fifty paces and turned. I knew I could hit the target from a greater distance but Raibeart's bow was not as powerful and I did not want to make my younger brother look foolish. I winked at him as he joined me. A crowd gathered behind me and Ywain said quietly, "That is much further away than they were standing."

I smiled, "Do not worry, my lord. When I aim and loose I hit the target."

I looked at Raibeart who nodded confidently and said, "We both do."

We both took aim and loosed an arrow each at exactly the same time. Both struck the targets in the centre thudding in unison. I heard the collective whistle of approval from the archers behind us. I decided to show off; father would not have approved, I know, but I wanted to show this young prince what we could do. I stuck five arrows in the ground. Raibeart grinned and did the same. "Sometimes, the enemy attacks so quickly that you have to loose quickly, like this…"

The two of us notched and loosed five times in quick succession. I knew that it looked impressive having watched my brother complete the same action himself. All ten arrows were embedded in the targets although not all in the centre. Ywain and Gildas rushed over to clap us on the back. "I think we have our two leaders of ten." He looked at me curiously, "Your bow has a longer range. How far away could you hit the target?"

"Raibeart, remove our arrows." I paced out another one hundred paces. Raibeart ran up to me and handed me my five arrows. He said quietly, "You can hit further than this, brother."

"I know, but we want these men to achieve this sometime so let us give them an achievable target." I chose my straightest arrow and I licked my fingers to smooth out the flights. I held up the wetted finger to ascertain the wind and then I notched it. I kept my breathing smooth as I pulled the bow back, almost to its maximum, and then I loosed. The arc of the arrow was true and it flew up into the air and then plunged down to strike the target dead centre.

"I think, master archer, that we will have your longer bows made for all of our warriors."

I shook my head. "It would be a waste of time until they are stronger in the arms and chest, my lord. My brother will be ready for one by midwinter for he has been training but the rest will take until spring. Do not worry. They will all improve."

The twenty men we had to teach were all attentive and desperate to learn how to be as accurate as we were. For the first afternoon, we concentrated on improving their technique. The strength training would come later. As we trudged back to the barracks we were tired but I felt a real sense of achievement. I was giving commands to men older than me but it did not feel strange; it was as though I had been born to do it.

Ywain and Gildas had kept glancing over as they trained the swordsmen and when we headed back they joined us. "You were sent by God to help us, Lann, and you, Raibeart. I always had a feeling that we could defeat the Saxons but, having seen your skill, now I know we shall."

"Have you fought the Saxons, my lord?"

I was aware that he was the same age as me but I suspected that he had not. "His red face confirmed it. "No, Lann, I have not, why?"

"I have fought three times and been lucky enough to kill the enemy but it is not as easy as hitting a target. You think you are going to piss or shit yourself when they charge at you and, until you have felt a man's blood spurt over you and watch his life ebb from his eyes then you cannot know how you will fare in a battle. Those archers we trained today will hit their targets but will they hit their enemies? Only our first battle will tell us that and the battlefield is a hard place to learn that lesson."

"Wise words from one so young and I will heed them, Lann the archer. Perhaps you can try out your sword tomorrow."

"I was going to suggest that the archers be trained with swords, my lord. If you run out of arrows on a battlefield then there is little for an archer to do but run, unless he has his sword at his side."

We did not get the chance to try our swords the next day for word came to us of a raid by some Saxons who were in the east and north of the Dunum. They were using the Roman road to come west. The war of King Urien and the Saxons would not now begin in the spring; it began when the skies were filled with clouds and the rain threatened to turn the roads into a morass. What was even worse was that the King had no idea of the size of the enemy warband. Two reports had reached him and the size of the Saxons varied from over two hundred to almost five hundred.

Our small army left the fortress taking all but twenty men left to guard the deserted fort. The three of us commanded forty archers and slingers while Ywain and Gildas had a further fifty armed with swords and spears. King Urien had his fifty horsemen and they led us along the road that the Romans had called the Stanegate, and we came to term it, the road to hell!

# Chapter 6

The three of us led our men immediately behind the horsemen. If we were ambushed then our task was to form a protective screen around the swordsmen and spearmen, thin the enemy out and then retreat behind their protective shields. Of course, the three of us marched with our own shields slung across our backs. The archers marched proudly behind Raibeart and me and I knew that they were envious of the wolf skins which marked us not only as warriors but hunters too. Aelle had quickly cowed the slingers with his skill and they were desperate to impress this warrior who was the only slinger they knew to have killed someone in battle. He had not had time to cast more of the round metal stones he had used against the Angles but it was one of the tasks he had set himself when we returned to the fort.

The first part of the journey was familiar to us as we had come along it but a few days' earlier. To the others, however, it was virgin territory and more than a little intimidating to them.

Raibeart was a thoughtful warrior, "It is a pity the King's allies did not join him."

I too wondered at that. Ywain had told us that Morcant Bulc's kingdom lay to the east of us. Admittedly it was further north but we wondered, at the time, why he had not come to aid us earlier. "Perhaps he could not gather his forces in time."

The King had scouts out and the dragon standard was furled. When the horsemen charged only then it would flutter above them, making its frightening, ghostly sound. The column was halted and the officers were summoned. The three of us stayed with our men but Ywain said, "No, we are all officers. You included. If the King gives instructions then we must all know what to do."

In truth, I wanted to avoid the baleful looks of Bladud but I would have to put up with it. "The scouts tell me that the Saxons are two miles up the road." He pointed behind him. "The fort we use is on that hillside. I will goad and provoke the Saxons into charging us. I want the archers and the rest of the army to form a battle line with your backs to the fort. We will bring them to you."

Gildas asked the question which was in all our minds. "Do we know how many yet?"

The King said simply. "They outnumber us." He rode off with the dragon standard unfurled and the eerie wail echoing down the road the ancient Romans had called the Stanegate.

We wasted no time but ran to the fort. Once again, I was familiar with it but the others were not. "Aelle, take your slingers to the left of the line so that you will be closer to the enemy. When they close with us, the slingers are agile enough to climb into the fort and carry on using their weapons from there." I know we both commanded ten but Aelle was used to following my orders. I do not know what would have happened had it been another officer. As the spear and swordsmen prepared I addressed our archers. "You loose on one command, mine, and you keep loosing until we are out of arrows. When that happens then those without another weapon join the slingers behind the walls, the rest will join my brother and me and we will fight alongside the others. "

I looked at Raibeart who nodded and said, "Put five arrows in the ground at your feet. It makes for faster and more effective use of our arrows."

I sensed the nervousness of the men around us and I understood how they felt. What was worse was that I did not know, or could not remember a single name. We had barely met them and the previous afternoon and evening had been spent answering questions about archery. I made myself a promise that, if we survived this first battle, I would find out more about the warriors I was leading. The King had a good eye for a battle and there was a ditch before us as well as a slope up which they would have to run. Our archers could see over the heads of those with spears and swords awaiting the attack. The only problem that I could see was running out of arrows. While Raibeart and I were well stocked, few of the men we commanded had more than fifteen and they would soon disappear in the heat of battle.

Ywain turned and gave me a nervous smile. "When will you send your first arrows?"

I wished that he had not asked me the question. If I answered truthfully it would affect the morale of the archers as I wanted to loose when they were as close as possible for they were not yet as good as they might be. "A hundred paces."

"That is close."

"By the time they are twenty paces from you, we will have loosed two hundred arrows." It was a confident claim but I knew that Raibeart and I could send eighty easily.

We heard the wail of the dragon standard before we saw the horsemen but when they did come I saw two empty saddles. They had not avoided casualties. The horses laboured up the slope in a wide line and behind I could see the enemy. They were better armed than the hunters we had ambushed and the ones who had chased us. These warriors were ready for war. There were many of them in mail and all had a shield and either an axe or a sword and, as they poured forwards,

I could see archers. "Aelle, take out the archers. Raibeart, try to hit the leaders."

When the horsemen cleared, I could see that they outnumbered us easily by as many as three to one. My first command could be a short one. As the horsemen cleared, I gave my first order. "Notch! Pull!" I paused to time it correctly. "Loose! Loose! Loose! Loose!" I noticed that the last flight had been ragged and the enemy warriors were closing quickly. "Choose your own targets!" I aimed at their archers and quickly sent five to their deaths. Unlike me, they were without armour and I felt some of their arrows clattering against my mail. My archers would be dying too. I saw the effect of Aelle's slingshots as the archers, the few who remained, fled down the hill to escape the rain of death. I switched to those warriors at the front of the wedge which was heading up the hill. They had their shields held tightly to their faces and I saw many shields with arrows embedded in them. I aimed at the eye of the warrior leading the wedge and, as he fell loosed a second at the man behind before he could bring his shield up. Raibeart, too, was choosing his targets wisely and his arrows were mortal. Unfortunately, the rest of the archers were hitting helmets, mail or shields. They were doing no good. "Archers, fall back!" I did not see how many retreated but I sent my last four arrows to good homes and then dropped my bow, swung around my shield and drew my blade. I stepped behind a warrior in the perilously thin second rank and Raibeart joined me a heartbeat later. "We thinned them out, brother."

"Yes, Raibeart, but they still outnumber us."

Aelle and his boys were still striking home and the effect was to make the vision of the advancing Saxons limited as they tried to protect more of their bodies and faces with their shields. It compacted the wedge and, as they approached the ditch, I could see that they would become disordered as they dropped down to the bottom of the defensive structure. I yelled, "Archers, loose!" The few archers who still had arrows sent a ragged volley into the air and were rewarded by eight warriors caught unawares. And then they slammed into our front line. I saw that they used their shields as a weapon, punching with them. The front ranks were so close that they could not move their arms and those with spears in our second file stabbed through the gaps causing many casualties. My sword was long and I saw a bearded giant with black holes for teeth and I stabbed forwards over the shoulder of the warrior in the front rank. He could see the blade coming for him but could not evade it and I twisted it as I pushed it through his eyeball and into his brain. He fell backwards into the crowd of warriors eagerly pushing forwards. Raibeart's sword was shorter and he had to wait his turn.

Suddenly the warrior in front of my brother fell to the ground, dead, and he stepped into the breach. I moved to the left to stand behind my brother. His shorter sword served him well and I saw the look of surprise on the blond warrior who was gutted from beneath. I stabbed at the warrior to Raibeart's right and this time the sword penetrated his ear and then he fell dead. I half saw an axe heading for Raibeart and, as I withdrew my sword from the man's skull, I parried the blow, catching the head on my guard. My shield was wrapped around my arm and I grabbed the axe and pulled it forwards. The man kept hold of the handle and pulled himself unwittingly onto the sharp blade which slit his throat.

I still could not tell who was winning. My sight of the battle was restricted to Raibeart and the two warriors either side of him. Then I heard the weird wailing sound and the Saxons before us looked up in terror as King Urien and his bodyguards plunged into the side of their lines. It proved to be too much for them. I heard Ywain roar, "Push them back!"

I put my shield into Raibeart's back and we both pushed forwards. The men before us tumbled into the ditch, falling onto the bodies already lying there. We stepped amongst them and stabbed and hacked them as they floundered like fish stranded by the tide. My arms felt as though they would drop off and then there were no more wounded. The ones before us were all dead and the whole army was cheering. Against the odds, we had won. I looked around to see that both of my brothers were safe. They smiled back at me. Raibeart had blood on his face but it was hard to tell just whose it was.

I clasped Raibeart's arm. "Let us go and count the cost amongst our men."

We found the bodies of eight of our archers who had fallen. One or two others had wounds but nothing serious. "Well done! Next time you will do even better but for now," I waved an arm behind me, "find swords from the dead Saxons, helmets if they will fit and shields. This will not be the last battle; we will need to be better armed next time. When you have done that then search the field and collect all the arrows, even the broken and damaged ones."

One of the men asked, "Just the good ones, surely?"

"No, all of them. Beggars cannot be choosers."

Ywain and Gildas came over grinning like children on baking day. "Your arrows and stones worked well. By the time they reached our blades, they had been thinned. Well done."

"How many did you lose?" I knew they had few to begin with.

"Too many. There are over twenty who are either dead or will never fight again."

We heard the dragon wail as the King returned. "Well done, my lords. You held them up well and made our task easier." He looked with dismay at the dead. "And now we must begin to build up our army again."

I bowed as he and his bodyguard rode off. I needed to find Aelle. He had done well and needed telling so. He and his boys were busy collecting their shot and any other metal they could find. "You did well, brother. Did you lose any?"

He grinned, "These boys of mine are too crafty and cunning to fall to an arrow. When we have collected metal we can make much better weapons."

It was too late to return to the stronghold and we slept where we fell; too tired to do more than swallow some water from the well. The King and ten of his men returned to Civitas Carvetiorum so that they could escort carts the next day to claim the booty. We had done well and over a hundred Saxons had fallen. The King had chased them east for many miles and they would be loath to return without a much bigger army than the one they had come with.

As we marched towards the fort the people came out to cheer us and praise us. Victories were rare and victories against the Saxons were even rarer. This was the beginning of a time of glory for Rheged and the people basked in our victories. As we entered the gates Urien waited for the three of us. "In honour of our victory I am slaughtering your sheep and you three shall be the guests at my table when we feast this evening. Use the baths to clean up and I will have some suitable garments sent to your barracks. Your coming was like the stone which begins an avalanche and I would have you share in my victory."

As we trudged back to our barracks Raibeart said, wryly, "Very nice of him to kill our sheep and then make it sound as though he was doing us a favour."

I shrugged. "He is a king; I suppose they do as they will. For my part, I am so hungry I could eat a horse, with the skin on!" We all laughed as that was one of our father's favourite sayings.

"Watch out, brother, you are becoming our father day by day."

The clothes he sent looked like booty from some other fight but we did not complain for they were clean. Ywain and Gildas took us to the baths the Romans had used. They were new to us and looked as though from another world. There were mosaics and pictures on the walls and the water was hot. Even the floor felt warm. They were not as clean as when the Romans had built and used them but they allowed us to clean off some of the dirt and begin to remove the smell of dried blood. As we walked through to the cooler room Raibeart asked, "How is the floor warm? Is it some magic of the Romans?"

The two lords laughed, "No, it is a fire and it is so built that the hot air rushes beneath the floor and keeps it warm."

Raibeart shook his head. "Where we come from, my lord, we call that magic."

We spent a long time in the baths and Ywain and Gildas told us of the Romans and how they had lived. When we were dressed I almost felt like a human again.

The room we ate in may have been Roman by design but the feast itself was less refined. There were huge jugs and jars of beer and the two sheep which had been slaughtered were jointed and laid on huge platters with other animals of varying sizes. The three of us were in the place of honour, to the King's right. The only other warrior, from the bodyguard seated at the table, was Bladud who kept casting us sinister glances which we soon ignored. The rest of the company was made up of the King's family and those who ran his fort. His wife, Niamh, was on his left with his other younger sons. Opposite were Ywain, Gildas, Brother Osric and the officials who ran the complex city. It was a little overwhelming for all of us. We were used to eating in a roundhouse with only the light of the cooking fire; here the King had lamps and candles to make it bright and cheery. Servants and slaves replenished the food and beer at regular intervals.

Once we began eating I relaxed a little and began to enjoy the event. King Urien leaned close to me, "We do not do this for every new warrior, Lann, son of Hogan."

I nodded, my mouth full. I quickly swallowed the lump of sweet and juicy meat. "I know, my lord, and I did wonder why three such as we should grace your high table."

"It is you and your sword which intrigues me. There is a legend that a warrior would come with a sword which would save Britannia."

I almost spat out the beer I was just swallowing. "And you think I am that warrior? I am a shepherd who can aim an arrow; that is all."

He shook his head. "No, Lann. That sword is no ordinary sword. I have only ever seen one of such quality and workmanship before and that one belongs to me."

I sat in silence for a moment taking in the import of his words. I could see that it was a special weapon. I had held other swords and by comparison, they were tools for the fields. "If the sword is so powerful or special then why did you not take it from me when we first met? There were but three of us."

He gestured towards the sour-faced Bladud at the other end of the table. "That is what Bladud counselled. He does not see you as a warrior."

"In that then we have an agreement. I confess that I have been lucky in my combats up to now."

"You call it luck but I call it divine intervention." I had noticed that Urien and his Christian warriors set great store by this god of theirs who seemed to be able to intervene at suspiciously crucial times. With our gods, you made an offering and hoped they would intervene. Sometimes they did and at others, as when my parents were killed, you were ignored. "My son watched you at the battle. You commanded easily and men followed you. When your arrows were spent you and your brother joined the line and helped to destroy the Saxons. Did you know that you and your brother killed more Saxons than the rest of those on foot?"

"How do you know?"

"We found your arrows in their bodies and my son watched you and your sword. You have yet to learn how to use your weapon but when you do then you will become a warrior to fear. You will become the warrior that the Saxons will dread to meet and you and I will drive them back from whence they came."

I was doubtful about his interpretation of the events at the Roman fort for they seemed confused, even to me, but they set me thinking. My brothers and I had been lucky when the Saxons had first come for, had we been in the stronghold, we would have perished along with my family and we would not have sought the sword. Then the thought struck me that I had not gone to the house seeking the sword; we had gone seeking shelter. It was *Wyrd* which had drawn me to the sword; perhaps the King was correct but I was too close to see it.

His voice lowered as he almost whispered in my ear. "You will become the champion of my people but first I need you and your brother to train up many archers. It was their success which won the battle. Then he can lead the archers whilst you and my son lead the foot. My horse warriors are feared by the Saxons but they know that if they use the shield wall then they are safe. The only way to break the shield wall is to use men such as you to smash into it and then my warriors can do what you cannot, we can run down the Saxons. Enjoy the feast and we will talk more in the morning but we will begin to train you with the sword."

Raibeart and Aelle had been politely talking to the others whilst keeping a sharp ear open for any of the conversation I had with the King. "Well?"

"Well what, brother?"

"What was all that about? I heard the word sword a couple of times but what was the King saying to you?"

I was acutely aware of the steely, hateful stares Bladud was giving me and I now had a better idea why; he coveted the sword and saw himself as the champion who wielded it. "We will talk when we are returned to the barracks. I promise I will tell all."

Now that I was no longer the focus of the King's conversation others came to speak with us. We were strangers and yet we had helped bring victory. Ywain, Gildas, even the Queen, Niamh, all wanted to know more about us. I was deliberately circumspect when talking of the sword for I was mindful of the King's words. It would not do to make too many enemies here.

When the King and Queen retired it was the signal for us all to return to our beds. As I was leaving Brother Osric, who appeared to have consumed much of the ale, took me to one side. "As you have been so successful at gathering booty I have taken the liberty of commissioning some yew for you to make bows as well as the ash for the arrows."

"Thank you, Brother Osric. That was kind of you." The Brother was obviously a man of influence and I intended to have as many allies as I could.

He waved away the compliment as though it was irrelevant. "I would, when you have the time, speak with you and view the sword." He cocked his head to one side and suddenly reminded me of a scrawny chicken we once had who had the same habit. "I am writing a history of the times and this would make a useful footnote."

I gave a slight bow. "I will make the time, Brother Osric."

As we headed across the courtyard I gave my brothers the gist of the King's words. Raibeart looked at me in amazement. "You, brother, a champion?"

"I know. We all know that I am no champion but it means the King thinks highly of us."

"Yes, and Bladud does not. Do not worry, Lann, we will watch your back. It will take more than Bladud to best the sons of Hogan."

The next morning, we wasted no time in taking out our archers and slingers to the north field where they could practise. Raibeart and I had adapted the way father had taught us. It was basically repetitive work; I wanted them to have arms like iron bars and the ability to send arrow after arrow at an enemy. Our skill on the battlefield meant that we had ready and eager learners. Aelle, for his part, merely had to give discipline to his brood although he too practised as often as he could with his bow. I gave my bow to Raibeart until his could be made when the yew arrived. He, in turn, gave his bow to the best archer we saw at the practice. I did not need the exercise although, as I write this down, I can see that it might sound arrogant but I was now taller than my father had been and I could send an arrow further than he. I also suspected, from my conversation with the King, that my days as an archer might be numbered.

We saw improvement by the afternoon and Ywain and Gildas joined us with their men. A trickle of new warriors was arriving daily meaning we never knew who we would have to train. Ywain strode over to me. "Can Raibeart handle the archers alone?"

"Of course." I wondered if this was to allow me to have a conversation with the King.

"Good. My father has asked me to give you the chance to work on your sword skills with me. These are from Roman times. They are heavy wooden swords. We found them buried beneath the fort when we took it over." I said nothing but it struck me as *wyrd*. "They make using swords seem easier after their heavyweight." He handed one to me. I did not say anything to the prince for fear of offending him but to me, it felt as light as a feather. "Here, try one of the oval shields we use. They cover more of the body."

As I hefted the shield I noticed how flimsy it was compared with mine. It covered more of the body but I wondered if it would stop an arrow as my own shield did. He looked apologetically at me as he said, "I have seen you wield a sword and know you know how to use one but the King insisted that you learn the correct posture and style." He adjusted his own stance and I copied him. It was little different from the one I had used although I saw that his feet were further apart. I felt better balanced when I emulated him. He grinned, "Now just try to kill me and don't hold back." He put his helmet on and I copied him even though I did not know why. As soon as we started I discovered the reason. I had barely fastened my helm when he swung the wooden sword at my head and clattered a blow which made my ears ring and head sing. Had I not had the helmet I would have been unconscious. He laughed, "Always be prepared for any trick."

"Thank you for the lesson." He advanced towards me and I punched with the shield and then smacked the side of the sword into his unprotected knee. He fell to the floor and I had the tip of the wooden sword at his throat in an instant. "Like that?"

He stood, ruefully rubbing his injured knee. "Exactly like that." He was warier now and circled me. I now knew that I had more strength than he did and as he hit my shield I had it confirmed. He had brought the wooden sword from a long way back and I hardly felt any impact. I swung my sword and hit across his shield. Once again he recoiled and barely kept his feet. I did not falter and I pushed with my shield as I hit his shield again. He had no control over the direction of the bout and was busy fending me off. As his shield dipped I swung at his head and, although he ducked, I caught the top of his helmet, which had a crest and it flew off.

"Either my son is a good teacher or you, Lann, son of Hogan, are a natural swordsman."

Ywain came and clasped me around the shoulders. "I have taught him nothing father. I am just glad that we were using wooden swords or my little brother would have been your heir."

I heard a snort and turned to see Bladud's sour face. "With respect, my lord, your son is a novice himself. Now if he had faced a real warrior." He pointedly emphasised the next words and stared hard at me, hate in every pore of his body, "Like me, then the outcome would have been different."

I knew that I would have to face him, one day, with a real sword but I was willing to try him with wooden ones. "If you would like to teach me then I am willing to learn."

Grinning he took the wooden sword and shield from Ywain who gave me a warning shake of the head. He had no need to worry; I would not underestimate this huge warrior. If he carried the standard into battle then he was both brave and skilled. I would have to use more skill and less brute force for he looked to be as strong as I was. I decided to let him attack and react to his blows. When he came at me I was surprised at the speed of his blows. Unlike Ywain, he did not try to hit my shield but swung at my head and sword. He used his shield offensively as I did. I kept my feet moving as I parried blow after blow.

"Getting tired, village boy?" He pushed his face close to mine. "Just slink back to your hole now and leave the sword to a real warrior."

He was trying to make me angry but, as I watched my brothers and my archers drift over to watch, I decided not to give him the satisfaction. I had observed that his blows came in flurries of five or six at a time and then he paused as though to recover. I used that to good effect. After the next flurry, I did not wait for his attack but instead swung a blow, as I had with Ywain, at his knee. He grunted in pain and his shield dipped a little. It was only a slight gap but I thrust the end of the wooden sword and it struck his nose full on. The blood spurted and he was partially blinded, I punched my shield onto his body and, already overbalanced, he fell. All of my archers cheered as did my brothers and Ywain. I turned to face the King who was smiling at me. I heard, "Lann, watch out!" And all went black.

*I was dreaming and I had lost my sword. I was searching for it and scrabbling around in the dirt. The dirt gradually turned into water and I was under the water. I could not breathe; I was drowning. Then I heard a voice, it was my mother's voice and I saw her long flowing red hair before me. "Reach for the blade and it will come. You and the sword are one; you were meant to wield the sword from the water." I suddenly felt calmer and I saw a sparkle in the black water. I reached out and touched the pommel. Then I heard another voice calling, as from afar, "Lann! Lann!"*

I opened my eyes and I was in a room which was painted white. Above me, I saw the prune-like face of Brother Osric. I tried to speak but he put his bony fingers on my lips. "Rest and let me heal you. Master Raibeart, your brother is awake."

The concerned faces of Raibeart and Aelle loomed above me. "We thought you had died. You have been out for most of the afternoon." I tried to speak but the words would not come.

Aelle held my hand. "It was Bladud, he hit you on the back of the neck when you turned to speak with the King. King Urien was very angry with him even though he said he was just doing as a warrior would do on a battlefield."

"Aye, and Ywain said that was a lie because if it was a battle you would have killed him while he lay like a fish out of water on the ground. Bladud was sent away in disgrace and we brought you to the infirmary and Brother Osric."

I heard the priest's voice. "You can rest here tonight and I will watch over you. He will survive. He has a head harder than wood, believe me. Say your goodbyes and he will come to you on the morrow."

As Raibeart and Aelle came closer to me I found my voice. "Mother came to me in a dream and she gave me the sword again but this time it was under water. I think the sword can be commanded."

Raibeart looked confused. "What? Is this the blow to the head speaking?"

"No, and I do not understand it yet but when I am recovered I need to try something with the sword. Do not worry; he has not taken my wits. Now go and watch your brother. I will see you in the morning but guard my sword."

"We will."

# Chapter 7

When I was released by the Brother I went immediately to the barracks. The priest rose early to say prayers to his White Christ and I was able to wake up my brothers. "What time of day do you call this?"

I kept my voice low. "The perfect time to test something about my sword."

Raibeart knew me well enough not to question me and he handed me the sword which I suddenly saw, as though for the first time. The King's words, Bladud's envy and the dream of my mother all made me curious. My brothers dressed and we left the barracks without disturbing anyone. We headed for the south gate and I could feel the unspoken questions from both of my brothers. We reached the gate just as it was being opened for the day. The guards looked at us curiously but said nothing.

Between the fort and the river was a small lake or a large pond. It was not perfect but it would have to do for the words of the dream came to me and the image of a weapon in the water. I took the sword off as well as my boots and I laid the wolf cloak on the ground. I just had the thin undershirt and leggings I wore beneath my armour. My brothers looked at me as though I was mad. I withdrew the sword and, without warning, threw it into the lake over my shoulder.

"Lann! Are you insane?"

I turned around three times and stepped into the water. If I could not find it quickly then the sword was not meant for me and my mother had been wrong. I knew that she was not wrong. When the water was up to my waist I stood and closed my eyes. I could see the pommel of the sword in my head. I lowered myself below the waters and I could still see the sword with my eyes closed; I knew precisely where it was. I reached out and felt the pommel and I lifted it and myself from the water. Later, when we talked of it, Raibeart and Aelle said that I disappeared for the briefest of times and then the sword seemed to erupt from the water drawing me with it. Raibeart wrapped the wolf cloak around me as Aelle helped me with my boots. Strangely I felt no cold; I felt elated. The power of the sword had been demonstrated.

As we entered the fort again, me dripping along the ground, the two guards looked at me with jaws dropping. "Did you just recover the sword from the lake?"

Pragmatic Raibeart just said, "Of course he did. It is a magical sword and returns to its owner." I nudged him in the ribs but the legend that became my blade was born at that moment for the tale grew in the telling. "You must name it."

Aelle ventured, "If it is a magic sword will it not have a name already?"

We walked across the courtyard and I left a series of wet marks where the water dripped from me. "Aye, but as the line is broken between father's grandfather and us we cannot know it."

"Saxon Slayer. That is its name for you slew Saxons with it."

"Let us just wait a while; the name may come, much as the sword came."

The name stuck and it remained Saxon Slayer for a long time and I did not mind the name for it spoke that which was in my heart and a sword is better when it is named. I had heard that, in the old days, warriors would have their blood forged in the steel with the sword and I could understand that. As I had held the sword and emerged from the water I felt such a rush of energy and power that I believe I could have fought a whole Saxon army. Perhaps that is folly for a Dane I met many years later told me of warriors who, when the rush of battle was upon them, would discard clothes and armour and fight naked until slain. It was battle madness. I hoped that the spirit of my mother would not allow that to happen to me.

The barracks was alive with the sound of warriors preparing for the day. I was greeted with cheers for the men we shared our hall with had fought alongside us and we were more than comrades. They also had an aversion to the King's bodyguard who looked down on the rest of the army as an irrelevance. My defeat of Bladud and his treachery had enhanced my status amongst the men.

After we had eaten our early meal we donned our armour. However, before we could organise the men two wagons entered the gate and Brother Osric waved us over. "Your wood for your bows and your arrows is here."

Raibeart and I had discussed at length the making of the weapons. He believed, as I did and our father had before us, that when a man made a weapon it became part of him and a better weapon because of it. The archers would make their own bows, under our tutelage, and then their arrows. The arrows were less urgent as we had neither tips nor feathers ready yet. The bow was the crucial element and would take many days to fashion. "Aelle, take your slingers out for some practice." I saw the disappointment on his face. "But before you do, take the first choice of stave for yourself."

The disappointment was replaced by joy. Not every yew stave is perfect; in addition, it should be the same height as the archer. As I waited for the archers to arrive he sifted through them, discarding the ones which were the wrong height and then eliminating those he thought were not perfect. Eventually, he had one he liked and it coincided with the arrival of Raibeart and our archers.

"My brother here has just chosen his bow stave. Notice that it is the same height as he is; see how the grain runs. He will make his own bow for he has been taught by us. We will give you your bow stave and, over the next two days, you will make, under our guidance, the weapon which will make you feared by the Saxons."

They were like children as they took their staves. I saw that Brother Osric had ordered plenty. When we had more recruits we would be in a good position to make the bows. "Raibeart, you start the construction. I will tell the King what we intend." I beckoned him closer, "Besides, he told me, the other night, that he wished to speak with me."

My brother, whose confidence had grown in leaps and bounds, said, cheerily, "Leave it with me, brother."

The King's chambers were in the same building as Brother Osric's. Before I went to find the King I entered his office which was bare and functional. "Thank you for the staves and the arrow blanks."

He looked up in surprise. "I am merely doing my job."

"I know but I am letting you know that I appreciate the speed with which you did it." He seemed, unusually for him, a little lost for words. "I seek the King, he said he would have words with me."

"He has left with some of his guards and gone hunting." He smiled maliciously, "it seems the disgraced Bladud has been given the task of the commander of the sentries for the next three days. How sad!"

I left and headed for the training ground. Ywain would be there and I could tell him. I did not want any to think I was shirking my job. As I left the gate I saw the men in two wedges. Gildas and Ywain were trying to get them as close as they could to each other. Even as I watched some of them fell over the feet of the men before them. The shield wall always seemed to be a simple formation but it required great skill to make it work effectively.

I hid my smile as I heard the King's son swearing like a blacksmith. "You dozy buggers! Cannot you stay on your feet? If we were Saxons then Lord Gildas and I could have beaten you on our own!!" He saw me and looked to the heavens in supplication. "Lord Gildas, carry on with the training while I go to talk to the swimmer." The story had been passed from the guards at the gate and was now all the way around the fort.

"I was looking for your father. He said he wanted to speak with me at the feast the other night."

"He went hunting. To be honest, Lann, he was not sure if you would be up and about today."

I laughed. "I have a hard head and it takes more than a blow on the back of the head to make me slow down. My men will be making longer bows over the next few days"

"Good."

I felt obliged to add a little more information. "I did not want you to think ill of me, that I was shirking my job."

He laughed and shook his head. "Did my father not make it clear the other night? You are a commander. As yet it is but forty men but soon you will be, as I am, the leader of a hundred. Then when I have a thousand men, should the army become that big, then you will command more. Yesterday did nothing to diminish your reputation. It was enhanced. Bladud has never been bested and you did it with consummate ease and little technique. I know, from our bouts, that I am not in your class but I can show you how to improve."

"I didn't know," I added lamely.

"There are quarters for you in the main building you know, with Gildas and me."

"Thank you, but I think I will stay with my brothers. I hope you are not offended."

He clasped my arm, "Of course not. They are family and family loyalty is more important than anything else. I know that. Soon my brothers will be fighting alongside me. When that day comes then no-one will stop us."

By the time the King returned the bows were all made and were maturing after being treated. We had taught the archers how to make arrows and, although they had only made two each, they had the technique and it was a job they could do in the long winter evenings which were drawing closer. We had also had many more recruits; these were men who had heard of our victory over the Saxons. After so many defeats it was a sign that the tide was turning at last. Our barrack block was full and a second was half filled.

I was summoned to the King's private quarters on the evening of his return. Ywain was there too and I stood awkwardly until the King asked me to sit. "I am sorry for Bladud's attack on you. It was uncalled for and he has been punished." I shrugged. "You should know that he is a fearless warrior and I owe him my life but he is, shall we say, strong minded. I have spoken with him and it will not happen again."

"It is forgotten."

"Good, now before I turn to the main reason, I wish to speak with you, could you tell me about this report of you retrieving a sword from the lake?"

I found myself blushing. At the time I had thought it necessary, I suppose I still did but I wished that I had been more discreet. "My mother was someone who understood dreams. When I was knocked out I dreamed she came to me and the sword was under water. It was lost. She told me how to retrieve it. When you told me the story of the legend of the warrior with the blade I felt I needed to test it and I did."

The King looked at me curiously. Those who worship the White Christ believe many magic things but not of people; for them, the magic is the work of God. My mother believed that people could work magic too. "Surely you saw where you threw it and then went directly to it?"

"Why would I do that? That would not prove anything would it?"

The King and his son exchanged an incredulous look. "You mean you risked losing the magnificent sword to see if your dream was true?"

"Of course."

The King shook his head. Ywain was more curious. "How did you find it?"

"I closed my eyes and saw it."

"How could you see it with your eyes closed?"

"It was in my head and I saw it as clearly as I see you now. I put my hand down and the sword awaited me. I now know that it is a powerful weapon. We have named it Saxon Slayer although there must be another name it was born with. That is now lost."

"May I see the blade?" I handed it to the King who took it from its scabbard. He hefted it from hand to hand. "It has a fine balance and I can see that it is well made. It does not look Roman."

"No, I have not seen another like it."

The King handed it back. "I have. There are swords like this one in Hibernia but none are as well made as this one." He shook himself as though to break the spell of the sword. "I know my son has spoken to you of our plans for you. I will need leaders when we fight larger armies. I need leaders on whom I can rely. We watched you in the battle against the Saxons and you kept your head and you led well." He glanced at his son. "We would make you a lord."

"Thank you, your majesty, but I need no title. My rank is enough. Will a title make men fight better? No, they will fight because I am one of them and they know me."

"Not the answer I expected but a good answer."

"What I would say, your majesty is that I would like my archers armed with more than just bows. There were times, at the Roman fort, when they were watching because the combat between the swordsmen was too close. We have few enough men to allow them to watch their comrades fight. The next Saxon helms we capture I would like for my archers. Six of the ones who died were struck in the head. Had they had helmets they might have survived."

"Very well."

"Can I ask if you have found any Roman arms in the fort?"

"Some, why do you ask?"

"I discovered boxes of Roman equipment buried beneath the fort on the Dunum. It would give all of our warriors helmets and armour."

"Then we shall explore that possibility. Brother Osric may be able to help. I am pleased that we spoke for I now know your heart and that makes me happier."

By the time the first snows had fallen the archers were fully trained and could send an arrow over a hundred and fifty paces and hit their target each time. They all owned a sword and a dagger and over half of them, the ones who had fought with us, owned a helmet. Aelle's slingers too were well trained. As we had a hundred archers and slingers I was now commander of a hundred and Ywain had five hundred men to fight in a shield wall. The King had managed to recruit ten more horsemen which swelled the whole army to six hundred and fifty. A sobering thought was that that army we had defeated was only a little smaller than that and it was one of the smaller warbands. We would have to rely on tactics and better warriors to defeat them.

Bladud and I had not seen each other since the bout. For my part, I had not avoided him but we just moved in different circles. I was busy with Ywain and the training of the army whilst Bladud and the King were frequently away showing the people of Rheged that they still had a king. Now that the days were shorter we spent less time training but Ywain and I used one of the empty barracks to practise our sword skills. Although I was much stronger than he was, he had more subtlety which I knew I would need. I also discovered deficiencies in my armour and helmet because the blow which had felled Bladud had been successful because he had no nasal and my armour, effective though it was, did not extend below my thighs. I knew that I would need more protection. The one aspect I was happy with was my shield. Despite Ywain's attempts to get me to use an oval one, I persisted with the one my father and I had made.

Eventually, I took him outside. "Go and set your shield and mine over there by that wall and then return here." While he set them up I went for my bow. I paced out a hundred paces and loosed an arrow at my shield and then one at his. I marched us forwards fifty paces and repeated it. When we reached the two shields and turned them around Ywain let out an audible gasp. The arrows had both penetrated his shield, one by three fingers but the other by a hand span and a half. "That would have pierced me."

"Or at least hit your mail." I showed him my shield; the second arrow had barely penetrated the shield and the first one had penetrated so little that I pulled it out easily. "It is the construction of the shield which gives it its strength. There are two layers with the grain going in different directions and the leather cover helps but the most important part is the large number of nails I have used. The arrow has more chance of striking metal than anything." I shrugged. "I agree with you that the shape of yours is better but mine gives me what I need, protection."

We carried the shields back to our rooms. "We have visitors next week, Lann, important ones. King Morcant Bulc and King Rhydderch the Generous are visiting for the Christmas celebrations." I gave him a blank look. He could have been speaking Greek for all that I understood him. "They are the two kings, one from north of here and the other from the northeast. They are allies of my father and they come to plan the spring offensive."

Ah, but what is this Christmas? Is it another White Christ thing?"

He sighed with exasperation. Despite the best efforts of the King, Brother Osric and Ywain himself my brothers and I were immune from the attraction of Christianity. "It is the celebration of the birth of Christ."

"Ah yes, like our Yule festival."

"No, nothing like that."

"So you do not drink and eat well."

"We do that, yes."

"You do not spend it with friends and family."

"Well of course we do but there is nothing similar otherwise." He reddened and I knew I had angered him. I enjoyed the game of baiting him about his religion. Brother Osric had explained well but I could see no advantage. I did not deny the existence of this White Christ but he did not appear to be any stronger than my gods. In fact, this turning of the cheek to enemies seemed like a real disadvantage to a warrior.

Rhydderch the Generous arrived first and I really liked him from the moment I met him. He was a huge red-headed bear of a man; he was already an old man but still hale and hearty. His lands bordered ours to the north but he was a staunch ally of King Urien. He marched down from his lands with his twenty bodyguards. All of them carried either a mighty war hammer or a double-headed axe. They were fierce looking warriors but, as I pointed out to Ywain, they could not defend themselves against arrows or a swordsman who was agile and swift. I did agree however that facing them might be a little frightening.

King Morcant Bulc was more of an enigma. He was younger than the other two kings and I judged him to be but little older than us. His kingdom was the most under threat from the Angles and the Saxons. His coast was constantly raided and I had heard that one of his island strongholds, Metcauld, had been taken. Now that the Saxons controlled the Dunum it was only a matter of time before they swallowed him up too. My problem was that I wondered why he had not aided us when we had fought in the autumn. Even though we had beaten the enemy it had been a close-run thing. That apart, he was like Rhydderch, a very affable and approachable man. I was introduced to them as one of the senior officers and they both expressed much interest in the story of the sword and the prowess my brothers and I had shown with bows. Neither king had a weapon which could match it.

At the feast we held to welcome them Rhydderch said, "My lads like to see a man's face before they smash his skull in." He looked admiringly at his bodyguards who were busy gorging themselves on venison, "Aye, they are fierce fighters."

Morcant Bulc was more amenable to the idea of bows. "I would use them if I had them. Perhaps, King Urien, you could loan me the brothers to train up men such as your archers?"

"Aye, well we will have to wait until my men are fully trained and ready for war and when we have finally defeated these Saxon bastards."

I then listened with interest to their ideas. Rhydderch seemed happy to go along with the other two kings' ideas but Urien and Morcant appeared to have slightly differing views. Morcant was all for a spring offensive against Metcauld but King Urien, wisely in my view, wanted to eliminate the enemies who lay before the island; those who had taken the centre of the land. "I would hate to be trapped against the sea with enemies in my rear for then we would have no escape."

"But all the time we delay they are growing stronger."

Rhydderch burped, "Aye, laddie, but we canna fight in the winter. It is not done. When the snows have gone then we can go."

Morcant was not convinced but he could see that he had been outnumbered. "I will have to harass them on my own then until your armies arrive."

"Don't waste your men uselessly." King Urien gestured towards me, "do as Lann and his brothers did. They ambushed the Saxons who took their land and they killed many of them before they had to flee. If three warriors could do that then perhaps twenty or thirty of your more determined men might do as well."

Although he did not say anything then I could see his mind working. He fixed me with a stare, when I saw it, he turned it to a smile and I wondered what was in his head. I was even more disturbed when I saw Bladud sidle up and speak privately with him. It did not bode well for me.

The feasting went on for days. My brothers and I soon tired of it. The bodyguards of the three kings seemed to enjoy trying to best each other in drinking contests. Ywain and Gildas were also weary of it but their relationship to the King meant that they could not escape their duties whereas we three could and we did. Winter has few animals to hunt but hunting is easier as you can see their tracks when there is snow on the ground. Using our wolf skins, we left the fort just before dawn with only the sentries to witness our departure. We had heard the wolves howling in the night and knew that there was a pack seeking food. Aelle often looked longingly at our cloaks and Raibeart and I wanted to hunt a wolf for him. We were close as brothers and, although it was a fancy, we all wished to dress alike. I had even begun to think about painting a wolf on my shield complete with red eyes. I wanted warriors who fought me to know who I was.

We tested the wind and travelled south with the wind in our faces. The hills to the south were filled with lakes and forests which were perfect for wolves but had few people and animals. The packs were forced to forage close to the houses and homes of our people and therein lay our opportunity. We had taken Wolf with us and he relished the opportunity to do something active once again. He had a fine life in the fort for he was well fed and given fuss by the archers but he was a working dog and he needed to do something. He quickly picked up the scent of the pack and, as the ground began to rise, we found the tracks. We strung our bows and each notched an arrow. Wolf's ears went down and he lay supine on the floor. The pack was close. I gestured for him to stay. A pack of wolves would tear him to pieces. Raibeart went to my right and Aelle to my left. It soon became obvious to me that they had retreated to their den which looked to me to be in a small dell hidden by a jumble of bushes and rocks. The smell of the pack drifted into our nostrils; it was a pungent mix and made us even warier. We needed to make them run; I mimed loosing into the air and into their den. They both understood and nodded. We aimed high and three arrows plunged into the den. Even as we heard a yelp, we had notched another arrow and waited for the pack to erupt. While most of the pack fled south two huge male wolves, teeth bared raced towards us. My arrow struck the second wolf in the shoulder while my brothers' arrows took out the first. My wounded beast still hurtled towards me and I dropped my bow and took out my dagger. I had my bracer on my left arm and I held that before me. The wolf's teeth sank into the leather, penetrating through to the skin but my dagger slashed across its throat and its lifeblood gushed over me.

My brothers were concerned about me and raced over to pull the dead wolf from me. Raibeart looked at my left arm. "You were lucky, brother. The teeth almost penetrated the bracer."

I took the leather bracer off and saw the teeth marks on my arm. Another few moments and he would have drawn blood. "You are right but it has given me a thought. Suppose we had bracers on both arms with pieces of metal sewn in."

Raibeart's brow wrinkled. "How would that help our archery?"

"It wouldn't but it would give us protection from sword and dagger blows. And it would not impede our arrows."

"If you had the same things for your right hand, brother, then it would protect it during combat."

"It would indeed, Aelle. I will try to get some soft leather which can be lined with iron. And now let us get these beasts back."

We gutted them there and we gave some of the offal to Wolf who voraciously consumed it. While he ate we sacrificed their hearts to Vindonnus and said a prayer of thanks to the god of hunting. Raibeart and I hefted the carcasses on our backs while Aelle, after retrieving the two arrows he could find, carried our bows and we made our way back to the fort. The sentries shook their heads as we entered. "You brothers, you are mad as fish. Who else would track a wolf pack on foot and then kill them? Mad!"

I detected the admiration beneath the jokes. "Well my little brother could not be the only one without a wolf skin, could he?" Their laughter was still ringing in our ears when we headed for the workshop close to the kitchens. There was a gully which ran under the walls and it was the area used for the butchery of animals. We could swill the wolf blood away after they had been skinned. I let my brothers skin the dead wolves for the last time it had been father and me who had done so. It was a skilful task, especially if you wanted the head intact as I had. It took some time and Ywain and Gildas wandered over their eyes and faces red and puffy from a night's carousing and wassailing.

"I see you have been busy."

"And productive." Ywain watched as Raibeart peeled back the skin. "This is so that Aelle can have a cloak, eh? I can see we will have to call you the brotherhood of the wolf." We looked at each other and nodded. The name seemed appropriate somehow.

"And why not? Yes, that shall be our name."

Gildas looked sadly at the spare skin. "I would like to be in the brotherhood."

Raibeart shook his head. "You have to kill your own wolf. This one will be a spare."

The cooks came out to see what we were doing. "What will you do with the meat? Feed your dog?"

"If you lads want it then you are welcome. Just keep the bones for the dog."

Wolf was a particular favourite of the cooks for he caught many of the rats who hung around. "Wolf knows he is always welcome here. Don't you boy?"

Ever the one to flatter those who fed him he rolled over on his back to allow them to tickle him.

We went to the nearby wood and cut two frames to stretch and dry the wolf skins. We were just finishing when the three kings wandered over. King Urien stood admiring the skins. "We heard that the three of you decided that drinking and feasting were not enough. You tracked these two, did you?"

"Yes, my lord. We knew there was a pack of them somewhere in the vicinity."

The King of Bryneich looked at the three of us in surprise. "Three of you hunted a wolf pack? Warriors indeed! Lann, would you come and hunt the wolves of the sea for me?"

I knew what he meant but I feigned ignorance, "My lord?"

King Urien put his arm around my shoulder. "The King has asked to borrow you for a couple of months to teach his warriors how to hunt the Angles who plague his coasts." There was a look of pleading in his eyes. He valued his two allies and my loan was part of the bargain.

"You are my lord. If you command, I will obey." My tone left no-one in any doubt that I did this out of a sense of duty and nothing more.

"Good then Raibeart can command while you are absent; for the King returns home to Din Guardi today. You will be serving the King of Bryneich for a while."

# Chapter 8

It did not leave me long to prepare and say my goodbyes. "If you will give me leave then. Brothers."

As we hurried to the barracks, I could see the worry and fear on their faces. This would be the first time we had been parted. "I like it not."

"And neither do I, Raibeart, but I am part of a pact. If I help King Morcant then he will aid our King and the end result will be dead Angles."

"I would come with you."

"And I."

"I need you two here, safe. If I am alone then I will only worry about me and I will return, that I promise. Keep Wolf with you." We hurried to the stables. It had been some time since I had ridden Blackie but I now had a sheepskin for added comfort. He had been well looked after and his coat had grown and his flanks filled out. He now looked healthy. I had cadged an apple from the cook on the way there. It was old and gnarly but he appreciated it and nuzzled my face. I was wearing my armour for I knew that we could run into bands of the enemy whilst crossing to the east. I had still to have a helmet made and so I took my old Roman one. The four pommels made loading Blackie easy. Once completed, I clasped my brothers' arms as we said our goodbyes. "Raibeart and Aelle watch over each other. Trust no-one. I believe the King and Ywain are honourable men as is Gildas but, until we have known them all longer, be careful and watch out for Bladud. I saw him speaking with King Morcant the other day and I fear he has had a hand in my departure. It may be for some purpose of his own."

"We will and watch over yourself brother, for now, we are the brethren of the wolf and you are our leader."

Laughing, I mounted Blackie. I managed it somewhat easier now than when first I tried. The King and his retinue were waiting for us. As I rode by Ywain, I said quietly so that only he could hear. "Watch over my brothers and I will be in your debt."

"I will do it as though they were my own blood kin."

Leaving Civitas Carvetiorum was like leaving home. I was also leaving my family and my newly acquired family. This was harder than I thought. I set my face into a mask and waited for the King and his bodyguards to pass me so that I could ride in the rear of the column.

"Lann, ride next to me I would speak with you while we journey to my home."

"Where is your home, your majesty?"

"Din Guardi. It is a mighty fortress on the coast of my kingdom. It is the safest stronghold in Hen Ogledd. The cursed Saxons have threatened it by capturing Metcauld. Tell me, how did three of you kill so many of the sea warriors and yet avoid wounds? Is it this magic sword?" He pointed at Saxon Slayer.

I shook my head. "When we fought the first time, we only had our bows. No, we killed many by tracking them as we would an animal and by knowing our land. Your men will be more skilled than I at that for they know the land."

"Aye, but they do not know how to be cunning. My warriors are all brave but there is recklessness with their bravery. They like to fight a man face to face."

"Then they will lose, for these men from the sea are like lice on a dog. There are always more of them. The only way to defeat them is to make them fear us. We struck in the night and in places they felt they were safe."

We spent the next three days, as we travelled east through the rain, sleet and snow, discussing ways to defeat the enemy and I found myself enjoying the challenge. I was not sure that we would have the same results as I was fighting with men I did not know but it would be a test of my leadership.

The land we crossed was a land devoid of people. It was a land of high moors and thick forests. There were few settlements and those we saw were palisaded and protected. The King visited each one, much as Urien had done, to show the people that he was still king. Finally, we reached the far side of the island of Britannia and I saw the mighty and impregnable stronghold from some distance. It stood on top of rugged rock and was surrounded on three sides by the sea. I could see what the King had meant. I could not see how it could be taken. The land before the castle which was not surrounded by water was marshy and swampy. There was a causeway which the King negotiated skilfully but I knew I would have struggled to find the correct path. The entrance to the castle twisted up and around a narrow path. The gatehouse at the top had a draw bridge, much as the one at Civitas Carvetiorum. There were many armed guards and sentries on the walls for the King had only brought his bodyguards and, as I discovered later, the rest of his army stayed within the walls of Din Guardi. The men at the gates were, however, a surly bunch and I was not made to feel welcome. Already I was wishing myself back in the west with my brothers.

The King wasted no time in putting his ideas into action. He gathered his leaders in his hall. This was the only stone part of the castle and the roaring fire made it a welcoming place unlike the faces of his lieutenants who seemed less than enamoured about being told what to do by someone who appeared to be little more than an overgrown youth. I could not see this working and that thought brightened my mood. If they would not do as I asked then I would have to return home again. The King, however, was in no mood for dissension. "Whoever succeeds in this task will be given command of my bodyguard."

I could see that the obvious bribe worked. As commander of the bodyguard the successful leader would be second only to the King and, as he had no children at the moment, it would put them in a powerful position. I saw the black look the present commander of the bodyguard gave to his king and I hoped that the King knew what he was doing. One of the younger leaders, Riderch, asked, "What does the warrior from the west plan?"

The King looked at me and nodded. "There are two plans. The first requires good weather. We will take a boat across to Metcauld at night and kill their guards."

There was silence and then an older warrior asked, "What will that achieve?"

I looked at the greybeard. "When you sleep in this castle do you feel safe and secure?"

"Of course, I do. What a stupid question."

"And if the sea warriors scaled the walls and slit the sentries' throats? Would you then feel safe?"

They understood my idea and the greybeard grudgingly nodded. Riderch asked, "And the other plan?"

"It is winter and there is a garrison on the island. They will need food. I would expect them to send foraging parties ashore. We find where they come ashore and we ambush them."

They were now intrigued although the ploy seemed obvious to me. "And how would we know where they had come ashore?"

I knew not if I was clever or they were stupid. "If they come from the sea then they are subject to the vagaries of the tide and they must cross the beach. We search the beaches after high tide and follow the footprints. If nothing else we can destroy their boats."

Riderch grinned. I later found him to be an impulsive warrior, "Or steal their boats. This is a good plan, I will go with the man with the wolf skin."

I was given quarters in the castle which showed me that the King, at least, valued my services. I was less convinced about his men and I began to see why he and his men had not aided King Urien. They did not want to take on the Saxons. Having seen their castle I could understand that they would believe that they could hold out and be safe from attack. That policy would not help the people of Bryneich, who would be treated as Monca and her family were, and they would become little more than slaves and thralls of the Saxons.

I dressed for war. The armour might be heavy but I had trained and eaten well. It would do me no harm to have to move long distances dressed as I was. I also took my bow. None of Riderch's fifteen men had bows and they looked at me in disgust for carrying what they thought was a dishonourable weapon; I now understood the King's words about the value his men placed on face to face combat. It did not worry me what they thought of me. My task was to kill Saxons and that I would do.

The first high tide was just after a late dawn and we left at first light to move down the beach seeking tracks. My unvoiced worry was that they would have left guards with the boat who would alert the others. We needed secrecy and surprise. I saw that the dunes extended down the coast.

"Riderch, let us walk among the dunes, it will give us cover and we will still see the footprints."

One of his men grumbled. "Let us walk where they cannot see us and then there will be no chance of combat."

I glared at the man. He was not worth my spit and I could gut him as soon as speak but Riderch restrained me. "It is just words. They do not know you."

Again I wondered at the leadership of these people, even Aelle would have had more control over his unruly boys than Riderch did. I could not see any discipline here and it did not bode well for combat. Once in the dunes, we were able to walk without being marked on the skyline. One of the sharp eyes of the men at the front saw the boat. Some of the men looked around with a look of grudging admiration that I had suggested this plan which might actually be working.

We worked our way down the dunes keeping out of sight until we reached the spot the men had come ashore. We could see the jumble of sandy footprints. Riderch was all for heading for the men but I said, "No. Remember you said we need the boat. Let us take it first."

"How? They will see us as we approach and row out to sea."

I shook my head and held my bow. "Bring your men with me. I might just convert some of them to like the bow." We reached the edge of the dunes and Riderch and I bellied up to the top. There were two men and they were seated at the prow of the boat. The range was a hundred and odd paces. I held up my finger to test the wind. "Now I will kill the men guarding the boats but your men will need to run as soon as I loose to stop the boat drifting off.

The grumbling warrior said, "How do you know you will hit them?"

"The same way I know that the only thing you have between your legs is some scraggly hair."

It took him a moment to realise I had insulted him but by the time he had leapt at me, my dagger was pricking a tendril of blood from his throat. "Go on, I have been itching to gut one of you."

"Back off!" The warrior backed off and Riderch grinned, saying, "You are not a man to cross I can see that." He turned to his men. "You heard the wolf warrior, as soon as the second arrow flies capture the boat and, of course, the first ones there get their weapons." The Saxons were known for fine weapons and that was incentive enough.

I stood so that the top of my head was above the dunes. To the men, I would have appeared as a rock for I had removed my helmet. I chose my best two arrows. I notched one and aimed, even as it sped aloft I notched the second and loosed that. I picked out a third and aimed but I saw the two men plunge over the side into the water and the boat began to ebb with the tide. The men had covered more than half the way they needed to and were able to beach the boat more solidly.

"That was incredible. You can do that every time?"

"Every time. I would have two of your men dress as the Saxons and wait here in case any evade us."

"Good idea." When his exuberant men returned he turned to the grumbling man and a younger version of him. "You two don the Saxon gear and wait by the boat. Kill any Saxons who come near." The grumbling man flashed me an angry glance and then put his finger to his throat where the blood still trickled and he thought better of making more of it. "Now what?"

"We backtrack them to the forest yonder. If they are any good they will have marked their trail to find the boat quickly. That is where we ambush them." Their trail was clear and easy to spot. The sand extended into the forest and I could see their footprints. I led the fourteen warriors into the trees until we were far enough in to be on pine needles. I examined the trees and saw the marks they had made to enable them to find their way back. I showed them to Riderch.

"Impressive. How did you know that?"

"I have used the same trick myself. Had they not used it then they would not be good warriors but we would have struggled to find them.

You take half your men on that side, and I will keep half here. I will step out and kill the warrior at the front and a second if I am able. Then we attack from both sides at the same time. The trees are narrow here and it will give us an advantage."

I looked at the men Riderch had given me. None of them inspired confidence. Some of them were the same age as me but they had pot bellies and the look of men who talk war more than they fight it. My archers were lean and hard fighters. These were not. I was beginning to appreciate just what I had on the west. I took out some dried venison to eat while I waited. Ambushes required patience and I could tell that these men had none and they were restless. "Keep quiet or we will not hear them. When I attack then you follow me." They were not happy but they obeyed me. Suddenly I heard something and I held my hand up. Thirty paces away Riderch's white face looked at me and I nodded. I notched an arrow and held a second in my teeth. I was ten paces ahead of my men and when the lead warrior was twenty paces away I stepped out and sent an arrow to bury itself in his throat. As he dropped I sent my second to kill the warrior following. I dropped my bow and drew my sword and shield I raced to attack the nearest warrior. "Attack!"

I plunged towards them. Their leader had not been one of the first two warriors. I knew he was the leader from the magnificent helmet which had a mask on it and the torc he wore around his neck. He carried a war axe and I roared up to him. He quickly organised his wedge and fifteen warriors who remained came straight for me. I deflected the axe blow with my shield and slashed across his shins with my sword. He screamed in pain. I punched him with my shield and then stabbed the man to his left through the throat. He gurgled his life away at my feet. I saw Riderch and his men to my right but my half of the band were hanging back. Suddenly I was surrounded! The chief was still stunned and so I smashed my shield into him and, as he stumbled, stabbed him in his thigh, a death wound. I felt something sharp in my back followed by a hard blow as though struck by a hammer and I spun around, smashing the edge of my shield, which was lined with nails, into his face. I saw another warrior looming up at me and I had no time to swing my sword and so I punched with the sword guard. I heard his nose break and as he recoiled I brought the blade down; he must have had a poorly made helmet for my blade went through the helmet and split his skull open. Then Riderch was next to me and the Saxons lost heart with the death of their chief. They ran.

"After them or they may escape!"

"Run! Do as the wolf warrior says!" I dropped to my knees. I felt weak. Riderch's face filled with concern. "What is it?"

"I think I was stabbed from behind."

He put his hand underneath my armour and it came away bloody. "Quick, take off your armour."

"No, let us get to the boat. I am not dying. I will follow." Pausing only to take the chief's fine helmet and his torc, I limped to the beach. The cut had not hurt me but the blow had. I wondered what weapon had caused it.

The Saxons fleeing to the beach had put up a good fight and, as we approached, the last of them was slain but there were the bodies of Riderch's men to show the battle they had given to stay alive. To see the way Riderch's men carried on you would have thought they had killed a whole Saxon army and not a mere handful of raiders.

Riderch was angry with his men and I knew why. The ones with me had held back and nearly cost me my life. "You five, go to the forest and bring the bodies, the raiders and ours." He looked at the others and said, "You four, strip the bodies of armour, swords and anything else of value. Put them in the bottom of the boat." Then he turned to me. "Now will you let me look at you?" He sounded like a mother scolding a naughty child and I smiled and nodded.

He pulled the armour off and gave it for me to view. I had been struck by an axe and it had given me the smack. The tip of the blade had penetrated and cut my skin but it was not a deep wound. I was certain that I had some broken ribs but my armour and the padding had saved me. "That armour saved your life. If it had struck my mail then I would be dead."

The men returned with the bodies and the booty. They had obviously raided a farming family for they had slaughtered a cow and a pig. It made me even angrier than I was before because those people had had no protection from these fat overfed warriors who were so reluctant to fight. "Who were the warriors who were supposed to follow me?" Three men looked shamefaced and one of them pointed to four of the bodies. "They did not deserve to live." I whipped out my sword and held it to the neck of the nearest one. "I should kill you all now! But you have no honour and do not know what you have done. You are not warriors, you are fat overpaid and lazy guards! You are excrement on my shoe!"

They recoiled and the man I had threatened fell to the floor sobbing. "My lord, forgive us, we were afraid."

I turned and said to Riderch, "Next time leave these women at home because they cannot be trusted."

As we rowed back to the stronghold the warriors were more subdued. Riderch spent the journey back asking me questions. "Where did you get the armour and the sword?" That and a thousand others poured from his lips. Although tired I felt I owed him the answers for he had been the only one of the leaders to volunteer to come with me.

"I can see that there is an aura about you. Perhaps *wyrd* brought you here."

"You are not of the White Christ then?"

"No, I keep the old ways." He leaned into me to speak confidentially, "I think our King keeps a foot in both camps if you know what I mean."

The King was delighted with our success and promoted Riderch immediately. Some of the other leaders questioned the losses. I was about to open my mouth and mention the civilian casualties but I refrained from doing so. This was not my land and soon I would be safely back home. The King showed his regal qualities and he firmly put those gainsayers in their place. "We have destroyed a whole band of Saxons. We have gained their boat and their arms and we have lost what? A handful of men and, from what Lord Riderch tells me," I saw him puff up at the first use of his title, "those four were cowards who deserved to die." He looked at his new deputy. "Tell me, Riderch, could you lead such a raid again without Lord Lann?" I didn't like to tell him I was not a lord. I just kept a stony, impassive face.

"I could, your majesty." His face broke into a smile, "Although I would prefer him to be with me for he is a fearsome fighter. He took an axe blow to the back which would have felled an oak and still killed four warriors who had surrounded him."

Even the gainsayers were impressed by that. "And that is the reason why I would like to husband his skills and learn more of his ways. He is to be with us for a short time and we need to make the most of his knowledge which," he gave me a measured look, "has exceeded my expectations I must confess."

After we had eaten he took me to one side and poured me a beaker of the local drink made with honey. "Lann, you did well today and I can see that you impressed my men. Why do you not stay and serve me as my deputy? Together we could conquer all that the Saxons took from us."

I was shocked. Riderch had risked his life and yet the King would give me his position without a second thought and he wanted me to betray my king. "I swore an oath to King Urien."

"On a holy relic?"

"No, I gave him my word."

He seemed relieved. "Urien is a Christian; an oath to him is not binding unless sworn on either a relic or one of the White Christ holy books."

"That matters not, your majesty. I gave my word and it is binding to me. I am Urien's man until death."

He looked amazed that I would not betray two men. "If you reconsider then let me know." He then dismissed the idea as though I would eventually come around to his way of thinking. "Now the raid on the island; I want you to lead it but not put yourself in harm's way. You are too valuable."

"May I speak honestly, your majesty?"

His eyes belied his answer, "Of course."

"In my experience, a leader who does not fight alongside his men is not a leader and his men will soon realise that. I will lead the raid but, believe me, I will return. I am not destined to die here. I will die far from here."

I had silenced him with my conviction. "You are a most interesting man and I look forward to getting to know you a little better."

When I was in my quarters I examined the damage I had suffered. My body would heal and the scar would be a small one. My ribs hurt, especially when I breathed hard, but they would repair. My wolf cloak had helped to save my life but I would need a new one. The armour was in urgent need of repair and that would be my task before I risked my life for King Morcant again. I spent the rest of the evening repairing my scales.

The tides and the weather were not right for a week which gave me time to heal and repair my armour and cloak. I also spent time with Riderch and the men who would be coming on the raid with us. We had supplemented our original band with another fifteen volunteers. I was interested to see that the keenest ones were the three who had failed me the first time. Riderch and I would take two boats; the Saxon one we had acquired and a similar one owned by the King. I would only take command once we were ashore for I was no seaman. Riderch told me that there was a causeway to the island which was heavily guarded. It was only usable at low tide but it meant we knew where the guards would be. We could see the stronghold on a clear day and they had built a formidable wooden fort on another crag similar to the one King Morcant used. Riderch knew the area well and we planned to use the side away from our castle for the approach. I knew that my bow would be crucial to silence sentries. We were taking flint and kindling for I planned to burn their boats. They could build new ones but it would take time and they would need to come to the mainland for wood and then King Morcant could bring them to battle. The one thing which worried me was how many men they had. No-one had bothered to count them. There might only be fifty or there could be a thousand. That was part of our task.

We set off after dark after a very short day. The men were all good seamen and they rowed us directly out to sea and then turned north. I could not tell where we were but Riderch and the helmsman seemed to be confident about our position. I saw the dark shape of the island on our left and we slowly made our way north. We were the lead boat and Riderch slowed down the strokes so that we were barely making way. I was peering into the dark for the tell-tale pinprick of light that would show where there was a fire. Eventually, Riderch seemed satisfied and we headed into the part of the island where it joined the causeway. He did not beach the boat but left three men with it and we slipped over the side into the bone-chillingly cold water. The second boat ghosted up alongside us and the other warriors joined us. I notched an arrow and followed Riderch across the swampy area filled with the Saxons' cattle. They barely made a sound as we moved through them and, in fact, they aided our subterfuge. Any guards watching from the ramparts would just see cows moving. I was now confident that the indolence of Morcant and his men had made them complacent and they only kept a desultory watch on the causeway.

We reached the rock and I was pleased to see that they had been too lazy to dig a ditch. We headed east towards the beached Saxon ships. Riderch and ten men were assigned to firing the ships while I had the rest in case we were attacked. Riderch and his men had been gone for moments when I saw something white on the ramparts. It was a guard. I could not see another but I knew that he could not help but see Riderch. I said quietly, "Prepare yourselves, we are about to be seen." I sent the arrow to plunge into his neck and I heard a thump as he fell from the ramparts. It would now be a matter of time before they found his body and knew they were under attack. "Spread out in a semi-circle with me in the centre. The guards from the causeway may come first."

As I glanced to my right I saw the three warriors I had berated. I smiled. They were trying to atone. Suddenly I saw torches and lights moving along the ramparts. I hoped that Riderch had managed to fire the boats or we would be in trouble and very soon. As soon as I saw a face I loosed an arrow and there was a scream and then silence. It was then I needed all my archers for a forest of faces appeared at the top of the rampart. I loosed four arrows in quick succession although only three found their mark but at least it kept their heads down and made them cautious.

Suddenly the sea behind us was illuminated by the eight boats set ablaze and pushed into the sea. Riderch raced towards us his face filled with excitement.

I could see that he was elated but I needed him to concentrate. "No time for congratulations, they are awake; back to the boats!" I did not want Riderch to get carried away with his victory. He nodded and raced past me. I walked steadily backwards watching for the Saxons who would flood after us soon enough. A sudden lightening of the walls showed me where the gate was and I killed two of the first four men who ran out. They seemed more intent with salvaging the boats and I kept retreating. I loosed two more arrows at warriors who had thrown caution to the wind and then I heard a shout behind me. "My lord, they are upon us!"

My three companions had stayed with me. I slipped my shield around to my front and put my bow over my back. Drawing my sword, I said, "Two of you stand on either side of me and one behind me. Keep your shields held tight together." I kept walking backwards as they joined me. Over my shoulder, I said to the warrior behind me. "Turn around and guide us. Prevent them surrounding us." I glanced at the two warriors who looked a little fearful as fifteen Saxons raced towards us. I gave them what I hoped was a reassuring smile, a smile I didn't feel. "Just keep together and we will beat them."

One of the Saxons saw the helmet I wore, the one I had taken from the dead chief. "So you are the dog who killed my cousin. Did you ambush him and stab him in the back?"

"No, Saxon, I faced him and his men tried to stab me in the back but Saxon Slayer will drink more Saxon blood this night."

The taunt worked and he threw himself at me. He had not bothered to don armour and it cost him his life. He smashed his axe at my shield and, as the blade bit, I stabbed him in the stomach twisting the sword as I withdrew it. His entrails spilled on the ground. The warrior on my left took the opportunity of smashing his sword on the unprotected head of a second Saxon whose skull was split open like a ripe plum. They were warier now, even though they outnumbered us. "How far?"

"Forty paces to the water, my lord."

"Can you see the boats?"

"No, my lord."

"Fear not, Lord Riderch will not desert us. When we are within twenty paces then tell me."

The Saxons suddenly launched themselves in a furious attack but there were too many of them to be effective. Some slipped in the mud and the gore, while others hit their comrades' weapons. We had the advantage that we could just stab forwards and whatever we struck was an enemy.

"Twenty paces!"

"When I shout go, push forward with your shields and then we run for the boats."

There was a chorus of, "Yes, my lord."

"Go!"

We all pushed and, as they pushed back, we were gone and they fell to the ground. I paused, took the axe from my shield and threw it in the direction of the band that chased us. *Wyrd* was with me as I struck one of those pursuing us and then I ran. I hoped that my judgement of Riderch was sound; otherwise, I would have a cold and watery end. The icy waters were around my thighs when I felt the wood of the boat nudge gently into me. Riderch's smiling face was above me as he and two others hauled me aboard. "So, my lord, you cannot fight just one man at a time, you have to take on a whole warband."

"Except that this time, my lord, I was not alone, I had warriors with me."

# Chapter 9

My standing rose considerably when we returned. The three warriors who had stood by me were now lauded as great warriors and Riderch was seen as a warlord. Half of the Saxon boats had been wrecked and burned. A couple had been salvaged and there were a few on the other beach but their raids would be hampered. The bad news was that we could now estimate their numbers and it was likely that there were six or seven hundred on the island. The King could now see the advantage of an alliance. Riderch was confident enough to take another band seeking Saxons. The parlous state of the Saxon stronghold meant that they risked the stormy seas and the ambushes to try to gather supplies. The sea took two boats and Riderch destroyed two warbands who tried to gather supplies.

By the end of the month, the King summoned me to his quarters. "You have fulfilled your part of the bargain, Lord Lann. Can I not entreat you to join me and my army? My men hold you in the highest regard. Together we could create a kingdom to rival that of Rome."

I worried about his ambition. It was all well and good to talk of defeating the Saxons on the borders of the kingdoms but it would take many years to build an army big enough to drive them home. "As I said, your majesty, when I am released from my oath by King Urien then I would deem it an honour to serve you but until then I must, perforce, rejoin my King and my brothers."

He reluctantly nodded, "But I have King Urien's promise that you and your brothers will come to train my archers. Your skill has impressed my men."

"Yes, your majesty and Riderch now knows how to make stronger shields. You have made a wise choice in him; he is a good leader."

The King was silent on the matter. I think he regretted his impulsive decision. Riderch had seemed like a keen and naive young warrior who could be dominated by the King but I had seen he had a mind of his own and, I had heard, the queen was now with child so perhaps he rued his rash promise.

I left the next day. I was touched by the turn out of warriors who wished to say goodbye. I was pleased that I had made friends. When the army of Rheged came east there would be one band of warriors on whom I could rely; the band of Riderch.

Blackie enjoyed the freedom of the road as we rode west. I regretted the lack of warm, dry beds. But I enjoyed the lack of responsibility. It also gave me the opportunity to examine the land we would pass through in the spring. I headed across the high ground for it was drier and there were forests which provided shelter. It was also further away from the Dunum; who knew if the Saxons had crossed it? I came across the old Roman road which still headed north. In places there were tufts of grass and weeds showing the lack of traffic but, almost five hundred years after it was built, it still stood testament to the skill of the soldier-builders. I saw another of the Roman forts. The soldiers of Rome had done their best to destroy the defences but they had built well and the stone bases still stood. If King Morcant Bulc had a mind he could easily fortify this one and it would be a defence against the Saxons, here on the western edge of his lands.

I completed the journey in two days. I was a more confident rider and I no longer feared falling off at anything more than a walk. Of course, I would not dream of fighting on horseback but I could allow Blackie to trot quite quickly and, occasionally, when I felt reckless, allow him to gallop. Brother Osric had told me that the Roman soldiers fed their horses grain. I marvelled at the luxury that had been Rome; they had so much food that they could give their horses grain. We had barely enough for the people let alone our horses but I did spoil Blackie and knew that if I came across some grain then he would have it.

When I reached the fort, I felt relieved. The sentries greeted me warmly although I could see that the garrison was not at home. The training ground, the area the Romans had called the gyrus, was empty. I stabled Blackie and told the stable boy to take special care of him. I had taken a bracelet from the dead chief and I gave it to the stable master. It was a blatant bribe but Blackie was valuable to me and I would have him cared for. After I had deposited my arms and gear in the barracks I took the helmet and the torc with me to the blacksmith's workshop.

Aed was a squat man, as broad as he was tall but he was a wonder with metals. "That is as fine a helmet as I have ever seen. Where did you get it?"

"A Saxon chief."

"Do you wish me to make more of them? It would take much metal and time."

"No, Aed, I have worn it and the eyepieces are too small. I would have them made bigger to enable me to see better and I have this." I gave him the torc.

"It is not gold."

I laughed, "I know but it is the colour of gold. I would have this melted down and used to reinforce the eyepieces, the crown and the nasal."

He nodded appreciatively. "That will indeed make it stronger and make it look magnificent."

"How much?" I knew he would do it for nothing but my father had taught me that a good workman was worthy of the hire.

"The metal from the torc that I do not need to use?"

I clasped his huge forearm. "Thank you, Aed."

My next visit was to Brother Osric. It would save me many questions later on. He looked up in surprise when I entered. "We did not expect you for another week at least."

"My job was done."

He leaned back and gestured towards the wooden seat across from his desk. "Tell me all." He took his quill. "I am keeping a record for future generations." I detailed all that I had done, omitting my opinions of both the Bryneicians and their king but I did give him a detailed description of the castle. When I had finished, he took a jug from beneath his desk and two beakers. "Try this. A ship was wrecked in the estuary and some jugs were washed ashore. I have not tasted the like for many years."

I sipped the red liquid, which looked like blood. "What is it?"

"It is wine. It used to be drunk all across the Empire but, now, sadly, it is reserved for kings and high churchmen. What do you think?"

"It is not as refreshing as beer but the taste is warming."

Brother Osric nodded enthusiastically. "Yes, it is a winter drink, especially on a cold day like this. Now your report was interesting but there were many things you left unsaid." His eyes felt as though they were boring into your mind, "Things to do with the King."

I started. Was he a witch? Could he read my mind? "I wanted to give you what actually happened at Din Guardi, Brother Osric, and not my opinion."

"Your opinion is valuable to me. Some men's opinion I disregard but you are an honest warrior and, more importantly, you are intelligent. That is a rare combination. You may tell me all and I will assess the importance of your words and your opinion."

I told him everything, including his attempt to subvert me to his side. "Interesting. Were you not tempted? From what you say you would have been rewarded with titles as well as treasure."

"I gave my word to the King and," I felt uncomfortable saying this, "I like King Urien and believe he is an honourable man. For me, he is the only chance this land has of freedom from Saxon rule. King Morcant wants, I think, power for him alone and thinks nothing of his people. He was not concerned with the raids on his farmers for he was safe in his stronghold. I do not think Urien would hide away if his people were suffering."

"You may be right, although kings sometimes have to act in ways which make the people suffer, for the good of the land." He looked at me shrewdly, like a thrush assessing how to get into a snail shell.

"You mean like leaving my home to be attacked because it was too far away to be helped?"

"I knew you were clever. I mean exactly that."

I nodded. "He could have done little save garrisoning our hill fort and my father and the others would have resented that. I think my home was destroyed because we did nothing to help ourselves. That will not happen to me."

"Well, I have enjoyed our little talk. The King took the army out on a march to prepare them for the coming campaign. They will return tonight." He looked out of the window. "Probably within the next hour."

I had no idea how he estimated time. I knew that the priests used candles and hourglasses to measure time but I did not understand it. He was like a magician who had knowledge hidden from us.

My brothers and Ywain were pleased to see me. Even as their men were making their weary way back to the barracks, they asked question after question. I felt as though I was being attacked by arrows not words. Later, when my brothers and I took a walk by the river I told them all that I had told Brother Osric. They both insisted upon seeing the wound in my back. "I was grateful for the extra protection of the wolf skin and I am glad that we have a spare. Make sure you both wear it over your mail for it will help to protect you. And how are the slingers and the archers coming along?"

"Much better. We have more recruits now and with many archers and more slingers; we are now a force to be reckoned with."

"I do not understand why the bow is not used more. Perhaps warriors just want the easy route of the sword."

"Is it easy, brother?" Aelle rarely used his sword.

"I find it so. It just seems to come naturally."

"Could I learn?" Although he was older than Raibeart something had happened when he was young to take all the confidence from him. Monca had never told us about just what the father of Aelle had done to them both but whatever it was, it had damaged Aelle. Perhaps she had confided in my parents; we would never know."

"Of course, and we will teach you."

The King sent for me the next day and I met him in Brother Osric's office. As there were just two seats I stood. It was obvious to me that he had been briefed by Brother Osric but what he had told him I did not know. "Did you see many Saxons, Lann?"

"Yes, but only on the island. The problem the King has is that come the spring and more clement weather they can raid all up and down the coast and the King…" I hesitated, unsure if I ought to carry on.

"Go on. I must have honesty from my men."

I bridled a little; I had always been honest with him. "The King seems happy to stay in his stronghold which overlooks his enemies. He can stop raids which are close to the castle but they can raid as far south as the Dunum. Once they learn that they can sail up that river then our lands will be in danger."

"Thank you. That is a worrying thought. Now, and tell me true, can we beat them?"

I smiled, "Easily. They have neither archers nor horsemen and even on their island, they are vulnerable. We raided and destroyed half of their ships with but thirty men. With an army, we could defeat them completely."

"Who is their leader?"

"He is a king called Ida. The King told me that one of the kings of the Saxons was called Ida but I am not sure if it is the same man."

"I am pleased that you are back; the men have missed their wolf warrior with the Saxon Slayer." He held up maps which I knew Brother Osric had been making for him. "We have begun to march the men to prepare them for a long campaign. Brother Osric told me the Romans used it as a way to toughen their men up. We will take them out again tomorrow and march to the coast and back. You say that you managed to travel across from King Morcant's land in two days?"

"Riding a horse, yes."

"Then we should be able to do it in three. I will send north for King Rhydderch and his army. They are stout warriors but they have neither horse nor archers. I suspect you and your archers will be in action more than the rest of the army."

"My brother has told me that they are trained well and have responded to their new weapons. They will not let you down."

"Good, but remember, soon I want you to take over half of the men at arms with Ywain. It is blade to blade which will win us this war."

I did not take Blackie the next day. There was little point other than to make me stand out from my men and I chose to march alongside them. I did, however, wear my new helmet. I picked it up from Aed as soon as he began work. He was proud of his handiwork and I was ecstatic. The new golden metal gleamed like gold. I knew that it was not, it was a mix of bronze, silver and iron but it made the helmet look magnificent. The enlarged eyepieces had been lined with the same metal and the face mask now looked like a face, complete with teeth and a grim grin. "You have excelled yourself, Aed. Was there enough metal left to make it worth your while?"

"Aye. I have used it on the new sword for the King." He showed me the King's new blade and the golden metal ran down the middle. "It is easier to engrave and the King would have words written on it." He looked to the heavens. "Brother Osric will have to write them and I will copy them for I can neither read nor write. It is your sword which made him order one. He says that two such swords will drive the wolves from our land."

I put the helmet on and was delighted with the vision I had. The first time I had worn it I felt as though I could only see ahead; now I had good vision all around but I had better protection. When I approached my men, I laughed behind my mask as I saw their jaws drop. My wolf cloak marked me as Lann but the mask made me something else. I removed it and the King and his men rode up. "A fine helmet; a trophy from the east perhaps?"

"Yes, your majesty, although it nearly cost me my life."

We marched along the old Roman Road with the wall and the river to our right. To reach the sea we would have to march more than twelve miles and the same distance back. If nothing else it would make the men fitter. My brothers and I had the advantage of caligae soles on our boots and the marching was easy. Some of the older men struggled with poor footwear. I regretted not bringing more of the precious footwear from the fort.

We were halfway there when the King halted the column and summoned his officers. I left Raibeart in command and hurried to his side. "The scouts have reported an Irish fleet in the estuary. It looks as though they have planned a raid. They are not expecting us. They think we will be safe in our stronghold." He threw me a knowing look. "I intend to use the Roman wall as our bastion and ambush them. We will let them land. I will take my bodyguard east towards the gate a mile down the wall. The rest will remain here under the command of Ywain my son. As soon as they land our swords and spears will form before the wall and the archers and slingers on the wall." I could see that he intended to use the same strategy which had worked against the Saxons. I thought it might well succeed against Hibernians who had not met it before. "We will then charge them from the flank and the only place they will have left to go will be into the river or the sea."

As he rode away I sent Aelle and his slingers to crawl on top of the wall and act as lookouts. Ywain and Gildas organised their men into ranks. We had devised a strategy which used the spearmen with shields in the front rank; those without shields in the second and the sword and axe men in the third. They stood behind the wall waiting for the command to take up their positions. Aelle slithered down. "They are almost ashore."

"Position your slingers in front of the spearmen and assault them as they advance. Then retreat to the flanks."

I nodded to Ywain. He roared, "Men of Rheged take your positions."

The two hundred men quickly climbed the wall and descended on the other side. I could hear the ping of stones as Aelle and his boys set to work and I was gratified to hear an occasional scream. "Archers, to the wall!"

Our men quickly took up their positions. Once at the top, I was daunted by the number of ships. There were twenty and each one looked as though it held thirty to forty men. We were outnumbered but they were not organised and all that they saw was the small number of spears and bows close to the wall. "Pull!" Each man now knew what to do and the bows came up as one. "Loose! Pull! Loose! Pull! Loose!" After three flights I looked at the Irish. They had been caught unawares. Many were killed as they struggled up the muddy bank while others had yet to don helmets or bring their shields around. The slingers were also causing much damage and the attack stalled. I wondered if the ships which had yet to disembark would turn and run but their leader was made of sterner stuff. I heard orders barked out and those on the riverbank formed a shield wall. It would stop casualties from a mass of arrows but my men could now aim.

"Archers! Kill them and show them how well my brother Raibeart has trained you!" I saw Raibeart look around in gratitude and the archers began to pick their targets. I saw the surprise on faces as arrows found the narrow gap between shield and helmet. Soon there was no gap but my men began to aim at the Hibernians' thighs. The range was only forty paces and the arrows did terrible damage. Finally, their leader had had enough of taking punishment and, as he now had over three hundred men ashore, he launched a wild attack. As soon as he did so my archers had easier targets but that meant they ran out of arrows quickly. I looked down at my empty quiver. "Raibeart, take charge of the archers. I will join Prince Ywain." He nodded and I saw that he still had six arrows. Either he had brought more or he had been more careful than I had. I joined the left-hand side of the front rank. It was the most vulnerable part of the line and I knew that while Ywain was on the right it was Gildas on the left and he was the less experienced of the three of us.

My archers still had spare arrows and they were slowing down the enemy. It would soon end. The screaming, snarling faces of the Irish were desperate to get to grips with the fleas and gnats that had irritated them and caused so many casualties. I drew my sword and I felt the line bristle as the men realised that the mystical sword was going into action. I watched as Aelle and his slingers fled to the security of the wall just behind us. They had plenty of stones and they would continue to hurl them at the enemy even when the archers ran out of arrows.

There was a clash and roar as the Irish hit our line. The spears might have shattered and broken but they caused many casualties amongst the brave warriors in the van of the Irish attack. I had no spear but I took the swinging axe from the tall warrior on my boss and twisted the shield so that the blade ended embedded in the mud. I brought the sword overhand and stabbed downwards between the shield and the helmet. When he tried to bring his shield upwards he just succeeded in directing the sword into his own throat and he gurgled his lifeblood away. The press of men was so great that it was a pushing match. We had the advantage that we had a wall behind us and still had men with spears who could jab and stab above the front line. The disadvantage was that when the men with the shields in the front rank fell then the warriors who replaced them were shieldless. Their leader was in the middle and he was a powerful warrior. Soon he began to drive in like a wedge, threatening to split our forces in two. "Aelle! Take out the leader!"

Suddenly stones and lead balls began to thunder and crash around the leader and the warriors closest to him. Most did no damage but at least five struck the warriors who were near to him and our line stabilised. I could see that the Irish were concentrating on the middle and I yelled again. "Raibeart, bring the archers to me!" They might have no more arrows but all had a sword and half had a shield. If we could pressure the enemy's right flank then the King and his horsemen might have a chance. I could not use my sword's blade but I could use the pommel and the guard. I was able to punch the warriors in the face. The ornate pommel had sharp edges and I blinded two warriors. They would not use the same technique on me for I had the face mask. When the pressure dropped on my left arm I punched hard with the shield and had the satisfaction of punching over a warrior. As I stamped on his nose I slid my sword in his throat and, for the first time, we moved forwards. "Gildas! Get to my right."

Gildas was a good swordsman but a little slight. He could stab while I pushed. I felt a shield at my back and then Raibeart stepped next to me. He grinned at me and I grinned back before I realised he could see nought but the mask. When I heard the ghostly wailing of the standard I yelled. "Now push. Let us drive them back into the sea."

I was determined to make my way to the leader of the Irish warband. If he died then the rest would lose heart. They still outnumbered us but I hoped that the attack on their flanks might make them return to their ships. The warrior before me was fighting a spearman on my right and I had no compunction in sinking my sword through him. I pushed so hard that the blade stabbed the man next to him and Gildas killed the man to their right. Suddenly there was a hole in their line and we had our own wedge, informal though it might have been. Raibeart pushed hard on my left as I punched hard at the warrior before me. I could hear stones crashing into the helmets and faces of the men before me and they held their shields up to defend themselves. They left themselves vulnerable and the shorter swords of the archers stabbed upwards ripping savage wounds in the Irish warriors' bodies.

The Irish leader, wielding a double handed sword, had managed to clear enough space to swing it around him and he was causing carnage amongst the spearmen. He was encased in mail, including his head, and Aelle's slingshots were having little effect. The warrior to his right, a bodyguard, turned to face me. I struck down with my sword; the blow was so hard it shattered his sword in two and continued to slice downwards from his neck, piercing mail and skin to lay him open like a butchered deer. He still had a surprised look as he fell dead at my feet. The huge sword was still keeping all at bay. I held my shield above my head and dived to hack at the knee of the leader. Although he had mail it could not withstand Saxon Slayer and I felt it bite into bone. He roared with anger and tried to smash his sword down upon my head. I lifted my shield higher and I was almost driven into the ground by the force but the double layers of leather and the iron held the blade fast and my sword came up under his arm to emerge in his neck. The spurting blood showered us all but a collective wail from the enemy went up as the huge warrior fell. His few remaining bodyguards gathered about the body, to become fodder for the angry spearmen and swordsmen, while those at the rear fled through the red waters of the river to reach the safety of their ships. The horsemen of the King drove the last remnants into the water where they were slaughtered before they could escape. All but two ships escaped but they had a skeleton crew on board. It would be many years before they risked a slave raid on Rheged's coast.

The aftermath of any battle is never pleasant and this one was no exception. The Irish, regardless of their wounds, were killed while those of our own too badly injured to be healed were given a merciful death by their comrades. We all had some skills with wounds and those with cuts and lighter wounds were dressed and bandaged. A fire was started to cauterize the deeper wounds and the King sent his bodyguard back to the city for wagons. I went over to Ywain. "It would be quicker to use those two Irish boats and row back to the fortress. It will save time."

"I will get men aboard them."

I took off my helmet. It had, undoubtedly, saved me from serious injury but it was hot wearing it in battle. Aelle and Raibeart joined me and we embraced. Every battle was your own personal battle and you saw only those men who fell around you. I was always grateful to see their smiling faces. "Thank you, brother. Your boys did well. I could hear the missiles striking them."

Aelle's face became serious. "We need more metal shot. They are more accurate and they cause better wounds."

I gestured at the battlefield. "Get your boys to gather up as much metal as they can before it is taken as booty." As he left, I said, "We had better collect any undamaged arrows."

Raibeart looked at the scene of devastation and carnage. "I think there will be precious few of those."

"You are right. We need to carry a spare quiver for each of the men on horses. We will use our four horses to do so. It almost cost us dear when we ran out."

When he had gone to organise the men, I walked to the river to wash my face. The water was a muddy red colour but I was beyond caring. I needed cooling down. When I stood Ywain and Gildas were next to me. "That was well done, Lann. I was terrified of having to face that huge warrior. Were you not afraid?"

"Shitting myself, I always am, but somehow that helps me to think a little clearer. I reasoned that once he began his swing it would be hard to reverse its direction and so it proved. Half the skill in fighting is letting your opponent defeat himself." I pointed to their swords. "You can, of course, make your weapons more effective. I punch with my sword guard and the sharp edges cause wounds. Notice on my boss, there is a nail protruding. I put a fresh one in each time I fight. But I have decided that I want two sheaths for daggers on the inside of my shield. When you are fighting close, sometimes you cannot swing your sword but a dagger could be used."

"Ah, there they are; my heroes who held the line magnificently." King Urien was obviously proud of his son and his nephew. He embraced them in turn and then hugged me. "When I saw the numbers and how you were pressed, I thought that all was lost."

"It would have been, father, but for the archers; when they ran out of arrows, they gave us extra numbers against their flanks."

"We will not run out again, King Urien. We will make more and carry them with us to the battle."

"Do not be hard on yourself. We did not know we would be fighting today."

"No, King Urien, but we were ready and I am pleased with that more than anything and," I spread my arms out, "we have more arms and mail as a result. This is a victory in every sense of the word. When we go to aid your allies, we will go as victors and not novices."

The King looked at me and nodded, "And we will go with a champion; a warrior who can beat the best that they have. We have Lann, Champion of Rheged."

All the men around who heard, cheered. All the warriors save one, Bladud, who cast me another hateful glance. I had made my enemy have even more reason to hate me.

# Chapter 10

The stronghold was a hive of activity over the next couple of weeks. Replacement warriors were sought. Although the numbers were short of what we needed we had volunteers at least, and new weapons were made. Our archers did not practise but made arrows and bows instead. Poor Aed was almost worked to death. Aelle took to making the shot for the slings himself. He used the forge and melted the metal while Aed grabbed some sleep. He had his boys make the moulds and they produced high-quality slingshot in short order. They seemed quite happy smoothing them off to make them polished. Aelle was a quiet, yet clever man. He deduced that the sand on the seashore and rivers was produced by rocks crashing onto rocks and he made a series of boxes which he filled with stones and his uneven shot. The boys shook the boxes and, after a few hours, what remained were smooth stone, shot and fine sand.

King Rhydderch and his army arrived just when the snowdrops were dying. Green was sprouting everywhere and we were as ready as we could be. His army was not impressive. There were five hundred warriors and they all looked like his bodyguards if a little smaller in stature. They favoured two-handed weapons such as axes and war hammers. Most of them did not bother with shields and few had armour. They seemed to regard the use of a helmet as almost dishonourable and cowardly! They were however brave and keen. The King assured us that they would never retreat. Part of me wondered about that; sometimes a retreat might be the right strategy. But I kept my own counsel.

Ywain came to see me the night before we left. "Bladud has been very quiet of late. I would watch your back."

I laughed, "I have watched my back ever since I met him. He just does not like me, does he?"

"I confess that I was always a little afraid of him. I feared he was such a powerful warrior that he would take the throne from my father."

"But your father is a great warrior. I have seen him on the battlefield and his bodyguards are devoted to him."

"Father's trouble is that he is too honourable. He believes the best in all men and he remembers how Bladud saved his life. He trusts him implicitly."

"Then we shall all have to watch Bladud closely."

"There is another thing." He hesitated as though unsure how to continue. "My father would like Raibeart alone to lead the archers. He wishes you to command the swordsmen while Gildas has the spears."

"But I am a good archer!"

Ywain shook his head ruefully. "You are the best but you are the most skilful warrior with a sword we have. However, more than that, the men see you as something of a symbol, the Wolf Warrior, the Saxon Slayer, the Mystical Sword. These are all names by which you are known."

"And what of you, Prince Ywain?"

He looked embarrassed and looked at the ground. "I am to command the whole army save father's bodyguard. He will command the combined armies."

I suspect he thought I would resent his promotion but I was delighted for him. He was a thoughtful leader and the men would not suffer. While his father lived the strategy would be the King's but he would lead the men well. "If I might make a suggestion, Prince Ywain?"

"Ywain, please. Of course; what is it?"

"We need a banner for the army. Somewhere we can rally around and a method of sending signals." He looked confused. "When your father rides to battle he has the dragon standard which all men see and hear but when we fight then you and I shout our orders. In the press and clash of battle, voices can be silenced by the noise."

It was as though a light had gone off in his head for he suddenly smiled. "Yes, and we need standards for the men; the archers, the spears and the swords." I smiled and nodded my approval. I had not thought of that but it would be a good idea. "I shall have a flag with a dragon on it."

"Like your father's?"

"Yes, but instead of a white dragon, I shall have a red dragon. And you shall have a wolf."

"No, I will let my brothers have a wolf for I am to fight with the swords, am I not?"

He nodded, it made sense and the archers would love the idea. We spent the next hour working out some simple signals. Once we were satisfied then we sought Gildas and my brothers. They had to be as confident about using them as we were. Ywain was so excited he sought his mother to ask her and the ladies of the court to sew two standards, a red dragon and a red wolf. My brothers and I went to the forge where we painted our shields with the red wolf. The Wolf

Brethren were going to war and their enemies would know who they were.

When we left the next day, the standards were still being made but Ywain left two of his younger brothers with their mother to bring the completed standards with them. The army looked magnificent as it set off. The two kings led the column: King Urien with sixty horsemen and King Rhydderch with fifty axemen. King Rhydderch's five hundred warriors followed and then the archers and slingers who were led by my brothers with their wolf skins gleaming. Prince Ywain came next on his white charger. I followed with my three hundred swordsmen; all of them proud to be following the Wolf Warrior and his Saxon Slayer. Lord Gildas guarded the wagons and spare horses with his two hundred spearmen. It was the largest army any of us, the King included, had ever seen, and we could not see how we could lose. We had servants and slaves this time with the horses and wagons. Our four horses carried spare arrows while armour, weapons and more arrows, as well as tents and skins, were in the wagons. I knew that the wagons would slow us down but I also knew that we needed the supplies they carried.

The King had said we would do the journey in three days- we took four. The wagons and the rains slowed us down but they did, at least, allow the standards to catch up with us. The two young princes both begged their brother to allow them to become the standard bearers. They were both still little more than boys but they were like their brother and they had true hearts. He could not gainsay them but he asked them to keep both the standards and their role quiet until he could tell his father.

Even though I had been honest in my description of the fortress of Din Guardi, the kings, princes and my brothers were taken aback by its site and the imposing nature of its defences.

"With that as my castle, I could hold the whole of Britannia."

We were walking up the ramp which led to the castle. "You would need to have other forts guarding the road, your majesty."

King Urien nodded at my words. "I see what you meant, Lann; this does give security to the King and his men. They would never fear being ousted from such a castle, made by God and improved by man."

The guards all recognised me and I was greeted with smiles and nudges. Prince Ywain said, "It seems that Lord Lann has a reputation on this side of the land too."

I just kept my head down. I did not take compliments well. Riderch almost ran up to me to embrace me. "We have captured two more ships and ambushed thirty more warriors and we now have some bows. We await the lessons from your archers eagerly." His words gushed out like a river over a waterfall.

The honest and open warrior was suddenly aware that kings and princes were watching him closely. He gave a slight apologetic incline of his head and I said, "Do not worry, old friend. They like to see an enthusiastic warrior." I lowered my voice. "A little different from my first visit, eh?"

"Do not remind me. I am ashamed of the way we behaved."

"You redeemed yourself tenfold as did your men."

We had a feast which was attended by just the kings, princes, champions, and commanders. Bladud had accompanied the King although Ywain said, somewhat petulantly, "It should just be you who is here. He is no longer the champion."

"Peace. I am not concerned. I know that King Morcant keeps a good table and the mead is fine. Just enjoy the evening and do not worry about one sour-faced warrior."

The feast was indeed gargantuan and King Morcant Bulc was going out of his way to impress his peers. Riderch made a point of seating himself next to me and he described, blow by blow, his victories. Ywain and Gildas seemed bemused by his enthusiasm. When the candles had burned halfway down King Morcant banged on the table and stood.

"Tomorrow we will speak of our assault on the island the Saxons have taken from us. But I know that, with the army we have, victory is assured." He waved his arm around us all, it seemed a trifle unsteady to my semi-sober eye, "Here we have champions and warriors who have fought the Saxons and defeated them before and we will do so again." Everyone cheered and banged their tankards loudly and drunkenly. King Rhydderch the Generous was living up to his name having brought some jugs of a fiery liquid they brewed in his land. We called it King Rhydderch's fire. It sent waves of heat through the blood and I had just had one mouthful. I wanted my wits about me.

As the evening degenerated into stories of battles past King Urien took my arm. "I have been watching you, Lord Lann," he insisted on giving me a title even though I had refused one many times, "you watch what you drink and you keep your wits about you."

I nodded. "My family was taken from me because we did not keep our wits about us. Besides, I do not want to spend tomorrow morning vomiting the good food we ate tonight."

"Each day I learn more about you. I think my visit to Stanwyck was the wisest move I made."

The next day was a dark day. I was one of the few who had a clear head. I had spent the night with my brothers in the camp eschewing the generous quarters provided by King Morcant. Part of the reason was that I did not want to spend the night listening to warriors empty the contents of their stomachs and the other was to talk with my brothers. The coming battle would be unlike any other we had fought. We would not be defending, we would be attacking and that had inherent dangers. I wanted them both to have a clear idea of what would happen for I knew that I would be leading the wedge when we did assault. Raibeart and Aelle were also concerned. They knew that they would be on the periphery of this battle, guarding the flanks, but their big brother, the Wolf Warrior, would be in the most dangerous place of all.

"When the arrows are exhausted my men will join you, brother."

"And we can never run out of stones, for we fight on the shore but we will stay close to you, Lann."

I smiled, "Then all will be well so long as the Wolf-Brethren are together."

When I returned to the hall the next day for the meeting which would decide the strategy I could tell that no one had had a good night's rest. Although the King had remained relatively sober his night's sleep had been disturbed and he was, unusually for him, a little grouchy. The kitchen had laid on cooked meats, bread, cheese and beer. However, apart from the King and I, no one ate or drank and there were some very green faces around the table. The champions were there as well as the commanders and the kings. Bladud's bloodshot eyes made him look even more sinister than he had the previous night. I wondered if I judged him ill because of his appearance but Ywain's words came back to me and I knew the truth.

As host, King Morcant began. "We will assault tomorrow. I will lead the armies across the causeway and drive the Saxons from our land."

I was not the only one taken aback by the effrontery of the young king. King Rhydderch and King Urien both raised their eyebrows and Ywain stared at me in amazement mouthing the word, "What!"

King Urien was nothing if not a diplomat and he was a kind man who, generally, thought the best of others. "It is a generous offer you make, King Morcant Bulc, but I fear that we will need to assess this island of Metcauld and decide on the best strategy, and as for leading the attack, with due respect, King Morcant, you are not well versed in war as yet."

King Rhydderch the Generous was a plain-spoken man, "And the other reason is, in case you had not counted, the bulk of the army and the better part of it is King Urien's. I am not sure that seasoned warriors such as Lord Lann would take kindly to being given orders by a novice."

Morcant Bulc reddened and, although the King had praised me, I wished that he had not for I knew that I would be put on the spot with the next utterance from the King of Bryneich. "Tell me, Lord Lann, do you agree with the comment from King Rhydderch?"

All eyes were upon me and I noticed a savage satisfaction in the red eyes of my enemy. "As I said before, your majesty; I am King Urien's man, and if he asks me to follow you then I will do so. It is my liege lord's decision. Not mine."

Morcant's eyes narrowed and he pursued the point. "You did not answer my question. Would you follow me?"

I could see no way out of this which would not result in the King being offended and so I made a joke of it. "Your majesty, I will follow any man who allows me to kill Saxons; even Brother Osric."

All but Morcant Bulc and Bladud laughed and the atmosphere was calmed but I could see that it was not forgotten. I had made another enemy although in truth I could not see how I could have avoided it without betraying my king. "So we will ride to the causeway and examine the defences and then we," he emphasised the 'we', "will decide the best strategy. I would suggest just the kings and their bodyguards. The other commanders will need to prepare their warriors for the assault."

As we left Riderch sought me out. "I am sorry that you were placed in such a position, my lord. I know your honour and your bravery." He looked darkly at the back of his king. "As do all my men. If you are chosen to lead the attack then we will not let you down."

I was touched by the young warrior's honesty. He was patently no diplomat. "Thank you, Riderch, that means much to me."

As I left the hall, I found Ywain waiting for me. "What does Morcant Bulc think he is about? He has less experience of leading a battle than Aed the blacksmith."

"He sees himself as the saviour of Britannia; the next Artorius."

"You mean Dux Britannica?"

"He does."

Ywain laughed. "That is ridiculous. If anyone has claim to that title it is my father and I know that he is far too humble to compare himself with Artorius."

"I am afraid that he has delusions of grandeur but we have more pressing matters to consider." Ywain's look was one of confusion. "When we attack tomorrow, we cannot use a shield wall for we will be attacking and, as far as I know, the men have not practised the wedge. We are going against hardened men who know their business."

"You are right but how do we know what the kings will decide?"

"No matter what their strategy it will involve men with spears and swords attacking across the causeway and that means a wedge."

"Which you will lead." It was not a question but a statement.

"If I am ordered I will do so but it is more than a decision about one warrior. We need to consider where we place the men. We have much work to do this day."

I had no doubt that the King would come up with a plan which would lose as few lives as possible. Equally, I also knew, from my own visit, that the only way, without a fleet of ships, was across the causeway at low tide and that would be a narrow, wet and deadly killing ground.

There was a high, dry although undulating piece of ground about a mile away and Ywain and I marched our army there. The other two armies just watched us with mild interest. As far as I was concerned the battle would be won by our men whom we would lead. The wind was blowing hard but the men could hear me as I gathered them around in a large circle. Ywain stood next to me, not that I needed his authority but I felt that, as he was the leader of the army he should be acknowledged as such. "We will be attacking that island," I pointed to the rocky island which dominated the bay. "Now there are well over five hundred Saxons there who will dispute that." I had no idea of actual numbers but that seemed a reasonable figure to me. For one thing, more men could not be brought into action on such a narrow front. I grinned at them and put my hands on my hips. "Now they have never fought us before; they fought against me and they didn't like that so imagine how they must be feeling knowing that there is an army of you, all as good a warrior as I am." They gave such a roar at the statement that the kings and their bodyguards on the beach looked over to us. "These Saxons are good fighters but," I tapped the side of my head, "they are a bit thick!" I received the laugh I wanted. "They don't have archers and slingers." I pointed to my brothers. "We do. The best in the whole land so when we go to fight them, we will have our brothers loosing arrows and slingshot to make their life a little uncomfortable and you know that these men can shoot the eye of a gnat at a hundred paces!"

They all laughed again and one comedian shouted, "Two hundred if the wind is right."

I had them now. They were eager and ready. "But we will need to practise fighting and working together. I want the spearmen to line up here, behind Lord Gildas and the sword and axemen next to Prince Ywain." They all shuffled into line wondering what my next instruction would be. "Now I want the tallest next to Lord Gildas and Prince Ywain and the smallest at the far end of the line." When they had done that, I saw that there were a number of men in both lines who were the same height as me. That is what I wanted. "Warriors of Rheged, put your hand up if you have fought in a wedge formation before." About twenty hands in total went up. I had never fought in a formal one but I had seen them and knew the concept.

I went down the lines touching men on the shoulder. "Those men I have touched come here." All the rest were fascinated. I had to take this step by step so that they all knew what we intended. When this was all over, we would have to use this as a regular training exercise. I placed the two tallest warriors next to each other. Behind them, I placed two tall axemen with a spearman between them. The next five were three spearmen flanked by two swordsmen. When I had finished we had a huge wedge with over three hundred men in it. The two hundred I had not used were disappointed. "You men will form the second wedge. First, you will watch how we work." I stood at the front and faced my wedge. "The warriors with the spears, you have been placed in the centre to protect the outside warriors. The most dangerous side is the right for you have no shield to protect you. It is up to the men with the spears to stop the enemy coming close. Keep your shield as high as you can and yet still be able to see over it. They have no archers remember that."

The next part would be the hardest. They would have to move without tripping over each other. I stood away so that they could all see me. I held up my wolf shield. "This side is wolf. All of you hold up wolf!" They laughed except for the two who did not and the ribald comments they received meant they would not repeat their mistake. I held up my sword. "This side is slayer. Hold up your slayer arm." They all cheered as they did it. "Good, now I am going to tell you which foot you will use for walking." I grinned at them. "I will be like your mother and teach you how to walk! I will hold up my sword and you will march on the spot. When I lower my sword, we will move forward until I hold up my sword."

I turned and nestled into the two warriors. I held up my sword and began to chant, "Wolf, Slayer, Wolf, Slayer." I heard the men chanting it too. "That's right, all of you chant it." When I was happy I lowered my sword and we set off. We marched forwards about a hundred paces and then I stopped them. The rest all applauded.

"Excellent, now we will work on attacking. We will turn around." It was harder than I thought to move three hundred men in a circle but we did it. "This time when I raise my sword we will charge Prince Ywain and the others but we will stop when I lower my sword." I had not told Ywain of the plan and his reaction would be interesting. They all chanted and we moved forwards. After fifty paces I raised my sword and I saw the look of horror on the faces of the prince and the men behind him when we charged. Some actually ran backwards but when I lowered my sword, my warriors all managed to stop. A little untidily but they stopped. In a real battle that would not matter for we would have struck their line and their shields would halt us.

"You had me worried there, Lord Lann."

"But was it effective?"

"Oh yes. I would not like to face your warriors in that formation."

"Lord Gildas, you need to form your men and do as we did. Can you do it?"

I saw a momentary hesitation and then he said confidently, "Of course."

We spent the rest of the morning perfecting the technique. I had the men practise pushing shields against each other and others supporting their backs with their shields. I was happy that we would be able to use the wedge formation in the battle if it came to one.

We had a break for a meal and then we gathered everyone around us. The two young princes, Rhiwallon and Rhun, who were the standard bearers, were brought out with the new standards. Ywain took them through the signals which were quite simple. The standard moved forwards meant attack. To the right meant a move to the right. To the left meant a move to the left and swung in a circle meant retreat.

As we trudged wearily back to the camp, ready for some hot food, I felt satisfied that we had prepared our men well. I was less sure of the other two components of our army but that was not my concern. Raibeart, Aelle, Ywain, Gildas and I hung back behind the men. "You two will have to advance with us, brothers, and cause as many casualties as we can. "

Raibeart had spent part of the morning looking at the causeway and the island. "The problem is, brother, that your wedge will take up the whole of the causeway and if we were at the rear then we would be too far away to see the falloff arrow."

Silence and depression consumed us. Then Aelle said, "Boats." We looked at him as though he had spoken Greek. "Lann, you said that you had taken two boats to attack the island, then fill them with archers and slingers and they can outflank the Saxons effectively."

It sounded like a good plan. "Unless they bring boats too."

Aelle gave me one of his really serious looks. "It seems, wolf brother, that you are the one who has been taking all the risks lately. I think Raibeart and I can manage."

The cooks had produced a rich stew made from fish they had caught from beach nets and shellfish which abounded on the shore. It was a refreshing change from either dried meat or game and there was a buoyant mood in the camp. When King Urien and Bladud entered the camp they both looked as though they had the cares of the world upon their shoulders. He gave us a wan smile. "It is good to see my warriors so happy." He looked at me and his son. "When I heard the cheers ringing out on the headland I wished I was with you. You do not need to tell me that you had a good and productive day."

Ywain could not help his enthusiasm. "We did, father, and I am certain that our tactics will defeat the Saxons."

"I am glad but I wished that I shared your conviction. The others are all for a direct assault on the causeway."

Our smiling faces made the King wonder if we had heard him. Ywain said, "We expected that and we have a strategy to make it work. We will have archers behind our assault wedge and slingers and archers in two boats which will harass them with missiles. Lord Lann will lead the first wedge and Lord Gildas the second. The other forces can follow it needed."

"Oh, that is a relief! And I dreaded to tell you the news. I thought the attack would be suicidal."

"We have practised father and we have the signals too. It will be a hard-fought day but we will prevail."

Gildas brought out an amphora of wine and we all celebrated our plan. The only one who looked put out was Bladud who kept casting looks of hate in my direction.

When the King returned the next morning he had agreed with the other kings the plan of action. King Morcant would provide the two ships and the crews. We would assault on the next low tide and the two missile ships would be rowed out on the high tide and wait. If the Saxons showed undue interest then the two ships would row inshore and we would evaluate our strategy. King Morcant was happy as his men would only be the rowers but King Rhydderch wanted his men to begin the assault. Eventually, he agreed that if we failed then his men would take up the attack. King Rhydderch was informed that if the attack totally failed then the men of Strathclyde would lead the next. He was placated.

We were up before first light as the low tide coincided with the dawn. My brothers had each taken command of the boats on each side of the causeway; both boats contained a mix of slingers and archers. As I waited on the mainland I looked at the two warriors who would be behind me, Scanlan and Tad. It was important that they knew their job. "We are the tip of the sword. We have to fight as one man. You, Scanlan, have the slightly easier task for you guard my shield side. You, Tad, have a more onerous job for you have to protect Saxon Slayer. Talk to me while we fight and tell me of any problems." I turned to the men behind. "You spearmen must keep the men from us. We have to penetrate as far as we can and those further behind let us know of any signals you see."

King Urien rode before us. "Today I cannot lead you for it will be up to your swords and axes. But you are well led and you will prevail. You fight for Rheged and freedom. May God be with you." I hoped that my gods, all of them, were with me and that my mother, in the spirit world, would do all that she could to aid us against those who had slain her and the rest of my family.

# Chapter 11

The King nodded and I said, "Wolf, Slayer!" The chant went up and I saw the king's look of surprise. The guards at the end of the causeway had seen us and there was no chance of surprise so our chant was a warning for the Saxons of the fight to come. Out of the corner of my eye, I saw Raibeart's boat glide alongside us, slowly and silently. I knew that they would all have arrows and stones ready to assault the Saxons and that gave me heart. Saxon Slayer was before me and, in the pale light of dawn, appeared to glow. I saw a brief flash of light as the gates opened and disgorged the Saxon shield wall which would face us. I concentrated on the man at the centre of their line. He would be my opponent. I saw that he had a helmet with a nasal and carried a sword and a shield. The shield had no boss and I assumed no metal. That gave me an advantage. I knew, without looking, that the boats were in position and I waited for my brothers to begin their attack. They would judge the moment well, that I knew. When they did loose their arrows and stones all that I heard was a faint whoosh and then I heard the clatter of metal on metal and the screams of men who were struck. Their front ranks crumpled and then the arrows and stones came a second time. More men fell and the ones who replaced them had their shields held high. It was our chance and I raised my sword. We ran. Three hundred men encased in armour and protected by wood and iron crashed into their lines. I thrust my sword forwards as we hit and the warrior I had watched had my sword driven through his mouth and through the back of his skull. The men behind me pushed and the wedge overran their front ranks. The warriors behind us were killing those who squirmed on the floor. I stabbed blindly and felt the sword strike something soft and fleshy and another warrior fell before me. The arrows and the slingshot were taking their toll and the two lines before us were crumbling. We had won and we had a victory.

Suddenly the men before us just ran and fled to the safety of the stronghold. We roared forwards, an uncontrolled mass of exultant warriors. Then we realised the trap they had set. The bridge over the ditch was raised, leaving forty or fifty of the last Saxons to be slaughtered like fish stranded on a beach. I halted the line. There was something I did not like. "Prepare for an attack." My men dressed their shields and prepared for the Saxons to come towards us. Suddenly King Rhydderch appeared. "You have done well, Lord Lann, but now is the time to attack."

"There is something amiss here."

"You are tired. Allow my men the honour of the final assault." He was a king and I was just a warrior. I could not gainsay him.

I turned to my men. "Take thirty steps to the rear and leave a gap for the men of Strathclyde."

The warriors of the King had obviously been watching us practise and they formed their own wedge with the leader of the King's bodyguard at the point. At a nod from the King, they roared into the ditch and attacked the wall. Suddenly a flaming torch was thrown from the ramparts and the whole ditch erupted in flame.

"Raibeart, Aelle, support the attack!"

It was a forlorn hope. The ditch was filled with faggots soaked in pitch and pig fat. The brave warriors of Strathclyde burned and roasted. Raibeart and Aelle kept the men from the walls killing those in the ditch but it would have been a mercy had they done so as they would have ensured a quick end. We waited to help out of the ditch those who were not badly burned but there were few of them. Ywain came to the King and me, "The tide is returning. We must clear the causeway or we will all perish too."

Reluctantly we turned and retreated. We had almost succeeded but in the end, it was a loss and could be viewed as a disaster. Had I led my men across the ditch then we would have lost the war there and then. The men of Strathclyde's sacrifice had saved the army.

In the camp that night there were no recriminations. King Rhydderch's name was justly the Generous. He knew that my caution had saved my men and his recklessness had cost him his. Over two hundred of his men had perished and it grieved him for he was a good king and he knew his men. We had lost barely thirty thanks to the accuracy of Aelle and Raibeart's men but we could not celebrate. We had the smell of human flesh roasting and no one was in the mood for food that night.

King Urien and his son came to visit me in the camp. "We so nearly won and it grieved me to have to watch those men die."

"The Saxons merely did what we would have done. They used every means available to them to destroy us and it worked. Until they set fire to the ditch we had killed more than they had."

The King looked thoughtful. Ywain knew him better than I. "Father, have you an idea?"

He did not answer but looked at me. "Could your men fire arrows which were burning?"

I had never done so but I saw what the King was driving at. "I think we could but we would need to devise a strategy to enable us to do so."

"Try."

"Father, what is your idea?"

"Use fire to fight fire. If we launched fire arrows at their ramparts then they would burn. It would make the assault much easier. Then we could surround the fortress and starve them out." He looked at me with a questioning look.

"I think it would work and, your majesty, it is worth a try." Raibeart gave me a weary look. He and I would need to devise a method of firing arrows.

King Morcant Bulc looked quite self-satisfied as he, too, visited our camp. "I am sorry for your losses, it was a valiant attack."

King Urien shook his head. "Commiserations should be given to King Rhydderch for his men suffered more grievous losses. We will attack again."

"My men will be ready to support this time for the King of Strathclyde has done enough. What do you intend?"

"We will surround them and then try to burn their walls. They lost many men today and now, I think, we might outnumber them if we can fire their walls."

That night I had to reorganise the wedge. It seemed likely that we would need to assault again for this time the Saxons would be desperate. As I was doing so Lord Gildas sought me out. "Please, Lord Lann; allow me to lead the attack tomorrow. I felt pained to watch you do all the work with your men while I stood idly by."

I knew not what to say. Ywain stepped forward. "He is right and we need as many men blooded as possible. There will be many battles before we have driven the Saxons from our shores."

Reluctantly I agreed. "I will support you on the morrow, my lord."

I walked with my brothers to the headland overlooking the beach. Wolf was with us sniffing for any rabbits in the dunes. We sat in the tussocky grass, in a sheltered dell. "It seems a waste of good arrows to set them on fire. We have precious few as it is."

"We could use the ones which are not perfect; after all, we only need to hit a wooden wall not a man."

"Even so, there would not be many of those." He smiled ruefully, "Our men are now accomplished fletchers."

Aelle was the thinker. "What about the arrows which were damaged and are unusable." Aelle had struck gold once more. Our archers collected every arrow they could find after each battle whether broken or not. The feathers and barbs could be reused even if the shaft was broken. When we had returned from the battle there were many captured shields brought back and many were studded with our arrows.

Raibeart brightened momentarily. "That would give us enough arrows for we would only need two arrows for each man but the range would be shorter."

"How so?" Aelle had a look of concentration upon his face.

"If the tip is on fire then we cannot draw the bow fully back for fear of burning the bow or the archer. We will need to be closer than we normally are and I do not know how we will make them burn."

"While you two discuss that I will go down to the beach and collect some pebbles while there is still daylight."

Aelle took his responsibilities as leader of the slingers very seriously. He disappeared over the dune. Wolf looked up briefly and then settled down again. There were no hares.

"You know the wicked drink that King Rhydderch and his men consume in such great quantities, King Rhydderch's fire?" Raibeart nodded, "well when they throw it on the fire it burns. If we soaked pieces of wool in it and wrapped it around the arrowhead then we could light it just before we loosed."

"Aye, that would work."

Just then Wolf's ears pricked up and he growled before ascending the dune and began barking. We knew that meant trouble. As we reached the top we saw Bladud, easily recognisable by his size, and two other men running towards Aelle, who could not hear them because the wind was coming from the east. Wolf raced towards the men. "I will go along the dunes and cut them off. Use your sling, brother."

I drew my sword as Raibeart and Wolf ran to aid our brother. He must have heard the barking for he turned when they were but thirty paces from him. Aelle did not have much time but he had enough to hurl a stone and strike the leading warrior. I could see that Raibeart was almost there as I saw the flash of light on his blade. Wolf fearlessly leapt up at Bladud's hand and I heard the scream as his teeth sank in. Aelle fell to the floor with the second warrior on him. I was forty paces away and I would not reach my brother in time. Bladud saw me and, hurling Wolf towards the sea, ran north back to his camp. The warrior's knife came up, poised to strike and Raibeart hurled a stone which struck the man's head and he fell over. The first warrior stood and drew his sword. I screamed, "No!" and pulled Saxon Slayer over my shoulder. I did not pause nor did I slow down, I swung the blade and his head flew off towards the incoming tide.

Even as the last warrior recovered and drew his own sword Raibeart plunged his blade into his neck. I looked for Bladud but he was too far away to catch. His reckoning would come another day. Raibeart was with Aelle as Wolf limped up. The blood on his jowls told me that Bladud had been injured. Aelle had a wound to his left arm but it was not deep and we bound it. He had been knocked about but he still smiled. He looked at us apologetically. "I did not hear them. Sorry."

"You have nothing to apologise for. I would say those three were hoping to catch me unawares." I looked at the two men. "Do you recognise them?"

Raibeart shook his head. He knew more of the army than I did. "They are not our men."

"And yet they look familiar." Then it struck me. They were Morcant's men. "They are from the castle."

"Why should Morcant Bulc wish harm to come to you?" I told them of his offer and how my refusal had offended him. "What do we do with the bodies?"

The water was already lapping around our ankles. "Leave them here and the tide will take them. They will be washed up on the Saxon beach."

"What will you tell the kings?"

"Nothing. I cannot believe that Bladud will say anything, neither will the King and I would not sow discord between the kings until this is over. We will watch Bladud even more carefully than before. At least it is out in the open now, between us anyway."

Aelle struggled to his feet. "I hope you are right, brother."

"So do I." In light of subsequent events, I think I was wrong but *wyrd* interferes in many ways; hitherto it had been to our benefit but now it was to cost us dear.

The tide was not low enough until the early afternoon which gave us the time we needed to prepare our fire arrows. Rhydderch made a joke of our request but acceded gladly. "A terrible waste of fine liquor. We will have to brew more when we return home. But if it pays back those bastards then it is a good use for it."

Gildas and his men spent the morning honing their formation. They had had the advantage of watching us fight and knew what the dangers were. I thought that we had done well but I too had learned much. When this was all over I would have a spear made for every man. A wall of spears would aid us and we would still be able to draw our swords. My shield had now been modified with two scabbards and the next time we fought I would have a surprise for my opponent.

King Urien and his bodyguards rode over and I felt great satisfaction when I saw his heavily bandaged hand. Wolf had been given some treats the previous night and I noticed that he growled as the standard bearer rode by. The hatred was even more visible but I smiled a greeting. The King dismounted and led me away from the men. "I see the Saxons are ready for us today." The Saxons had two boats filled with warriors on either side of the causeway. If we attempted the same tactic then the archers would be attacked.

I grinned. "A good job we are not repeating the same attack today then."

The King nodded and looked to the empty headland behind us. "King Morcant is a little tardy. It seems strange when we are here to regain him his kingdom and yet he is the last one to present himself."

"Perhaps we should let him lead this attack."

The King stroked his beard. "I had thought of that but Gildas would take offence at that and I would not dampen his enthusiasm."

Just then the army of King Morcant Bulc arrived. "Hail King Urien. Today we defeat them, eh?"

"Aye, King Morcant. We were just discussing if you and your men would like to assault in the second wave."

Everyone knew that I was to lead the second assault and the Bryneician king said, "Why, is the Wolf Warrior afraid?"

My hand went to my sword but the King restrained me and his voice was cold. "There is no need for an insult such as that. Lord Lann has shown to all, especially you, that he is the bravest of warriors. I was just wondering if your warriors need blooding."

The insult was thrown back and Morcant Bulc reddened. "My men will lead the assault if you wish!"

King Urien had regained his composure. "There is no need for that, Lord Gildas is in position and the tide is right."

Gildas turned to us and Ywain ordered his brother to lower the standard. They set off with the same chant we had used. Their feet splashed in the water as the tide receded but Gildas kept up the same pace. The archers under Raibeart were behind them, as close as it was possible to walk. Aelle's slingers would have to wait until Gildas had taken the other side of the causeway. It would be a hard fight. This time the Saxons were not attacking the wedge, they were waiting for it in a shield wall. King Morcant's men also formed a wedge but I could see that they had not perfected it for it was neither tight nor uniform and, as they followed the archers across the causeway it became even more disjointed. Riderch gave me a wan smile as they trudged forwards. It was obvious that he was not happy about the ragged formation and I hoped that his brave life would not be wasted.

I turned to my men. Ywain was next to me, his mail gleaming. "Stand eight men wide behind us." With the proud Rhun between us, holding our new standard, we stepped onto the causeway the men chanting "Wolf" and "Slayer." It was most effective as it made the whole column sound like a fell beast tramping towards the Saxon lines.

I could not see the front of the battle but I saw Raibeart's arrows showering the Saxons and I saw spears thrown back and then I heard a clash of metal on metal and metal on wood. It was a terrible noise punctuated by shouts and screams. I slowed up our advance for I could see that Morcant's men had also slowed. I looked at the sea next to me and I could see Rheged and Saxon bodies floating on the ebbing tide. I was grateful that the Saxons had no archers for if they had then the boats could have decimated us as we marched ever closer.

Suddenly we were on dry land! We had crossed the causeway. Ywain said to his brother. "Signal the withdrawal. Lord Gildas has done all that he can. Now it is Bryneich's turn." It seemed to take an age but the survivors of the attack made their way around the edge of the Bryneician wedge. I was relieved to see Gildas, although bloodied, had survived and was grinning. "Form up behind us."

"I will, cousin."

"Aelle. Take your slingers forward and order the men to bring the urns with the fire." At the rear, eight men carried four urns filled with burning coals. They would provide the fire for the arrows. "Shield wall!" My men spread out in two lines on either side of Ywain and me. Rhun proudly held the dragon standard high.

I drew my sword and held it aloft. All of my men roared, "Saxon Slayer." Aelle and his slingers cheered as they ran to take their place on the flanks where they would keep up a constant storm of stones and slingshot. The number of arrows had diminished as Raibeart conserved his stock. He knew that he needed many for the attack on the wooden walls. The wedge ahead of us was struggling and they began to push back against us. Their lack of cohesion meant that the Saxons outnumbered them and they were losing heavily. When some of the terrified warriors turned to try to force their way past us, I shouted, "Make a passage in the middle." I stepped to the left and Rhun and Ywain to the right and suddenly the Bryneicians fled accompanied by the jeers from the Saxons.

"Lock shields."

Ywain turned to his brother. "Signal the advance and then take your place behind the rear rank." He looked as though he was going to argue but the fierce look from his elder brother made him obey. We stepped over the bodies of the dead and I could see a knot of warriors still gathered around their standard. Riderch was still alive. I dropped my sword and the whole line raced forwards in perfect time. The Saxons who had surrounded the survivors were so busy trying to despatch them that they did not see us coming until it was too late. They thought that they had won and the whole of our line had retreated. It was understandable, two wedges had failed to break them. My sword smashed down the back of a warrior; the blade sliced through the mail and opened his backbone as though by a butcher. Ywain and the rest of those who were close to the Saxons did the same and we saw the grateful faces of our allies. "Let them pass through!"

We turned sideways, still presenting our shields to the enemy but leaving space for the men to squeeze through. The last one to pass was Riderch; his cheek sliced open to the bone by a sword. "Thank you, my friend. I thought I was going to meet my father."

"Not yet, but thank you, and we will now finish what you have started." The Saxons were dismayed. They thought that they had won and now their tormentors from the previous day, the warriors with the dragon standard and the men of the wolf had returned and were fresh. We had seen our comrades and allies hurt and killed and we were ready for revenge. We had watched the men burn in their ditches and now we burned with the desire to end this. "Halt!" The men stopped and I steadied the line. The Saxons waited. Stones still flew from the flanks and I saw that all of the enemy had their shields held tightly to protect them. "Ready! Charge!" We had but ten paces to go but we threw ourselves at the enemy. I saw a spear hurled and I flicked up my shield and it pinged off and flew behind me. The warrior who had thrown it did not have time to draw his sword and Saxon Slayer took him in the throat. I twisted as it went in and it slid out with his lifeblood. The warriors behind us were all armed with spears which stabbed over our shoulders so that each Saxon faced two enemies and they fell like wheat to a scythe.

"Push them!" I could see the ditch some twenty paces behind them and we pushed, punched and stabbed them relentlessly so that they had to gradually move backwards. I smashed my sword down so hard on one shield that it cracked and I saw the terror on the man's face. I punched him with the boss of my own shield and, as he fell at my feet stamped down with my nail-encrusted caligae to crush his face and brains into a bloody mush. The ones at the back fell into the ditch and that was the signal for them to flee towards the safety of their stronghold.

They hurtled towards the gates and I saw men on the ramparts with spears ready to slaughter any of us who tried to follow. That was not our plan. I nodded to a grinning Ywain who shouted, "Rhun! Halt!"

The whole line stopped and I could see the Saxons wondering what we intended. I heard the sound of hooves and I turned to see the three kings with their bodyguards and the survivors of the attacks forming up behind us. They would be the final assault once Raibeart had performed his magic. Ywain shouted, "Raibeart!"

Raibeart and his archers ran around to stand before us. The eight men placed the urns at regular intervals and after the tops had been removed, they began to blow on the coals. I could see the glow. I nodded at Raibeart and he and the men nearest him went to the urn and dipped the end of their arrows into it. It came out flaming. I was worried for my brother; we had never done this before and it could end up a disaster. They all brought them up and Raibeart shouted, "Loose!" The flaming arrows arced into the sky and plunged onto the walls. Raibeart's second flight also struck the walls and they even managed a third. The walls were soon ablaze and the Saxons had no water ready to douse the flames. They had been unprepared. Aelle's boys kept hurling stones at any face which appeared over the ramparts and Raibeart and his men were quickly gathering spent arrows from their earlier attack and were loosing them at the enemy. Now was the time for patience but, as I glanced over my shoulder, I saw that we had made a momentous cast of the dice for the tide had covered the causeway. We had nowhere left to run. We would either defeat them now or we would all perish on this little island which was now covered in blood, the dead and the dying.

"Raibeart, see if you can set the two Saxon ships alight."

My brother grinned as he and his archers took their last soaked arrow and lit them. He split his men into two groups and soon the two Saxon ships which had been filled with observers were turned into funeral pyres as they erupted in flames, the crews jumping overboard to save themselves. Those who were not pulled down by the armour and struggled to the shore were slaughtered by the waiting men of King Rhydderch, eager for revenge on these Saxons.

King Morcant Bulc suddenly launched the attack of his men into the stronghold. King Urien should have ordered the charge but King Morcant wanted some glory for himself. The others all followed. We were weary and we just waited and tended to the wounds of our comrades who had been hurt. We could hear the clash of arms within and Ywain gave the order for us to follow. The fires had quickly consumed the wood and we were able to enter almost anywhere we wished. I kept together with my men as I did not wish to be surprised by the cornered rats in their hole. There were dead and burning bodies everywhere. Some men had been struck by the fire arrows and the smell of roast flesh was all around us. It was like marching through a mortuary and we headed up the sides of the mound to their keep where the kings and their bodyguards were busy destroying the last of the defenders.

"The ships, Ywain, they will try to escape."

"You take the north of the island and I will take the south."

"Aelle, go with the Prince. Raibeart, follow me!"

We found that there were many men, women and children trying to board the boats. There was no time for discrimination and we waded into them killing any we saw who still had weapons. The warriors tried to face us and help their families to escape but it was fruitless. I stabbed, hacked and punched all who stood in my way. I suspect that my accomplishments on the previous day had marked me, because of my helmet, as a fearsome warrior who had killed their champion and every man who faced me had that look in their eyes which admits defeat before he has struck a blow. I felt someone behind me and I swung my sword. I managed to stop it before it hit the young woman and the crying child. Her face implored pity and I thought of my mother and Monca. I could not kill this woman and I sheathed my sword and reached an arm out of her. She looked afraid and I said, in Saxon, "I will not harm you. I swear it." Perhaps the words helped because she gave a wan smile and allowed me to raise her up. A wild-eyed warrior lunged at her and I batted his sword away with my shield. "Enough!" I could see that they were defeated. "Take prisoners!"

I helped her from the water and found my brothers and Wolf. They were bandaging wounded warriors. They saw me with the young girl. "Watch her. There has been enough killing of women before now."

"Aye, there has. I will watch them for you, brother."

I went around the water restraining warriors who had the blood lust and escorting the grateful women and children back to my brothers who soon had a clutch of survivors. Night had fallen and I was weary but I did not stop until all that remained were the dead. I returned to my brothers. My men had gathered there and as I approached, they roared, "Lord Lann the Wolf Warrior and the Saxon Slayer." They all began to bang their shields and roar my name. I held up my hand to silence them.

The first woman I had rescued looked up at me in amazement. "You are Lann the Wolf Warrior? We heard that you ate babies and raped women."

My brothers shook their heads and Aelle said, "No. He is a fierce warrior but he kills only men. He is honourable."

"I am sorry, my lord. I meant no disrespect."

I smiled and cupped the chin of the child. "You are the first women we have seen and the first we have captured. This is new to us all." I turned to the men. "Let us get inside the stronghold for shelter and food."

My men surrounded the prisoners and we made our weary way inside. When we reached the middle the bodyguards of the kings were hurling the bodies of the Saxon warriors into the remains of the burning keep as a giant funeral pyre. King Morcant Bulc, his face flushed and red, rode up to my men. "Who sanctioned these prisoners. I said that all should be killed." He raised his sword and the women recoiled in fear.

I stepped forwards. "I did! No-one said we were to kill women and children."

"I did and this is my land! I will do as I wish!"

I was ready to draw my sword and end this petulant king's life when King Urien's quiet and calm voice said. "This land of yours was bought with the blood and lives of my men, and King Rhydderch and I did not sanction the killing of women and children."

Morcant Bulc looked angry and he whipped his horse's head around and galloped off. As he did so, Raibeart said, "He does know this is an island? Where does he think he is going?"

I took off my helmet and shook my head, "I do not care so long as it is away from me. I weary of him." The King and Ywain approached me. "I am sorry if I did aught I should not have and put you in a difficult position, your majesty."

He smiled that gracious smile we all loved. "No, Lann, you did exactly as I would have done, and tomorrow, when we can, we will return home and give these women and children our protection until we have decided what to do with them and I can get the taste of death and King Morcant Bulc out of my nostrils.

# Chapter 12

When dawn had finally arrived King Morcant began to clear the debris left from the previous day's battle. We had persuaded him that he should fortify it himself and garrison it; if only to stop the Saxons reinvesting it and making us take it once more. It had cost too many men's lives to take and it would be foolish to throw away the hard-won gain. King Morcant was stiff and formal when taking leave of his brother kings. It still rankled that King Urien had overridden his edict. I think too, he had been unhappy about the fact that the victory had so obviously been won by the men of Rheged. While they said their goodbyes I sought out Riderch. He had a fine angry looking scar which now ran from his eye to his chin. "At least I shall frighten my enemies now, Lann."

"You did well yesterday in your first battle."

He shook his head. "We were an ill-disciplined mob. You and your warriors showed us how it should be done. The King has told me I can train our men in your style of fighting."

"Good." I took him out of earshot of his fellows. "And I would train archers. There must be, among your people, those who use slingshots and bows for hunting. Use them as the basis for a supporting band. You saw how effective our men were."

"Aye, and I will do so, and Lann," he came really close to me, "beware for you have made enemies. Two of the king's bodyguard disappeared the other night and I fear they may be hunting you."

I was intrigued although I was not afraid for those men were now dead, "How do you know?"

"I heard the King talking to them and he pointed you out. The look they had on their faces was not one of friendship."

"Thank you for the warning and I will heed it."

Ywain's voice drifted over, "The causeway is open."

I clasped his arm in a soldier's farewell. "Goodbye and may Belatu-Cadros be with you."

"And may the White Christ watch over you."

Keeping the captives securely within a ring of my best warriors we headed west, first to the mainland and thence home. It would be a long journey, burdened as we were by women and children but at least we knew that there were no Saxons to hinder our passage. We had said farewell to King Rhydderch the Generous soon after leaving Din Guardi. He still grieved over the loss of so many warriors but he was happy that we had succeeded. "If you ever need my help, Urien, then just ask but I will not be coming again to help that ungrateful whelp."

He was a generous man as his name said but he did not suffer fools gladly. This was the only time his men left their home for he died a few years later when the Irish raided his lands. I was sad because I liked him. He was honest and he was brave; what better epitaph for a warrior.

I rode next to the King and Ywain as we headed for the high passes. I gestured back to the captives. "What would you do with the prisoners, your majesty?"

"I have given that much thought since we left Din Guardi. It goes against my nature to make slaves of women and children. I would have done it with any of the warriors who survived but..."

Ywain nodded, "I agree, father, and having saved their lives I feel obligated to protect them."

We were crossing yet another Roman road and another deserted shell of an outpost. The Romans had spent many years in this land and their buildings and roads were like a skeleton they had left and yet they had left something else behind, their blood. My father's grandfather had been a Roman, or at least a British Roman. They remained within all of us who were not Saxon. "We could do as the Saxons do." Both King and Prince knew me well enough to listen to my words, no matter how ridiculous they sounded at first. "Well, what I mean is how the Saxons take over a place. Aelle had a British mother and a Saxon father. The women and their children will become the people of Rheged if we allow them to."

I could see King Urien considering the idea. "That is worth thinking about, Lann. They have skills and they are fertile. Our people are dwindling and this may be a way to ensure the survival of the people of Rheged and Britannia. I will think about it as we ride homeward."

I turned and rode to the rear where my brothers and Wolf led our men. My warband had gained much fame and honour with their brave deeds and actions. Over fifty had paid with their lives but we were now all richer having looted the stronghold and the bodies of the dead. Many of my men had more treasure now than many lords. I would have enough to build my own home in stone if I chose. As I rode up they all gave a cheer. Raibeart and Aelle smiled. They never begrudged me my fame and honour for they knew that they, too, were highly regarded, not only by their peers but the officers and leaders of Rheged's army.

Aelle, thoughtful as ever, asked, "What will happen to the prisoners and captives?" For Aelle, the son of a captive, this was the most pressing issue.

"I think they will not be made slaves if that is what is worrying you."

He blushed and Raibeart laughed, "I think, brother, that he has an eye for one of them; that first one who spoke with you. He has the puppy eyes when he sees her."

Aelle punched his brother in the arm. "You are soft in the head."

Raibeart looked at me and said seriously, "He has ridden next to the woman you rescued, Freja, many times and she has smiled at him, brother."

"I think it is a good thing, Aelle. We should all think of taking a wife for our father sired me when he was younger than you, Raibeart." I waved at the men who followed us. "Think how many good men died without issue. We carry on as our father would have, even though he is gone. That is how we will live forever through our children and I know that father would be proud of us and our deeds."

I saw them both smile at the thought. It had not occurred to them but, as the eldest, I was acutely aware of my responsibilities and I felt closer to my father now that he was dead than ever, I did when he was alive. I found myself dreaming of him and in my dreams, I spoke with him. I regretted, more than anything, that I had not spoken with him more; just talked of his life and his plans for us. The Angles had robbed me of that opportunity but I would talk with my brothers every chance I had.

Civitas Carvetiorum looked even more welcoming than it normally did as we entered our fortress. It seemed as though we had been away for a year and yet it had been a much shorter time. The threat to our neighbour had gone and that meant that the threat to our southern and eastern borders had also evaporated but the Saxons were still out there, close to our lands, and they would return. We had not scotched the snake; we had just driven it to a deep hole. I resolved to make the men I commanded even better over the next few months. We would not campaign again until either the Saxons returned or the spring and that gave my brothers and me the time to forge a weapon which would halt and then destroy our enemies.

Brother Osric greeted us when we arrived and cast his birdlike eyes on the captives. He looked at the captives with a strange look on his face. "Are these to be sold, your majesty?"

King Urien returned the priest's stare. "No, Brother Osric, house them, for the moment in the spare barracks."

I had begun to recognise the different expressions on the priest's face and I knew that he was pleased that they were not slaves. "From the wagons and carts, I assume you have profited from your labours and I have ordered replacement ash, feathers and yew. I hope that you have provided the iron?"

I grinned, for I knew the question was directed at me. "Of course. How could you doubt it?"

He walked off mumbling, "Yes, but you also brought more mouths to feed."

The King turned to face the army. "You have all performed as I knew you would, honourably, bravely and in the spirit of Rheged. You are all granted the time to visit with your families and return after the harvest when you will all be paid your reward for the campaign and we will begin to train again for next year's travails."

Every warrior cheered. Life did not get any better than this. They would all have three months to bask in the glory of the defeat of the Saxons. The crops and animals would be harvested and when they returned, with their wives pregnant, they would be ready to prepare for war again. The King was kind but astute. By dangling their pay when they returned he ensured that his army would be as large next year as it was this and he would not have to pay for his men's food for three months. I was learning how to be a leader each day I spent in the king's company.

The barracks was emptied by dusk. The bodyguard of the King remained as did the single men who had neither wives nor lovers but we three enjoyed the solitude of each other's company. We used the spare bunks to lay out our gear and all went to the bathhouse to cleanse ourselves of the smell of blood, death and sweat. Aelle's wound had healed well but, as we lay, naked in the baths, I brought up an idea I had had when we campaigned.

"Leather armour would suit the slingers and the archers. It is lighter, it would have stopped the knife slicing your arm, brother, and it would stop a spear penetrating too far."

Raibeart nodded his approval. "And it would make movement easier. Mail and armour are fine when you are standing in a shield wall but we are just extra bodies, used to stop you warriors from being outflanked."

"But helmets, even leather ones, would help."

"You are right, Aelle. We have plenty of time to get the leather and the deer hide and prepare the armour."

"Do you three brothers never talk of anything but war?" Ywain, Gildas and the two prince standard-bearers had entered.

"We are warriors. We are not princes who fight for the fun of it. For us, it is our livelihood."

Gildas nudged Ywain, "I think Aelle thinks of things other than war. A little bird told me that his loins are stirring and he has his eyes on a mate."

Aelle reddened and left. "You should not tease him, Gildas. I, for one, am pleased that he is thinking of a wife. I said to Raibeart that we all should."

"And that is where you are lucky, Lann. You can choose a woman because she makes your dick bigger. Even Gildas has that choice but I must have a wife who will be a future queen. My wife may be a fat and ugly milk cow but as long as I can provide my father with an alliance then that it is whom I shall marry!"

I could not believe that King Urien would do that. "You do not believe that, Ywain. You know your father would consult you, besides, can you think of a kingdom other than Rheged which is so powerful right now? Elmet, even Bryneicia, has not the army that your father has. Every king who has a presentable daughter will try to marry her to you."

Ywain had been drinking. "And damned lucky to get me she would be!"

We all fell about laughing and then Rhun said, "My father, the king, asked if you would join us tonight for food." He waved his hand at Raibeart and Aelle, "All of you."

"I would have thought that time away from the queen would have made him desire a quieter evening."

Ywain shook his head. "You do not know my father. He is single-minded about being king. He sees himself as the servant of the people."

"As opposed to Morcant Bulc who does not give a shit about his people."

"Raibeart!"

"Sorry, Lann. I forgot myself. Forgive me, Prince Ywain."

"No, you are right. I was most disappointed in King Morcant Bulc. I had thought, from his reputation, that he was a noble king and he isn't. I think my father was disappointed too. Well, we had better get dressed. Father is quite casual about these things but not so my mother."

We left quickly. Queen Niamh who had been a Welsh princess, the daughter of one of the Welsh kings, was known to be a stickler for protocol. It would not do to upset her.

It was quite a cosy affair. The royal couple along with their four sons were there as well as Brother Osric and my two brothers. We were all on our best behaviour for it was the first time we had all dined privately with the royal family. Queen Niamh, however, went out of her way to be pleasant. "I am grateful to you three warriors. From what I have heard you have helped my husband and my son to achieve greater success than if the King had not happened upon your settlement." She crossed herself, which I had learned was a White Christ action. "Praise be to God."

Ywain gave an apologetic shrug but I did not mind. I never objected to anyone's religious beliefs so long as they did not try to convert me. My mother had strong views about her religion too. "We are glad that the King rescued us. We believe that we were meant to serve Rheged and fight the Saxons."

The King stood and held his goblet out. "A toast to chance, and the fates which brought us all together." His wife threw him a black look but smiled and raised her goblet too.

The meal had been planned and devised by Brother Osric and was magnificent. He had acquired, no one knew how spices from the east and the food tasted exquisite. None of us could quite explain the range of tastes which exploded in our mouths but we all knew that it was a unique experience. After the delicate sweets, we had at the end of the meal Queen Niamh stood. "Once again I thank you three for your support for my family, I am deeply indebted to you." She held out her hand for us all to kiss. When we had all done so she said, "And when you are all converted to Christ then I will be even happier."

She left, as she had entered, majestically. Ywain said, "Sorry about mother, she has her opinions."

"Do not apologise, Prince Ywain. I like people to believe in something. It may not be what I believe in but I can respect it."

The King nodded at Brother Osric who disappeared briefly and then returned with an amphora. "This, Lord Lann, is the same wine I gave you last year. I have acquired some more and the King thought that this would be an appropriate occasion to taste it; especially your younger brothers, who are now men and worthy warriors."

Ywain, his brothers and Gildas all banged the table and the King frowned and then smiled indulgently. "I give you a toast. The future."

I had tasted it before and knew the power of the deep red liquid but my brothers had not and I smiled at their expression as they drank for the first time. They went to take a second swallow and I said, "Slowly boys. Trust your big brother. Slowly does it."

There was a moment of silence as we all enjoyed the taste. Even the youngest son of the King who was but ten years old had been given a small goblet. The King looked around the table. "I have been thinking, for some time, how we might make the kingdom more secure. Lann, it was not until your coming that I saw how this might be achieved. You are a leader whom men follow. But you are not alone; your brothers have the same qualities. And Gildas, you showed that you too have those qualities. My sons have them, that goes without saying, and they will inherit land but only Ywain will be king. I want all of you to benefit from our success."

He nodded to Osric who stood. "Each of you is to be made a lord. There are seven of you, which is, in pagan terms, a magical number. As a Christian, I cannot subscribe to magic but I cannot deny the power it has over men. You will each be given a settlement to rule and to protect. You will each raise the men from that area to serve in times of war." He smiled indulgently at the youngest son of the king. "Some of you will need my help, at least for a while. For the rest, you need to make your settlements defensible. The people in your care will be taxed to enable you to run an effective defence. The King trusts all of you and knows that this is the most equitable way to ensure that fairness and the rule of law flows through Rheged."

I did not know what to say and nor did my brothers. Ywain saw our confusion and he continued. "It was father's visit to Stanwyck that set him thinking. There was a perfect place to defend, and had there been a leader appointed by King Urien who could enforce the king's will then it could have held out against the Angles until help arrived." He saw my face cloud over. "There is no disrespect intended to your father. He could not make the others make the fortress defensible. You said yourself, Lann, that it took the death of a young couple and a baby before the others even blocked the gates."

The King shook his head sadly. "I had thought that my bodyguard alone would be enough to defend the land but I can see that the people must be made to defend their land or they will lose it. These invaders want the best land and our people live there."

Brother Osric chimed in, "It is simple economics. If the people want to use the best land then they must pay for its protection and participate in the defence of the land or they will lose it, along with their lives."

The King stood, "Come and bring your wine. It would be a waste to let it turn sour." We went to the next, smaller room in the old Roman fort. Brother Osric lit the lamps. There, on the table, was a deer hide with a map painstakingly drawn upon it. The King smiled and gestured towards the priest. "Brother Osric's work while we were away."

He snorted, "That and a hundred other matters!"

The sea was marked in blue and the land left the natural colour of the deer hide. There were places marked in red with writing next to them. None of us could read and we waited for the explanation. The priest took a pointer. "Here we are in the centre of the kingdom. There are old Roman forts nearby and they were chosen by the Romans to protect the land. Some of them are close to settlements where our people live while others are isolated. We have chosen six for you to occupy." He smiled at Pasgen, the youngest son of King Urien, "When Prince Pasgen is of an age he will be given his own fiefdom." Pasgen looked disappointed and his father ruffled his head. "Here in the north, the safe fort, if you will, for it borders the land of King Rhydderch, is Blatobulgium." He saw our puzzled expressions. He sniffed contemptuously, "Had you all learned Latin as did the King then you would know these names. This land is rich farmland with many people living there and it will yield many warriors. Prince Rhiwallon, this is yours to manage. Here on the coast is the port of Alavna. This is vital for the fish it brings in is a great resource and the fishermen are hardy warriors. It is most important, Prince Rhun, that it is defended from the depredations of the Hibernians." The two princes nodded very seriously.

Brother Osric then turned his gaze to Gildas. "Fanum Cocidii is north of the wall. It is protected to the north by King Rhydderch, to the west there is King Morcant Bulc. The stronghold is important; it protects the Roman Road. There are not as many warriors and settlers there but it is vital that it is held to protect the capital." Gildas too gave a serious nod and I could tell that Brother Osric was building up to the most hazardous postings. Ours!

The King put his hand on Brother Osric's shoulder and the priest moved away from the table and drank a little more of his wine. The King pointed to the land south of Rheged. "Once all this was ours but now it is disputed land and the Saxons to the south will be heading north for the land of the lakes is rich in game and fish as well as the best pastures for cattle and sheep. There are three forts which are in the way of any army coming north. Here, at Glanibanta, on the lake called Wide Water, is a fort which has fallen into disrepair but there are many people here. Aelle, we would like you to hold this for the king."

"I will do so, your majesty."

I almost smiled at the serious expression on my little brother's face but I was proud of the man he had become. Now scarred, he was a doughty warrior who was adored by his slingers. I knew that he would win over the people of the lake.

The King smiled and nodded, "I know you will." He pointed to a fort not far from the capital. "Here is a Roman fort on the old wall,

Banna. It protects the road and the wall. Like Blatobulgium, there are few people there and it will be hard to defend but the walls of the fort still stand and it will be yours, Raibeart, to protect."

Raibeart leaned over to look at the map. Although he found it hard to understand, as well all did, it gave the relationship of the places to Civitas.

"Finally, Lord Lann, we have the most exposed fiefdom. Brocavum is the furthest east. It is but twenty miles from your old home of Stanwyck. When the Saxons come from the south or the east you will be the first to know. You are the most remote and furthest from help. The southern Roman road passes by the fort which has fallen into disrepair but there are many people who live and work there. You must make them into a force which can hold an enemy up until we can reach you."

He paused to allow it all to sink in. I was a little intimidated. I had been fighting the Saxons for some years and I had led men for almost as long and yet this would be new for I would be alone. I knew that my brothers would be feeling the same. Prince Ywain must have sensed our doubts for he spoke and there was warmth in his voice. "You should know that I will not be idle. I will be forming my own bodyguard which will be, like my father's guards, mounted. Our role will be to travel around your forts regularly. We need the people of Rheged to know that they still have a king who rules and will defy the Saxons. This is a good time for us. Our warriors have returned to their homes and they will be telling their communities of our success. There is a dawn of hope and there is a light shining here in the west. My father, King Urien, is the light of hope."

We all raised our goblets impulsively and toasted the King who beamed at us. "I have my seven lords before me. You are the Seven Stars of Rheged, you are the new equites."

Aelle looked puzzled. Brother Osric tutted. "If people only learned to read Latin." He sighed and then explained, "The equites were the high-born Romans who rode horses and led their armies. You are the equites now and you have the titles which go with that."

King Urien went to a casket and opened it. "And here are your chains of office." He took out seven chains. They were made of bronze and from each hung silver encrusted crosses. In the centre of each cross was a polished black stone which I knew came from the east coast. It was a precious metal called jet. "This stone was believed in the old times to bring luck." He smiled at the three of us who were still pagans. "The cross is for my sons and the black stone is for you. We are combining pagans and Christians and together we will prevail."

Brother Osric placed the chains around our necks and we became the Seven Stars; the equites of Rheged.

As we walked back to the barracks, I was not certain if we were drunk with the wine or drunk with joy. Aelle, of all of us, was the most serious. "It means we will no longer be together."

"Not true, little brother, we are together here," I tapped my heart, "and here." I tapped my head. "We have been placed close to each other. I am in the centre, Raibeart to the north and you Aelle to the south. I intend to visit just as soon as I have discovered what my land is like. This is not the end of something, this is the beginning."

The next day we were summoned, all seven of us, to Brother Osric's office. He had in front of him seven piles of coins. Ywain went to touch one and the priest slapped his hand. "The King has deemed that we need coinage. Thanks to the booty that has been accrued we have minted coins with the king's image upon them. These seven piles represent the bulk of the money in the kingdom. Use them wisely. They are sound coins." He took one and bit it. "This is what the people will do and it will prove their value. You all need to have a defensible home. For some of you, this will be easy for there will be a fort. For others, it will be more difficult as the locals will have taken the stone for their own use." He looked at us all and I could see a paternal look upon his face. He looked like my father when one of us had done something of which he was proud. "Today the King will escort his two sons and Gildas to their forts. Tomorrow Prince Ywain will escort," he smiled, "the Wolf Brothers to theirs. You have four months to establish your lands and then return here to begin training the army for the spring. I am sure that the Saxons will have flexed their muscles by then."

As we left, with our bags of coins, Aelle drew Raibeart and me apart. "Lann. I would like to be wed before we leave the fort."

I looked perplexed. "Good."

"No, you are the head of our family and I need your permission."

I grinned. "You have it. Freja?" He blushed and nodded. "Then you will also need the king's permission for they are his captives."

"Would you ask him for me?"

"Of course. I will do so now."

Leaving my two brothers to return to the barracks I headed for the king's quarters. As I entered Bladud left. This was the first time we had been this close since he and his men had tried to hurt Aelle. "Is the arm healed, Bladud?" I asked innocently.

He snarled his reply, "You were lucky but you will not always be so and you will die by my hand."

I was not afraid of him and I closed up to him. "Any time you wish to try it, Bladud, I am ready and I will even pay for your funeral." He was used to warriors backing down and he brushed past me angrily. Somehow it calmed me; now it was in the open. I knocked and entered the king's quarters.

"Has Brother Osric given you the coin?"

"He has and we thank your majesty. I come on behalf of my brother Aelle. He would marry one of the captives, the woman Freja with the young child."

He stood and embraced me, his face alight with joy. "This is a sign, Lann. Our peoples, the Saxons and the Celtic peoples are joined and we can survive. I am even more grateful to you and your brothers now."

As Aelle and Freja were pagans the ceremony was conducted before the captives and us. However, Brother Osric, the King and his sons also attended. Aelle and Freja had become close on the journey across the land and I was pleased that she was happy with the union. Monca, Aelle's mother, had been forced. We did not need to do so. I wondered then just how many others would take a Saxon bride.

# Chapter 13

We had taken Raibeart to the windswept hillside on the wall first. I found it hard to say farewell to him; even though we would see each other again, this was the first time he been on his own, without his big brother watching over him. When I had gone east, he had had Aelle and the rest of the army for company. I could see emotion filling his face as he stood in the ruins of the fort of Banna. The departing soldiers had done their best to render it indefensible but the locals had not robbed all of the stone and it could be repaired quickly. It all depended upon the people who lived close by.

Ywain looked unhappy too. "I will send you each a warrior and a cleric to aid you. This is too much for one man." We had many clerics. King Urien's generosity meant that we had priests seeking sanctuary with us. There were also many soldiers who were not in the bodyguard and had no families. It would make us less isolated.

"Send them to my brothers first." I grasped Raibeart's arm. "We have done well, brother, already, and I know that father would have been proud." He nodded, unable to speak. "I will visit as soon as I am able." Aelle too just embraced his brother and his eyes were heavy with tears.

Turning Blackie's head I followed Ywain and his bodyguard, beneath their dragon standard. Aelle and Wolf followed behind and the two wagons, one with Aelle's new family and his equipment, and one containing mine. The road south rose and fell through small valleys and I could see that it was not the country for horses. We stopped on a ridge and I saw Brocavum across a shallow valley. It was a good site for a fort. It was on a small rise above a river and the road crossed a bridge over the river. Whoever held the high ground would control the road. Ywain rode next to me. "This is Castle Perilous, Lann. It is the only way from east to west and north to south for many miles. If the Saxons come…"

"You mean when the Saxons come."

He inclined his head and nodded. "Then they will have to reduce this fort. You will have to buy time for the rest of Rheged." I could see that the fiefdoms had been allocated with a view to each lord's strength. "My father has complete faith in you, as I do."

As we rode across the bridge I could see that the walls were lower than those of Raibeart's Banna, Someone had stolen much of the stone. There would not be enough to make the walls as they once were. I would have to compromise. They unpacked the wagon for me and covered everything with deer hides to protect them from the weather. I walked over to Aelle and his new wife. "Be safe, little brother, and look after your new wife. Freja, I am happy that you have joined our family and Aelle's mother is smiling now on this union."

"Thank you, brother, and I hope to be half the warrior that you have become." I hugged Freja and saw that she too was filled with the emotion of the farewell.

Wolf came over to nuzzle me and I stroked him. "Go with Aelle and look after him and his family. The obedient sheepdog trotted off with his ears down and his tail between his legs.

When they had all left I felt quite lonely. Blackie snorted and threw his head back. "I know I still have you. Let us begin to make something of this mess, eh?" I took off his saddle and let him wander to graze the grass which looked to have been untouched since the Romans left. I found what had been the gatehouse. The huge wooden doors had been pillaged long ago as had the walls on either side but one of the towers still looked usable. I found the door which needed repair but was functional and climbed the stairs. There was a guard room which looked as though it would make a functional bedroom and then I opened the door at the top and found myself on the ramparts. I had a good view across the bridge and the road. Behind me, the hills stretched away but I was still afforded a fine view. I could see why the Romans had chosen this site; it controlled the land for many miles. I had my home. The ground floor would make a secure and dry stable for Blackie and I began the arduous task of carrying my armour and weapons up to the first floor. I put everything I owned in there, even though it filled the space. I would organise it later. I went into the other tower and saw that, although the roof had been destroyed the walls were still sound. It would make a serviceable kitchen.

Leaving my towers I walked the perimeter. The ditch still functioned but the walls had been robbed. I walked up to the remaining stones. I could build a turf wall upon them and then build wooden palisades. As yet I had no warriors but when I did we could rebuild and defend. The ditch would need deepening. All that it required was hard work. I returned to my quarters and laid out my bed. Along one wall I placed my armour and weapons and on the short wall, my spare clothes. I carried the cooking implements down to my new kitchen; that done I led Blackie to the river to get water. While he drank, I filled my two buckets with the sparkling river water. When we returned to my kitchen, I found some loose stones and constructed a fire on which to cook. I had some oats which I would share with Blackie. He would have his raw and I would cook mine. It would not be tasty but it would stave off the hunger pangs until I could hunt. While that was cooking,

I repaired the door to the ground floor. I would, at least, be able to bar it from any predators, human or animal.

After my frugal meal, I retired to the top of the tower. It was a clear night and I looked for the seven stars. Seven was a magical number among my people and it was said, by some, that the stars could foretell the future. I lay back and stared into the black night sky and the twinkling stars. What did they portend for me?

Suddenly Blackie whinnied; a sure sign of danger. I went to my quarters and grabbed my bow. I returned to the tower and peered cautiously over the top. I knew I would see nothing immediately. I would have to let my eyes adjust to the dark first. I detected movement. There were men and they looked to be three warriors; I could see their spear points. They were armed. The question was, who were they? I did not have a clear target and I watched the shapes as they moved up from the bridge towards the ditch. When they crossed the ditch then they would die. Whoever they were they were good. They kept a low profile and used whatever cover they could. When they neared the ditch they split up and I had the problem of choosing the best target from amongst them. Had I seen them more clearly I would have chosen the leader but I could not discern, in the dark, any difference between them. I put down the bow and slipped down to the room where I drew my sword. They did not know that I had spotted them and I would have the advantage. I would not die in this tower; that much I knew. I stroked Blackie as I passed my horse, munching oats, a rare treat for him. I slowly unbarred the door and crept around the side of the tower. I held a dagger in my left hand and my sword in my right; I was calm and I was ready. They had split up which gave me the advantage. They would come at me one by one and, thus far, even champions did not worry me. I could handle three rogue warriors.

I saw the first blade appear around the edge of the gate and I swung the sword around. Just before it connected with the warrior's throat I recognised him. It was Garth; it was one of the warriors from my shield wall and wedge. He dropped to his knees. "My lord! I am sorry. We thought you were a Saxon."

I burst out laughing, "And I thought that you were three assassins."

The other two stepped from the shadows and I recognised them as more warriors from our warband. "Come, let us go from the shadows. I am sure I have something to drink and to celebrate this reunion." I opened the door and Blackie gave us a bored look and went back to his oats. I found flint and lit a tallow candle which gave off a smoky yellow light. I led them to my quarters and found the jug Brother Osric had given me. I searched around and found three beakers. I poured a little into each one and held the jug up. "Here is to the victors of Metcauld." I swallowed from the jug and they quaffed their beakers.

"What are you doing here, my lord?"

"I am the new lord of this land. The King has commissioned me to raise a force to defend this land from the Saxons."

The three of them cheered. "That is the best news we have heard in a long time, my lord, for the Saxons, have raided here many times and taken away slaves."

"You live here?"

"Aye." The three of them were young warriors although they were large men and had shown great skill in the wedge. "Our families all have farms hereabouts."

*Wyrd*! Once again forces greater than I could comprehend were working in my favour. "Would you like to be the start of my army?" Their faces gave me their answer before their answers confirmed it. "Good, then return to your homes and tell your families that you will be stationed here. You are the first warriors in my warband." Had I given them a box of gold I could not have had a better reaction. I had been worried that I would be alone here and now there were four of us. Not much of an army, but a start.

The next morning there were not three warriors but ten. I frowned. I did not want to take away workers who would be needed to tend to animals and look after the land. I looked at Garth. "Are these men not needed on their farms and in their homes?"

Garth grinned and shook his head. "They will return home to work on their farms when you do not need them, my lord, but when they heard that the Wolf Warrior with Saxon Slayer was the new lord, they could not wait to serve you."

"In that case, they are welcome but I am aware of the needs of families. I want you all to return home and give your parents this. It is compensation for the loss of your labour." I gave each of them one of the silver pennies with King Urien's face upon it. They looked at the silver in amazement. Some of them had never seen coins before. "I will pay for all goods and services hereabouts. I am here, we are here, to protect the people, and not to rob them." It was only much later that I realised that the simple act of giving the coins embedded me in the community faster than a victory on the battlefield. No one had given these people anything before. Others had taken and this was a change. King Urien had brought hope.

We decided to improve the tower with the damaged roof and repair the gate first. That way the garrison of ten men would have somewhere to eat and to sleep. We moved my improvised kitchen to what had been the blacksmith building close to the walls. I delegated that task to Garth and I took the opportunity of riding around my new fiefdom. It seems word of my arrival had spread quicker than fleas on a dog and everyone greeted me by name. Many of the men touched my sword for luck and I could see that King Urien's plan was working. When I returned I took Garth to one side. "Do you know of any of the women hereabouts who have skill with a needle or can weave?"

"Aye, my lord. Carlin's mother is a wonder with both."

"What I want is a standard with the same design as my shield." I held up my shield although I knew he knew the design. "Could she do that?"

He grinned. "Let me borrow your shield and you shall have it." I gave him a silver penny which he was reluctant to take. "She will gladly do it."

"Garth, this is silver taken from the Saxons. Give it to the woman. We take nothing and we pay for all."

That simple act reaped dividends far in excess of the one coin. Men from the surrounding villages and farms came to deepen the ditch. I had hunted and I gave them a dinner of roast venison. As we enjoyed the food after a hard day's work I addressed them. "I lived as you did with my family and the Angles came and killed them. The King has sent me here to stop that happening to you. If the Saxons or the Angles come, and I believe they will, then bring your families here and we will defend them. But more than that you will all need training as warriors." I spread my arm to include Garth and his nine companions. "These warriors will be the nucleus of my army but eleven men cannot defeat a Saxon warband, even if they do have Saxon Slayer." They all roared and cheered. "I want you all here on the holy day so that we can teach you how to become warriors."

One greybeard asked, "But we have no weapons."

"You will have. While my men repair the walls of the fort, I will bring you weapons so that when the Saxons come, they will feel Rheged steel and they will find easier victims to plunder!"

I saddled Blackie the next day and left Garth to improve the defences. He had to cut down trees and make ramparts behind which the people who lived nearby could shelter while their men killed the enemy, and I was going into the land of the enemy to find those weapons. I was returning to my secret cache. My men would be as well armed as the Romans were and the Saxons would learn to fear the warriors of the wolf. I did not take armour nor did I use my helmet. It would be my bow, sword and wolf cloak which would protect me.

I worked out that I was less than forty miles from the Roman fort on the Dunum; I could not get there and back within a day but I could make most of the way back and be closer to home. Not that that would save me if the Saxons pursued. In that case, I would have a lonely and unmarked grave. I risked the road to make the quickest time. The Romans had built well and the gentle turns took the pain from the climbs. When I reached the windswept tops of the hills I could see the land of my birth nestling fifteen miles ahead. I hoped that the Saxons had no-one watching the road or this could be a short journey and a savage death. I had with me some sacks which would carry whatever weapons remained. It was worth the risk to give my new warriors weapons which could hurt the enemy.

When I neared the river I left the road and walked Blackie. He would need a rest from my weight anyway. I gave him a bagful of oats while I scouted the bridge. The enemy were there. They had occupied the bridge and were denied passage. I could not dig up any of the other treasure and I would have to rely on the goods I had stashed years before. I walked Blackie and soon found my spot. It was undisturbed. I dug up the weapons and found that they had begun to rust but it was superficial. There were ten swords and ten daggers. I put them in sacks and balanced them on my saddle. There was one mail shirt which I laid across Blackie's flanks and there were twenty javelin heads. Those I split between two bags. I was torn between the nails and the caligae for I could not bring both and eventually settled on the nails. At least they would come in useful to improve the defence of shields and in the making of arrowheads.

I walked away from the river with Blackie. I would ride him when we reached the road. We were not far from the road when he whinnied. It had to be the enemy. I was too far from friends. I tied him to a tree and took out my bow. I saw three Saxons searching the ground. They had found my tracks. They were a hundred paces from me and they would inevitably find me. Blackie was in no condition to gallop anywhere. I had to stop them from finding me. I stabbed three arrows into the ground. I drew my bow. When they were eighty paces from me, still peering at the ground I loosed. Before I had struck the lead warrior I had drawn and loosed a second. Both men died instantly but before I could loose my third the last warrior dropped to the ground. I smiled to myself. It would be a blind shot but I knew where he was; I loosed and then, drawing my sword, I ran. When I reached him I saw that I had pinned his shoulder to the ground. He was bleeding to death but slowly.

I spoke to him in Saxon. "You are dying." He nodded. "I can give you a warrior's death if you answer some questions." I drew his sword and held it in my hand.

"What do you want to know, Lord Lann?"

"You know my name?"

"Every Saxon knows your name; the warrior with the wolf cloak who killed King Ida's champion. We were hunting for you. King Ida has put a price upon your head."

"Who is King Ida?"

"He held Metcauld until you took it."

"And where is this lord now?"

"He gathers an army in the south and next year he will come north to kill you and all the men of Rheged."

"Thank you." I took his sword and ended his life. This was news indeed. I stripped the swords, daggers, spears and helmets from the dead and loaded Blackie. I would need to walk further!

My warriors met me on the road the next day. They had been worried when I had not returned and I was touched. I gave them the first choice of weapons and Garth appreciated the mail shirt and the Saxon helmet. The spare weapons and spearheads were reserved for the men of the community.

"Garth, I will ride to the King on the morrow. Continue the work."

The King was not in the fortress but Brother Osric was. I explained to him what I had discovered. "That is worrying. The King had thought that the defeat of this Ida would have dented his ambitions but it seems not." He smiled at me. It seems you are always surprising us."

I shrugged, "I just do what I feel is right."

"And it is always the correct decision. I have some bow staves and arrows, would your new fellows like them do you think?"

"I think we could make use of them but I could do with a spare horse."

"We can manage that too. And your cleric is here. Brother Oswald fled the Saxons to the south. He is a young man and will work hard."

Brother Oswald was a happy, cheerful priest. On the journey back to Castle Perilous I discovered that he did not mind me being a pagan just so long as I didn't mind his trying to convert me. I wished him luck with that enterprise. I found that he had some skills with healing which would be useful. He told me that Brother Osric had impressed on him the need to take all administrative burdens from my shoulders. He grinned as he told me, "Brother Osric said you are a warrior from your toes to your head. He said you are the consummate warrior." I had wanted to ask him what the word consummate meant but I assumed it was a compliment.

When I reached my castle I was a satisfied man. My men had made the gatehouse into a stronghold with a deep ditch which had an ankle breaker at the bottom. They had lined one side with stakes and made the wooden walls firm and easily defended. They had roofed what I assumed had been the Principia so that we had a room we could use to eat and meet, leaving our towers as our barracks. Brother Oswald found a small room which suited him as both an office and cell. From the look of the debris in there, I deduced he was hard working!

On the first morning after the work was completed, I gathered my men around me. "We are a small company. We cannot just use one method of fighting." I held up Saxon Slayer. "In a shield wall this is unbeatable...unless, of course, we are heavily outnumbered but we can reduce the numbers of our enemies with this." I held up my bow. "Three of you have witnessed its power but, by the time winter is upon us, you will all be proficient archers and the Saxons will fear us."

I was kept busy training my men as archers and the local men as part-time warriors but it was worth it. More men came each holy day and we soon had forty men. They were rough and ready and they would not stand up to a Saxon horde but they could defend my walls and they would kill Saxons and that is all that I could hope. The nails I had brought back were used to give my warriors better shields and we encouraged our other soldiers to make a shield, however rudimentary. All had a Roman sword, a dagger or a spear. I promised them that, after our first battle, we would have more. Brother Oswald kept a record of their names and their families. I felt that was important. If they died then we knew which families would need our help.

As the harvest was collected in I prepared my warriors to march to the king's muster for winter training. The headman of the nearest village, Ambrosius, organised a rota of my part-time soldiers to garrison the fort while we were away and they would be supervised by Brother Oswald. They were honoured and proud to be given the task and I knew that, when we returned, it would be in better condition than when we left it. Finally, as we left, Garth carried my Wolf Standard and I thought that we looked like real warriors. They walked behind Garth and me like legionaries from the Roman Imperial army and could not wait to meet the Saxons in battle.

Civitas Carvetiorum seemed bigger and more solid after my time in the shell of my new home. Garth and the two warriors from my shield wall had been there but the other seven looked at the imposing walls in amazement. I could hear their words as we approached along the Roman Road.

"The Saxons could never take such a castle."

"How did they make the walls so high?"

"Look at the men on the walls. King Urien must be the greatest king in the whole of the land."

I smiled to myself; it was almost the same conversation my brothers and I had had when we had first seen it. The sentries stood aside as we entered. "Garth, take the men to the barracks and then stable our horses. I will join you later." Garth strode confidently towards the barracks, smiling at the naïve young warriors who were so intimidated by the experience thus far.

Brother Osric barely glanced up as I entered the Principia. "You are not the first to arrive this time. Lord Gildas is with the King already." He finally put down his quill and looked at me. "He was disturbed by the intelligence you gave him. He has had the news confirmed by other refugees fleeing the invader." He actually looked concerned as he put his hands together and said. "It is highly likely that you will be the first to know of any attack. How are your defences?"

I shrugged. "I have fifty men. Only ten are warriors but we can protect the people from the area. I am not sure that I could deny the Saxons the passage of the bridge and that is the point of the castle is it not?"

"That is the king's worry too but he will tell you of his plans, I doubt it not. Fortunately, the muster is going well and the King is pleased." He looked at me, giving me the scrutiny he always did. "How is Brother Oswald working out?"

"He is, as you told me, hardworking and he fits in well."

"Good, I am afraid we have not been able to procure a warrior to help you."

"Do not worry. I have enough local men and I would prefer to have men with something to fight for."

The King, Gildas and Ywain were gathered in his hall with the map of Rheged before them. Their smiles told me that I was welcome and I did feel at home. These were men I trusted and I felt sorry for Riderch serving such a devious man as Morcant Bulc. King Urien's men fought for more than a man and a country, they fought for an idea.

"Welcome, Lord Lann, and thank you for your news, however grievous and worrying, it has allowed us to plan."

"I explained to Brother Osric that, while I could protect the people, I cannot stop an army invading. There would be too many of them."

"I know, and Ywain has a solution."

"My bodyguards have spent the autumn learning to be true equites and we can now fight from the back of a horse. We can cover great distances on horseback. If we alternate our patrols from here to your fort and here to Raibeart's it means that we will be within a day of you both at any time. We could summon the army. You will have a patrol every three days."

"But if they come from the south, through Glanibanta…"

"Then your brother Aelle would be in a worse position than you for he is the most isolated of the outposts."

I looked at the map and the extensive land that was Rheged. The mountains and lakes made travel difficult, especially from the south. "You need riders in each fort. Not warriors but young boys who ride fast ponies and horses. If each fort had three or four such riders then they could bring daily despatches to Brother Osric."

Gildas scratched his head. "And how would that help us?"

"If you had news then it would reach the King quickly and if a rider did not arrive then it would be an instant method of alerting the King to danger." They nodded at the sense. "There must be many ponies which are too small to be used for war and there must be many young boys who are too small and young to fight. I know that I have at least six who could carry out the task. As Prince Ywain says, no fort is more than a day away from here."

"When all the Seven Stars are here we will tell them and then we can begin the training. We will only keep the men for two weeks. I fear the Saxons may try a winter attack."

Gildas looked at his uncle in horror. "But they have never fought in winter before."

"I know, which is why they may try it. They know that we have no standing army and it may be the trick that will capture this kingdom for them."

"In which case, we would have to let the land fight for us. Winter is harsh here and the Saxons will find it hard to move when the snows come."

It was good to see my brothers. Aelle looked as though he had suddenly become a man and he had the confident look of someone who has had his life changed. "It is Freja, brothers. She is with child and she makes me happy. It seems that she was taken as a slave when the Saxons raided Elmet. She was only a child and she learned their language. She had no choice of her husband." He blushed, "She said that she had longed to choose a man for herself."

"And she chose well, brother. How is your fiefdom?"

"It is a rich land. The fort is now repaired and we have over a hundred men who can fight although they are not warriors and would not stand in a shield wall." He grinned and was suddenly my little brother again, "but they are excellent slingers and archers."

"With you as their teacher how could they be anything else and you, brother, how is life on the wall?"

"The fort needed little repair but there are few people who live there. I only have twenty men who can fight but they are tough men. They have to be to live on the wall."

I had told them about my news. "We three will be the first to be attacked if the Saxons come and you, Aelle, are the most vulnerable."

"I know, but there is a mere to the north of us and an island is on that water. I have had boats constructed. If they come then I can send my people to the island where they can hide and be safe from attack. My men will fight harder if they know their families are safe. My fort is not large but it has water on three sides. There are many places between here and there where a determined force could halt them because the valleys are narrow."

"Aye, but come they will and the King worries they might come in the winter."

The training was a success. We learned to fight in a battle line which now had horse warriors on both flanks. We had better weapons and arms than when we had gathered before and we had a much bigger army. When we paraded before the King, we had over seven hundred and fifty warriors. It was not the largest army but it was the largest one I had ever seen. I noticed the envious glances from my brothers when they saw my wolf standard. I knew that when they returned home they would also order the making of their own rallying point. We departed just when the first snows came. Brother Osric had procured the requisite ponies. Six for each of us and I felt better knowing that we now had communication with the King and each other. The three of us shared the road east from the capital for we were loath to part. The time we had spent apart had made us somehow closer.

"Remember, little brother, tell us when you are a father, we would both like to wet the baby's head."

He blushed. "I will, but Freja's daughter, Anya, calls me father now." He shrugged, "And I did nothing for that one."

We left each other ten miles along the road. Raibeart, north, I went east and Aelle and his handful of warriors had the longest road, south."

# Chapter 14

We had many offers to be despatch riders. I used Garth and Brother Oswald to help me choose. Garth knew which families needed the extra hands on the land and Brother Oswald would be dealing with them on a daily basis. I remembered when we had lived at Stanwyck there were always tasks for the three of us. Eventually, he found four. We would only need three initially but the fourth was probably too small and young to be used, however, they all needed work. None could ride and that was my task. Having taught myself I knew how difficult it would be. There was a leather worker in one of the nearby settlements and, in exchange for some of my nails, he made three simple saddles. While they were being made, we gave the boys some slings and taught them how to use them; they were young and quick learners. There were few enough warriors to fight the Saxons without discarding the young. While I taught the four boys to ride, Garth and the rest of my men worked on enlarging our hall under the supervision of the quick-witted Brother Oswald. It was crudely built, using the stones of the Roman Praetorium, but we had used wattle and daub and turf buttresses to make it stronger. Aelle's island refuge had set me to thinking; we needed somewhere for the people to shelter with their livestock when the Saxons came. We had plenty of water but not enough accommodation. By enlarging the hall, however crudely, we would save lives.

As a precaution, Garth or one of the other senior warriors took to riding a twenty-mile loop around the area to look for sign of tracks. Blackie was a quiet and reliable horse and he gave the novice warriors a gentle ride. When I could, I would get a second horse for Garth. Ywain and his patrol came every third day and, as the White Christ's birthday approached, I felt sure that the Saxons had yet to make an appearance.

Once they were ready the three chosen boys could not wait to make their first journey. We had made them a tabard with a wolf's head emblazoned upon it. It served two purposes, it told the guards at the fort where they came from and it gave them some extra protection from the biting cold. The ponies which had been a little thin when they arrived had benefited from the fine grazing on the river bank and their winter coats shone in the snow. We watched with some trepidation for the return of the first rider. When he did there was an audible sigh of relief. The messages were oral of course because neither the boys nor I could read. The first message was banal and yet a relief. "No sign of the Saxons." They soon developed a close relationship with our cleric.

Once the system worked I could return to my main job; watching for the Saxons. The two days when there was no patrol I would take out five of my men. While I was away Garth or one of the other senior men would remain at the fort. I rotated the men for I wanted to know their mettle. I was pleased with what I saw. They were all keen and willing to learn. They all had bows and I combined the patrols with foraging for food and soon we were bringing game back every day. Sometimes it was merely hares, rabbits and squirrels but it supplemented the diet; at other times we managed to bring back a deer. So far the wild boars had eluded us but I was a patient man. The community also brought their surplus; sometimes some old apples or plums or vegetables which would not last the week and sometimes surplus meals, about to go off. We learned to make sustaining stews on the pot which we kept constantly bubbling. My mother always maintained that a truly hungry man would eat anything.

Garth and I were on patrol and I had left Blackie at the fort. It did not seem equitable to ride while my men walked. It was not as though we could go any faster. "Are the people pagan or Christian, Garth?"

"They are a mixture. Why do you ask, my lord?"

"I was wondering if they celebrate the White Christ's birthday or the winter solstice."

"They do both but their celebrations tend to be on a small scale. The people hereabouts are poor."

Then I had an idea. "They could come to us. The men will want to be with their families and we could hold the feast in the fort. If we hunted on the days of Prince Ywain's patrol, then we might bag some larger game."

The look on Garth's face told me that it was a good idea. "They will all bring what little they have and it will be a good way to celebrate our first winter in the fort."

Garth was the bearer of the good tidings and I sent a message to Brother Osric asking for some wine. I made sure the messenger boy explained why I had made the request and when he returned, he was grinning. "The Brother said that if it was just for you then you would wait until hell froze over but as part of the King's initiative, he would send a wagon tomorrow."

The days until the festival flew by. The offer had been greeted with joy and gratitude; if only for the fact that they would have shelter and be feasting on the shortest day of the year. Osric did more than send the wine; he sent some onions and garlic from the fort's supplies as well as a small jug with King Rhydderch's fiery liquid. Brother Oswald had embraced the idea and had suggested that we make it a two-day feast or they would have to leave in the dark and the wolves had been howling again. I did not mind and I made sure that the warriors had cut plenty of wood for the fires. It had ten days to dry out and would provide a cheery atmosphere. As we went hunting, all my warriors and the three despatch riders, I felt strangely sad. I would be the only one without his family but that came with the title; my new family were my people.

We had a successful hunt. Having so many hunters we were able to spread out further and we managed a wild boar, two small deer, a dozen rabbits and five brace of wild birds. We would eat well whilst we feasted on the shortest days of the year.

The farmers and villagers began to arrive with their families just after dawn on the shortest day of the year. Some must have begun walking in the middle of the night and they were grateful for the blazing fire my men had lit. Every family which arrived brought something, either food or a bowl they had made or something they had woven. Some even brought their animals. I did not mind. There was room aplenty in the fort. Soon the smell of the roasting meat wafted across the land and the community began hurrying in. It was an emotional time for some of them lived ten or more miles from the fort and had not seen their sons and brothers that were my warriors. The mothers of the despatch riders wept openly when they saw how much their bairns had grown. As the sun began to dip behind the western hills we began to eat. Brother Oswald and the Christians all said prayers to their God while we pagans saluted the gods who had delivered the bounty. I had watered down the wine to make it go further but added a small amount of King Rhydderch's fire and we all drank a toast to King Urien. Before I could start to eat Garth stood, "And a special toast to our lord, Lord Lann the Wolf Warrior and the Saxon Slayer."

I was touched by the response which was as warm as the fire which blazed merrily away. I sat back and watched the scene, happy and sad at the same time; this was the time I missed my family. I listened to their songs after the food had disappeared and we had eaten the puddings and treats that the women had brought. I knew some of them but others were strange to me. Some were so funny that I wept with laughter while others evoked a sad memory of my mother and father and I wept with remembrance. Most had never had wine and they all fell asleep as the fire slowly slumbered to a glowing pile of ash. Like me, Brother Oswald had not had too much to drink and we walked the fort, making sure that the gates were secured. "It was a good day, Brother Oswald."

"Aye, my lord, and it is a good thing that you have done." He looked at me with a mischievous look upon his face, "And a very Christian thing too, my lord."

I peered out at the stone covered land and listened to the wolves howling. "I will ride out just after dawn and do the patrol alone. The men will appreciate the time with their families."

Garth had been dozing next to us and he had heard me. He slurred, sleepily, "I will come with you, my lord."

"You have a family too, and besides, I can cover more of the land on horseback than you can on foot."

There was a warm fug in the hall and huddles of bodies beneath blankets. The snores and flatulent noises spoke of people who had enjoyed themselves. I led Blackie from his stable. Garth stirred himself. "You could have slept on."

"No, my lord, I will bar the gate after you have gone and I will light the fire. We have more feasting today before they depart."

I shook my head. They certainly knew how to enjoy themselves. I had my bow with me and I looked towards the river as I crossed the bridge; it was bubbling away well which suggested there was rain or melting snow on the hills. Any kind of game would come in useful but, more than that, it kept up my skill with a bow for I did not want to lose the skill I once had. I saw little and the fresh snow covered the ground completely. I could see no tracks which boded well for that meant the wolves were not close to the fort. I swept south for a few miles and still saw nothing and then I spied a dirty patch of snow. From a distance, it looked like a herd or a pack had crossed that way and I urged Blackie on to investigate; if I could get a couple of deer then we would eat well for a week. His ears pricked and that told me that the smell in his nostrils was either wolf or man! When I saw the tracks, I knew what it was; man! The Saxons were here. I could see from a quick look that there were many of them for the snow was quite deep and they had marched three or four abreast. The ground was visible as a muddy morass. They were heading for the road.

I jerked Blackie's head around and rode back the way I had come. I did not want to come across them while I was alone and before I could warn my people. When I judged I had travelled far enough north I turned west and really gave Blackie his head. The soft snow made life easy for him and he flew. I felt relief when I saw the walls of the fort still stood. Garth had posted sentries and they waved cheerily as they opened the gates for me. "Bar the gates and stand to. Saxons!"

I dismounted and called over one of the despatch riders. "Ride to the capital and tell them there are Saxons near to the fort."

He looked terrified but he gritted his teeth and went for his horse. I regretted their youth for I would have loved to send one to Aelle to warn him but it was too dangerous. The trail south ran perilously close to the place I had seen the tracks. As a second boy took care of Blackie, Garth strode up and he looked concerned too. "Is it true, my lord? Saxons?"

"I crossed the trail of a warband. Arm as many of the men as we are able, and man the walls. Get the women to bring food to the men on the wall. It will keep them busy and it will help keep up the men's strength." Not all the people round about had come to the fort and we had fifty men only. There were boys who could help but only thirty-five of the men had been trained as warriors. Until we could count them, we were blind. "Keep watch. I will go and arm. Unfurl the standard above the tower." I wanted the Saxons to know who they fought.

Brother Oswald came over. "I will prepare hot water and get the women to make bandages." He cocked his head to one side, just as Brother Osric did, "It will keep them busy and stop them fretting." He was young but he was wise beyond his years.

When I returned Garth pointed to the south. "Look, my lord." There was a plume of smoke from the south. They had raided a farm.

"Who lives there?"

I breathed a sigh of relief when he pointed to a greybeard on the wall, "Tan." He saw the question on my face. "And his family and animals are within."

"Good, then the Saxons will be disappointed." I looked to the skies. Whoever had put the thought of the feast in my fort had had the gift of prophecy for there would have been at least one dead family had I not done so. The villagers and farmers soon heard of the danger from the busy scurrying of my warriors and the arming of the men.

"Over there, my lord. Another fire." Further to the north and east of us, another plume of smoke arose.

I turned to Garth who anticipated my question. "They are here too, my lord."

"Good. Go around and make sure our warriors are evenly spread out with the farmers and others between them. Put the boys with slings around evenly and make sure that everyone is armed. Even if it is just a hatchet or a knife." We would die hard if that was our fate.

I stood on the top of the tower closest to the bridge. The Saxons might be making for the fort but the bridge would make just as good a target. One of the women climbed up the ladder with a hunk of cold boar meat in a wooden bowl and a beaker of river water. "Here you are, my lord; Brother Oswald thought you might be hungry."

I was not hungry and I needed to focus but this woman had been kind enough to bring it to me. "Thank you, I am ready for this."

I took them from her and she bobbed her head. "Will they come for us, my lord?"

"They might come for us but so long as I wield Saxon Slayer, they will go away empty-handed, that I promise you."

Her smile beamed like a flame in the night and she descended. Some other women must have been below for I heard her say, "We will be safe Lord Lann has promised me."

I shook my head. How could they have so much confidence in me? I was much younger than the old woman who had brought me food and the greybeards around me knew much more of life. I glanced down into the fort and saw the woman and her friends watching me. I bit into the pork. Surprisingly, I was ready for it and I wolfed it down quickly and drank the water. I must have pleased them for they all smiled and went about their business. As I watched, another spiral of smoke climbed out of the grey sky to the northeast. It looked to be close to the river. I knew why they had confidence in me, I was a warrior, I was a killer and I would kill for them.

Garth came running down the ramparts. "That is the home of Scanlan and his wife. They are old and chose not to come in. She sent the apple pudding you enjoyed." The look on his face told me that he knew them well. They would have died but, they would, if they had been captured, have told the Saxons of the fort and the warriors; if King Ida wanted my death, he now had the means.

"Prepare the men; it will not be long now." I hoped the despatch rider had made good time but it was a long ride to the King. I just prayed that they were celebrating the White Christ's birthday.

I saw some movement in the trees to the east and one of my warriors at the far corner yelled, "Saxons!"

I strode down the rampart to see with my own eyes how many men we faced. By the time I reached the corner, they were streaming from the woods. It was a large warband but it did not look to be an army. The leader wore a helmet similar to mine but more plainly decorated and I saw a torc around his neck. They halted three hundred paces from the walls. At first, I wondered why and then I saw them pointing at the standard above the tower and then at me. They knew who they fought and they remembered my arrows. This was good. It would buy us time. What I did not want was a night attack for that would only serve them and not us.

"How many, Garth?" I had counted but I wanted a second opinion.

"Over a hundred." He grinned. "The odds are in our favour, my lord."

I laughed and strung my bow. They were three hundred paces away and thought that they were out of range but I was high above them and they were tightly packed. "Let us test their courage, Garth." I drew back and let fly. The arrow soared high into the air, disappearing against the white. Then it plunged down and, fortuitously, it must be admitted, it struck a warrior in the neck and he fell dead. The effect was instantaneous. The rest all fled to the safety of the trees, all that is, except the leader who steadfastly stared at the walls.

The effect on the garrison was also immediate. They all cheered as though I had slain a hundred men rather than the one. "I want no one trying to emulate me. We loose the arrows on my command."

The Saxon leader turned to his men and I could hear angry shouting. They emerged reluctantly and held their shields before them. Urged on by their chief they raced across the snow towards the walls. The snow was our ally that day for it hid the traps in the ditch. I knew that we did not have a great supply of arrows, that task was to have been the work of the winter, and so I waited until they were thirty paces short of the hidden ditch. "Loose." We had but fifteen bows and yet they were effective. Even the ones who took arrows on their shields had a greater weight to carry. The boys with the slings were even more effective as they had a direct trajectory and were able to score hits on many of the Saxons. The barbarians closed up behind the shields and pushed on. I was aiming my bow carefully and each arrow found a victim. My men kept pulling and loosing until I knew their arms were aching fit to drop. Raibeart's men would have halted the attack. These were not archers; these were farmers with a bow. When they reached the ditch I heard the screams as some had their ankles broken by the fall and others stood or fell on to the spikes we had cunningly laid there. Even there my novice archers and slingers caused casualties. When the raiders tried to clamber out, they found the banks a slippery morass of mud. We constantly wet it. The men found it funny each night and each morning to piss on the bank and now they laughed as the Saxons struggled to climb up the treacherous slope.

Their leader was a foolish man. Had he spread his men around the walls then he would have suffered fewer casualties instead he concentrated on one wall but now, climbing over those dead or wounded, his warriors steadily approached the walls. Here they were a danger. "Get ready with your spears!"

The bottom part of the wall was stone-faced with turf and they began to clamber up. Once they reached the wood, they had a problem for it was too high to climb. The noise of the battle stopped me from hearing the chief's words but suddenly pairs of men held a shield for a third warrior to climb upon. They were now the same height as those men on the ramparts. "Archers to the towers!" The towers were both higher and the archers could continue to rain death upon the Saxons but now it was down to the work with swords and axes and these Saxons were all warriors.

I laid down my bow and drew Saxon Slayer. I descended the tower and stepped onto the rampart just as a farmer was pushed to the ground below. I had the advantage for my opponent's sword was on the rampart side and he was forced to bring the sword down to allow him to make a thrust. I had no such obstacle and I swung my blade upwards to sever his leg above the knee. He fell to the floor of the fort where the angry women, literally, tore his body to pieces. I saw a Saxon head appear above the wooden walls and I swung the sword to take his head but now the rest were pouring over the walls and my men were falling to the superior weapons and armour of the Saxons. The boys were still causing men to fall with their stones but, my three trained men apart, we were ill-matched. I stabbed a Saxon through the spine as he tried to decapitate Garth and then I leaned over the wall to put Saxon Slayer through the neck of a man who was about to be launched over the wall.

"Now I will claim the reward from King Ida when I bring back your head in a bag." I sensed the weapon striking my unprotected back and I thrust my shield around. The axe bit into the leather and was held tightly by the nails. I stabbed below his shield into his knee and twisted the blade as I removed it. He screamed. Regardless of the result of this combat, he would be crippled for the rest of his life. "You have no honour, Wolf man!"

"I fight honourably against honourable warriors not Saxon shit like you!"

He pulled hard on his axe to remove it from my shield and almost overbalanced. I stabbed forwards and felt the blade cut through his mail shirt and along his side. It was not a killing wound but it would slow him up. I almost slipped on the blood which was flowing freely from his knee but I kept my balance. Suddenly one of the boys in the tower shouted, "Lord Lann! Duck!" I quickly lowered my head as the stone flew from his sling and struck the warrior behind me full in the face, throwing him to his death. The chief was becoming reckless and he swung his axe at my head as I raised it. Had it struck me I would have died instantly but the edge of my shield caught the handle and the blade flew harmlessly over the top of my helmet. The momentum carried the blade around and I took my chance; I stabbed my sword into his neck, below his facemask. The axe fell and he crumpled to the floor.

Before I could turn to face another warrior I heard a voice from the tower. "It is the Prince. He comes!"

I looked over the walls and saw Prince Ywain and sixty horsemen plough into the Saxons waiting to climb into the ditch. With their chief dead and enemies to their rear, they fled, pursued by Ywain. Few would return home. "Garth! Finish the wounded Saxons!

All around me were the dead Saxons. None lived. I looked over the wall and saw that the survivors had all fled. We had survived. I looked to see how many of my men still lived. It was hard to tell. The women were tending to their husbands, brothers and sons and that meant that more of the wounded would survive but it had been a close-run thing. I could see Brother Oswald calmly bandaging a man's arm. He caught my eye and smiled; I thanked Brother Osric for sending me such a reliable cleric. I picked up the chief's dagger and went up to the tower. "Who shouted the warning?"

They all pointed at a boy who stood grinning. "I did, my lord."

"And what is your name?"

"Tuanthal."

"Well, Tuanthal, I am in your debt, and when you are big enough to wield a sword I would have you join my warriors but, in the meantime, here is the chief's dagger and two silver pennies."

They were both gifts which the boy did not expect. The dagger was ornate with a magnificent scabbard and a bone handle and he had obviously never had coins before. "Thank you, my lord, but I did not do it for the reward."

"I know, which is why the reward is well earned."

Four of my warriors and another eight of the men who had come to the Castle Perilous for the feast had died. As Garth pointed out, had the Saxons been loose in the valley then all would have died along with us in the fort. The Saxon dead were stripped and piled outside the fort. We used kindling and wood to make a bonfire of their bodies. The smell of burning flesh was a savage reminder of how close we came to dying. The Saxons had lost over a hundred dead. All of the men wounded in the ditch had had their throats cut by men eager to vent their anger upon them.

It was dark when Ywain and his men returned. The women had cooked up the remains of the food and the weary horsemen were greeted with hot food as they stabled their horses and warmed themselves in the now overcrowded hall.

"We chased them until we could no longer see them. On the morrow, we will find and strip their bodies. What were your losses?"

"Not as many as it might have been but too many to be acceptable. Do you think this was the invasion?"

He shook his head. "No, there were not enough of them. The leader, what did he look like?" I showed him his helmet and torc. "These look like a minor chief. I think they will come but in greater force. We have been lucky."

"I believe the gods of this land protected us with the snow."

He smiled, "Perhaps the snow is the sign of the White Christ and perhaps he saved his people."

"Let us agree that it was the gods of all the people who helped."

The families were reluctant to leave the next day. Ywain came over to me. "They will have to go back now, Lann. It will be safe for them. The Saxons are dead."

"And yet I can understand their fear. Leave it with me, Prince Ywain, and I will devise something." They all cheered Ywain as he left. Brother Osric would be happy with the booty. I put my men on guard and then Garth and I addressed them with Brother Oswald looking on. "I know that you are reluctant to return to your homes. You are welcome to stay here. We are not throwing you out but I will tell you that it will be safe for you to return home. I also promise that, if there are four or five families living in a village we will come and build you a ditch and a wall such as we have and you can take arms we captured from the Saxons. You are not being abandoned, and should the Saxons return then you are welcome inside my fort at any time."

One of the older men said, "Lord Lann is right. If we leave our land then they have won. I will return." He picked up a sword and a shield from the pile outside the hall. "But I will be prepared and I will learn how to use a bow." He laughed, "Then I can kill as Lord Lann did!"

His words were the stone which starts the avalanche and they picked up weapons and helmets as they left the fort. Garth looked ruefully at the diminishing pile of weapons. "There go our spare weapons, my lord."

Brother Oswald said quietly, "Regard it as an investment. They will look after their weapons and learn how to use them. You lost three brave men yesterday but through this, you will gain many more recruits."

As I looked around, I saw one young woman who had not moved and she was alone. I looked at Garth who said, "That is Aideen, her husband and father both died. She is alone."

Brother Oswald looked like he would speak with her but there was something about her and I shook my head. And, although I could not tell the priest, I heard my mother's voice in my head exhorting me to comfort her. He nodded goodnight and headed for his cell.

I went down to her. She looked to be the same age as Raibeart and she looked to be in shock. I had seen the same with warriors after their first battle when they have survived and cannot believe it. The villagers had taken their dead with them to be buried near to their homes. There were two bodies covered with cloaks and I assumed they were her husband and father. I was better speaking with warriors than men. This needed Aelle for he had a way with women and knew the words to use. "I am sorry for your loss."

She stood and threw her arms around my waist and wept. Garth and my warriors watched with interest. They could see that I knew not what to do. Garth mimed putting my arms around her shoulders. I did so and she began to sob, her whole body shaking. Garth waved the men away I heard him mumble something about jobs to be done and then he too went to check that the gate had been fastened.

After a while, her sobs subsided and she pulled away. Her face was red and puffy. "I am sorry, my lord, but I am alone now and when I saw you there, I thought you reminded me of my father and..." she threw her arms around me and began to cry again. I could see this was going to take some time and then a picture of a terrified Monca and a young Aelle came to mind. If all I had to do was to stand there and let this young woman cry then I could do that. This time when she stopped, I held her at arm's length. Now, Aideen, what would you like us to do for you?"

It was obvious that she had not thought beyond the next moment. "I have no home now. Our animals are there." She pointed to a milk cow and a couple of goats. Her eyes filled with terror. "Do not send me away I beg you, my lord!"

"You heard my words. No one has to leave and you are welcome to stay here but we have things to do." There was no easy way to say what I had to. "We needs must put your father and husband beneath the ground. Would you like them buried at your home?"

She shook her head violently, "No, my lord. I do not want to return to my home, ever, it is far from here and we have no neighbours. Could we bury them here?"

My men were already digging graves for their comrades and two more would not inconvenience them. "Of course."

Garth had been close by and obviously listening. "I will see to it, my lord."

I picked up a discarded cloak, "Now wash your face and put this cloak about you. We will honour your family and then we will talk of your future." It was as though I had lit a lamp in a dark room for her face lit up with hope.

When we had laid the bodies beneath the ground and covered them with stones Brother Oswald said some comforting words to send them beyond our world and then we re-entered the fort. "I have arranged for the men to guard tonight in pairs." Garth smiled. "I think our boys did well enough today and need to sleep."

"Do not forget to rest yourself, Garth, for you did well today. You all did." He inclined his head and went to the tower. We needed a couple of dogs. The men could sleep at night and the dogs would act as sentries. I thought of Wolf. Aelle would be reaping the benefit of his alertness.

Brother Oswald said, "Good night, my lord; I will complete an inventory tomorrow and send a despatch rider to Brother Osric for supplies."

I went into the hall where Aideen sat next to the blazing fire. During the battle, the women had tended it and it now burned well. The room seemed empty now with just the two of us. I took off my cloak. I could have done with taking off my armour but I could not leave her alone yet. She turned to look at me. "Can I stay here, my lord? I mean beyond tonight."

"It is a fort filled with men you know. There is no female touch here."

She suddenly smiled and I was reminded of my mother. "If I am here there will be a female touch. I can make cheese. That is what we did with the goats and the cow and I can cook. And I can sew and I can clean."

I held up my hand. "Enough! You can stay and we will make some quarters for you."

It was as though a great weight had been taken from her and she hugged me and placed her head upon my shoulder. I did not know what to do, and so I sat there with her head on my shoulder and her hair smelling of rosemary, and then I felt her body moving slowly and she was asleep. I laid her down gently and covered her with the wolf cloak. *Wyrd* was working hard this night.

# Chapter 15

Aideen proved to be a hard-working woman who made excellent cheese. Her cooking was an improvement on what we had had before and her presence improved the behaviour of the men. I realised that we had needed something like this and I was not displeased. I also found that I liked her laughter and her songs. I woke up and looked forward to the food she would bring and the sing-song greeting she would give. Brother Oswald also took to her for he loved his food and he learned, from Aideen, how to make cheese. I knew that while I was away she would have the kind company of Brother Oswald. As the days lengthened and we settled into a routine of making arrows and repairing the fort I found that I had time to talk with Garth, Brother Oswald and Aideen. I was in a happy place for I could talk of war and strategy with Garth and of domestic matters with Aideen. With Brother Oswald, I could learn much for he was a wise and well-read priest. I was happier and calmer than at any time in my life.

We had found a horse wandering in the woods soon after the battle and we assumed it was the Saxon chiefs. It gave Garth and me the chance to ride further afield and check for intruders. We found three bodies which the Prince had overlooked, although by the time we reached them the wolves and the rats had taken most of the flesh but it afforded us more weapons.

"We have weapons aplenty but what we do not have are the men to wield them."

"Perhaps, my lord, when we begin the training again, we can ask if there are any volunteers, and some of the slingers look to be ready to use swords."

"Good idea, remind me to visit the farms and tell the men when we are to start our practice again."

That night we all sat in the hall and ate the stew Aideen had prepared. It was good to finish off the meal with cheese and she had brewed her first batch of beer. It was not the best but, as Garth said, and he was the beer expert, "Winter is the wrong time of year for good beer." Brother Oswald had also solved the problem of its poor taste by heating a sword in the fire and plunging it into the beer. It transformed the taste. We were living well.

Aideen sang a song of a shepherd falling in love with a maiden and we all enjoyed the fire. I did not notice the men drifting off or Brother Oswald give me a wave of goodnight for I was watching the flames flicker and burn. I saw cities and towns, dragons and mythical beasts. I was suddenly aware that my arm was around Aideen's shoulders and she was looking up at me, her mouth slightly open and smiling. I still do not know what made me do it but I leaned down and kissed her. I had never kissed before, and when her mouth opened and her tongue darted into my mouth, I thought my head would explode. I pulled away slightly. Her smile widened as she murmured huskily, "Do not fight it, my lord. It was meant to be."

Later as we lay naked beneath my cloak, I felt complete. I was far older now than my father had been when he sired me and I wondered why I had waited so long. As I looked at the sleeping Aideen I knew why. I was waiting for her. My mother still influenced my life though long dead. She walked the spirit world and waited for me.

My men were discreet the next morning. Garth organised the food and the guards so that when we arose it was to order and organisation. "I have sent the despatch rider, my lord."

Aideen clung to my arm. "Thank you, Garth. Aideen will share my quarters now." She smiled up at me as did Garth. I think I was the only one to be embarrassed by the events. Then I remembered that Garth knew Aideen and her family. She was only a stranger to me. "I will ride to the fortress today," I looked at Aideen, "I have news for the king."

Aideen stood on her tiptoes to kiss me on my cheek. "And I will clean your ... sorry our quarters. I am sure they have not been cleaned since you moved in." And so my life changed. I went from the lonely life of a lord to a warrior with a wife and soon a child. Still, as I rode down the snow-covered road to Civitas Carvetiorum, I felt I had gained more than I had lost. I now had something else to fight for, my wife, Aideen.

Blackie made good time and we soon caught up with the despatch rider, Adair. He looked disappointed. "Does this mean I have to return to the fort, my lord?"

"No, Adair, although I would have thought you would have wanted to avoid the journey through the snow."

He grinned and I saw that there was still much of the boy in him although he would soon be a man. "No, my lord. Brother Osric always has something for me and the cooks keep a bowl of something good to eat."

I should have known that the kindly priest would enjoy spoiling the boys. They were the children he would never father. The sentries saluted as we entered. "See you later, Adair. I will be returning later and I will accompany you."

"Thank you, my lord. I will wait by the gate." He looked at me seriously and said, confidentially, "they have a brazier there and it is warm." He might be a boy but he was learning the ways of the warrior.

Brother Osric was surprised to see me and his hand covered the honeyed dried plum he had on his desk. "Lord Lann, I was expecting a rider but not you."

I smiled, "He is coming along soon and you can give him his treat then."

"They have a hard journey in the snow and they are little more than boys…"

I held my hand up. "You have no need to explain, Brother Osric, but those boys fought a hard battle against the Saxons and one of them saved my life with a stone."

"Like David from the Bible." I looked confused and he sighed. "The book of Christ and God. He was a shepherd boy and he killed a giant with a stone."

"Well the Saxon was no giant but his axe would have taken my head. Is the King at home?"

"Yes, Ywain patrols today." He paused, "You and your people did well the other day. Prince Ywain said that, had the warband descended into the valley then there would have been much slaughter."

"It is why we are there, Brother Osric." I shrugged. "The sacrifice of ten warriors to save a kingdom is a small price to pay."

Brother Osric suddenly looked concerned. "Do not throw your life away cheaply, Lord Lann. You have much to do in this land and the King depends heavily upon you."

The King looked up from the list he was studying and I thought he looked older. Of course he now only had Ywain and his young son at home and he would be missing his other sons and, I suspected, Gildas and myself. "Does this visit mean trouble?"

I smiled, "No, your majesty, but I have news which I had to deliver to you first, as my liege lord."

"That sounds serious."

"I am taking a wife." His face split into a grin and he beckoned me to sit. I explained to him the circumstances of Aideen's widowhood but I omitted the details of our liaison.

"That is good. I am pleased that two of the wolf brothers are married. Rheged needs sons of fine warriors to continue the fight against the Saxons. You and your warriors did well."

"We were lucky. Had I not brought the people within the fort then all would have perished."

"Perhaps that is something to consider for the future. We cannot protect all the people but those close to the forts can, at least, have winter protection. I am glad that you are here for I can bring you up to date with events in the rest of the kingdom." He took a breath and looked me in the eye as he said, "The Saxons tried an attack on Glanibanta." My heart sank to my boots; Aelle! He saw my concern. "Do not fear your brother survives. He had made the defences even more secure than yours and he did not lose a man. They withdrew. He said that the lake helped them."

I nodded sagely, "Erecura came to their aid as she did to me."

He shook his head and laughed, "I believe it was the White Christ but we can agree to disagree. Someone aided us in our fight against these invaders."

"Agreed."

"When the crops are in and the spring animals are born then we will ask our men to rejoin us. We will muster this time close to your fort for that is where they are most likely to attack. I believe that the raids were Ida's way of testing our defences. He lost many men and many weapons; next time he will try to find a softer way in and I think it will be north of the wall. There are few roads there and the only defence we have is your brother Raibeart."

"What of King Morcant Bulc? If they came up the east then they would have to defeat his armies."

"I have heard that he has made the coastal defences stronger and left the people beyond the coast to their own devices. I fear he is not the King I took him to be. But the last message I had was that he would come to my aid if I needed him."

"By the time we send for him, it may be too late. And how is Prince Ywain enjoying his equites?"

"He is grateful to you for the arms and armour he gathered after the battle. He can now equip his men as mine are, in full mail with lance, shield and sword. He and I hope to have a hundred men each by the spring."

That was the best news I had had in a long time. "The Saxons fear your men, your majesty. That may be the turning point in this war. If my shield wall can halt them, and our archers weaken them then your horsemen can destroy them. I will take this message of hope to my people and it will make their hearts glad."

"You return today?"

"Yes, your majesty."

"Then I will give you a gift before you leave."

I returned to Brother Osric who cocked his head to one side and his piercing eyes bored into me. "And just when were you going to tell me that you had taken a woman? Or was I to be the last to know!"

"I am sorry but I had to ask the King first."

He sniffed which was his way of accepting the excuse. "Here." He took from one of his cupboards a sweet-smelling bag. "Give this to your wife as a wedding present."

"What is it?"

"It is a mixture of dried herbs and petals. It makes rooms smell pleasant. You warriors do not know how to bathe; goodness only knows how the poor woman will survive. And I have some more ash and yew. I assume you would like to make more arrows?"

"It looks like we are going to need them but I now believe we can defeat the Saxons."

"With King Urien at our head we can but if aught happened to him…"

I was shocked. I had never considered that the King might not survive a battle. "He is well protected."

"Aye, he is, and yet one lax moment and he could die. You of all people should know that. Had that boy not shouted at the right time and slung his stone then I would be talking to a ghost now."

As I went to the stables to pick up Blackie and the pony laden with wood, I realised that he was right. We lived a parlous existence. The royal couple awaited me and Queen Niamh held a bundle. It was a fur but it was tied with rope implying that there was something within.

The Queen stood to kiss me on the cheek. "I am glad that you have taken a wife." She wagged an admonishing finger in my face. "Look after her. The fur will keep you warm and within is a dress for the day she marries."

"She has a dress!"

"Men! It is the day she marries and to a woman that is an important day. She will appreciate it even if you do not!" I noticed that the King and Pasgen were hiding their grins and enjoying my discomfort.

"I will do as your majesty says and I thank you for the gift."

She softened and put her hand to my cheek. "Take care. I know that you are in harm's way and we survive here because of your vigilance. May God protect you." She then made the sign of the cross; I noticed the Christians did this many times and had decided it must be a spell they were casting.

As we rode home Adair was quite chatty. On the journey out he had been quiet, almost intimidated, riding with his lord but now he was almost garrulous. "The men in the fort said that you are the greatest warrior in the kingdom. Better even than the king. They say you could defeat any Saxon they send against you."

"Don't always believe what soldiers tell you, Adair. Your own eyes are a better judge."

He looked at me curiously, "Then I will say the same, my lord, for I saw you when we fought the Saxons at the fort. You killed more men with both your bow and your sword than any other."

I could not argue with that. "And what would you be, Adair? Would you be an archer or a swordsman?"

"I would be as you and Lord Raibeart. I would use both!"

I laughed. "Then you had better start building up your body for my brother and I began training for the bow when we were younger than you."

He looked crestfallen. "I did not know."

"Many men believe you just have to pick up a weapon and you will become a warrior. It is not true; your body must be strong to enable you to use the weapon and then you must train long hours to become proficient. The best warriors never stop training."

He said, very seriously. "Then I will begin when we return to the fort."

Aideen rushed to greet me, as though I had been on campaign for the winter. Garth hid his smile as he led the pony and Blackie off. I had carried the Queen's and Brother Osric's gifts with me and, after she had tried to crush the life out of me and we were stood by the fire, I said, "This is a present from Brother Osric."

She held the bag to her nose and whooped excitedly. "What a kind man! This will make your quarters smell better."

"And this is from the Queen."

Her jaw dropped, "From the Queen? For me. It is a lovely fur."

"That is just one of the gifts. There is something within. Open it."

She laid the fur down and carefully untied the knots. There lay a delicate, gossamer thin, white dress. It looked highly impractical to me. It would not keep her warm but she burst into tears. "It is the most beautiful thing I have ever seen."

The Queen had been right. Aideen had seen more in the dress than I had. "We will be married on the morrow. Will that suit?"

She kissed me. "At noon. I will need the morning to get ready."

Many of the nearby villagers, told no doubt by my garrison, turned up for the ceremony. Unlike the Christian wedding, this needed no-one apart from the couple and a witness. We had many witnesses. I spent the morning training with my men; I daresay the Queen would have been appalled. I had decided to marry by the river, Icaunus had always been good to me and Erecura would smile on the union too. I waited with Garth and my men. He had insisted that I wear my wolf cloak and carry Saxon Slayer. "It is who you are, my lord. You are telling your bride and the world that Wolf Warrior has taken a bride."

Although it was still cold and there was snow on the ground, the sun shone and, when Aideen appeared through the gate with the sunlight behind her, it looked as though she glowed. Brother Oswald led her out and, he too looked happy. Aideen's hair was braided and set in coils on her head. Interwoven in the chestnut strands were snowdrops, rosemary and mistletoe. In her hands, she carried a garland of holly and ivy, symbols of birth after winter. She looked beautiful and my heart filled with joy. I could almost hear my mother's rapturous tears. She came to me and we faced each other. I placed my sword and scabbard on the ground. It could have been any piece of wood or straight object but Garth had said that the sword would have greater power than any wood. Holding Aideen's hand, we stepped across the sword, I kissed her and then everyone erupted with cheers, throwing flower petals over us. Brother Oswald mumbled some words in Latin and made the sign of the cross. It did not matter; so long as all the gods protected us then I was happy.

We retired to the hall where we ate the food Aideen had prepared the previous day. When everyone had gone and I lay with her in my arms I knew that another phase of my life was beginning. The first phase had been as a carefree boy in the bosom of his family. The second had been when I learned to be a warrior and now the third was my life as a husband, a father and the champion of Rheged.

As late winter and early spring passed so my wife grew in size with my child. She had wanted to remain at Castle Perilous, as we had named it, but I would have none of that. I would need my guards for the coming campaign and so we escorted her to Civitas Carvetiorum. Brother Oswald would look after our home. He said he would enjoy the peace and the solitude and he could perfect his cheese making. We reached the citadel just as Aelle, his wife and daughter arrived. It was a joyous meeting for us all and the Queen looked as proud as any mother. Having only sons she could enjoy the pleasure of children who would be as her grandchildren and Aelle and I were happy that, no matter what happened on the field of battle, our wives and children would be safe. The King was leaving all the older warriors and those who had suffered wounds to guard his home and family. We had had more men come to join the King's army; success breeds success and we had yet to be bested.

We all set off to return to Castle Perilous. Raibeart and Lord Gildas would meet us there but we had a fine army to seek the Saxons. Once again King Urien led and Ywain brought up the rear. My little brother, not so little any more, rode next to me. "I have a good fiefdom, Lann. When the Saxons came, they could not get close to my walls. The lake covers three sides and I devised a moat around the fourth. It is a temporary structure and I use lake water. It means that, in times of danger, we can stay within the watery walls and be safe. The fort is even large enough to house the local population. I believe you did the same at your castle?"

"True, but had the prince not arrived when he did we would have been destroyed. The Saxons, brother, are well-trained warriors. We fight them with farmers, fishermen and herdsmen. Our men are brave but lack the skill. It is the King and his bodyguard who keep the Saxons at bay. They do not like to face men on horses."

He looked at me shrewdly. "You could fight on a horse you know."

"I am not so sure but that is irrelevant. The King cannot defeat the Saxons without a shield wall to hold them up and that is my job. I am the dam to hold them back while your men whittle them down and then the King destroys them."

"Yours is the most dangerous role."

I shrugged. "I am happy enough. The shield wall is safer than fighting elsewhere. I nearly died in the attack when a warrior got behind me. Tuanthal managed to save my life and now he is one of my warriors."

The spring had brought another crop of despatch riders who now accompanied us on their ponies and would act as mobile slingers. The original three had now become warriors and I went to war with fifteen warriors; all armed with a shield, a spear, a mail shirt and a helmet. The winter battle had been productive. They all had a bow and I had given Aelle five spare quivers, arrows my men had made in the winter. We had learned from the problems at Din Guardi.

The King and the lords stayed in my hall while the men camped in the meadow by the river. We ate well and the men enjoyed practising with other warriors. This time was vital to rekindle old friendships and teach the newer warriors how to stand in a shield wall. Garth carried my standard and stood to my left in battle. The princes and Aelle had their own rallying standards and this campaign would see us more organised than we had been before. It would have been the best of times had it not been for Bladud, who seemed to blight the mood whenever he entered a room. He never said anything but I could sense him glowering at me. Wolf growled each time he approached us and he soon learned to stay on the far side of a room. He was leaner than he had been and I learned that he had been training hard all winter. Aelle was wise beyond his years. "He will come for you one day, brother; mark my words."

Raibeart and Gildas arrived on the same day. They had travelled together for security. Raibeart still only had ten warriors, sound looking archers, but Gildas had thirty men. His fiefdom was rich and it was safe. We three had not met since the autumn and I went with my brothers to the top of my tower where we could have privacy and a good talk. Wolf waited below, guarding us against interruption.

Raibeart looked at Aelle. Like me, he could not believe how much he had grown. "Married life suits you, brother." Then he punched my arm, "and I hear that you have a bride and I am sure that you will sire a son. I can see I will have to look around for one such as you two have found. If you two ugly buggers can win one then I should have no problem."

"Seriously, Raibeart. How is it on the wall?"

"It is bleak and it is cold and there are few people around but I have been luckier than you two. The despatch riders told me of the attacks. How desperate was it?"

"Had Ywain not arrived then I do not know if we could have survived but, you know, I believe that our mother had something to do with it for out of the pain and the death I won a bride and I know that mother would have approved."

"She would indeed, brother. Raibeart, she is beautiful. Freja is a beautiful woman but she appears dowdy next to Aideen."

Raibeart glanced down and caught Bladud looking up at us. "I see the ugly bastard still lives."

"He does and I told Lann that he will come for our brother one day and he had best be ready."

Raibeart grinned. "In the heat of battle, I could send a shaft into his back and no-one would be any the wiser."

I snorted, "The finest shot in the army hitting one of his own men by mistake? I think you delude yourself. Besides, we kill Saxons and not the men of Rheged, no matter how much they deserve it."

That evening the King had his Seven Stars sat in my hall while he spoke of his plans for the campaign. "I think that we will take the war to the Saxons." We all became animated. This was what we had all secretly hoped. "Lann, you and your brothers know the country around the Dunum and the Roman Bridge well. If we can defeat the Saxons there then we can head south and reclaim the old fortress. If we have Stanwyck in our hands once more and defend it, as well as the bridge, then we can control the eastern side of the country. Lord Aelle has shown us how to protect the south. One determined leader and a well-defended fort can thwart an enemy."

Aelle looked proud and I clapped him around the shoulders. Ywain said, "And what of King Morcant Bulc?"

"He has promised me aid and if we fight in the east then he is more likely to give it."

"If he gets off his arse and leaves his castles by the sea." All of the lords, except the King laughed at my comment. "Sorry, your majesty, forgive my attempt at humour: I know he is an ally."

"But you may be right and I do not intend to rely on aid from that quarter. When we defeat the Saxons, it will be by our own efforts." We all banged the table enthusiastically. "I intend to use our despatch riders as scouts."

"Isn't that a little dangerous. They are young."

"I know, Gildas, and yet they have spent a winter putting themselves in danger and learning to live on their wits. I think that they may well be of more use than you can imagine. There are over twenty of them, and if they work in pairs then they can cover a large area." He stood and raised his beaker, we were using my crude wooden, hand carved beakers and I felt a little ashamed of them but the King seemed not to notice. "Here is to the Seven Stars!"

"And King Urien the Good!" we chorused. The next day, we went to war.

# Chapter 16

The King was as good as his word and he gathered the scouts about him the next morning before we left. He gave them an inspirational speech about their role in the coming war and they all rode away riding a little taller in the saddle. They were to be a line five miles ahead of the main column which lumbered along the Roman Road. As we passed all the forts and the defences, most of them now in ruins, I wondered what it would have been like had the Romans remained. Would they have fought the Saxons as we did for I now believed that it was inevitable for them to come to the land of the Britons? We were rich and we were prosperous and they were pirates and parasites who preyed on the weak. The Romans had done many good things for us but taking our soldiers away was not one of them.

We camped the first night by the Tyne. The Roman fort there was on the river and had a bridge. I learned from King Urien that it was called Chesters, the name coming from the Latin for camp, Castra. Little remained of the stone from the walls but we had passed many stone buildings along the road; the locals had obviously robbed them. The scouts returned that first day with no news. When we ate that night the King approached me and my brothers. "You and your brothers have skill in tracking, have you not?"

I nodded. It was not arrogant to acknowledge the truth. "We had to or we would have been killed."

"Tomorrow I would like you each to take out seven despatch riders and teach them how to scout. Lord Raibeart can take north of the river. Lord Aelle next to the river and the road and Lord Lann, south of the river. I am not sure that the scouts did not miss tracks. I find it hard to believe that they found no sign of Saxons."

We grinned at each other. We craved action and this would be like the old days when we were boys. "We would be delighted!"

With the whole army on the road, the King had ordered some wagons for spare arrows and supplies. I put my armour in the back of one of them along with my shield. If any of us needed armour on the patrol then we had failed. I knew that I had the most difficult patrol but it just added to the excitement. I only knew Adair from the group of scouts I commanded and he looked as proud as a new father. I winked at him. "Have you bows?" Four held up bows. "Slings?" the others held up slings. "There are some instructions you need. If I hold up my hand you stop. If I dismount you do not. You watch with weapons ready and you attack any who surprise me. If you see any sign then signal to me by waving your right arm back and forth. We are looking for sign and that means any sign; a footprint, a hoof print, a broken branch; any evidence that the Saxons are here."

One of the boys stared incredulously at me, "A broken branch?"

"Trust me, it is signs as small as that which will tell us we are close to the enemy and remember to smell." Even Adair looked confused at that instruction. "Saxons do not smell as we do. And watch your ponies. They have good senses and they will hear and smell the Saxons before you do. Do not ignore whinny or pricked ears. It may mean something."

I led with Adair and the others were split into three pairs. I was pleased that they were scanning the ground as we rode south towards Stanwyck; it showed they had listened to me. I was going home again although it had been Saxon for some years now. We passed the wood containing the hidden house and I paid particular attention to the boggy ground which led to it but there were only the signs of deer and wild boar. I headed up the ridge towards the settlement. I held up my hand and they stopped. I could smell wood smoke. I slid from Blackie's back and notched an arrow. Holding the reins in my left hand I made my way to the ridge top. There were trees and bushes and I tied my horse to the trunk of an elderberry tree. Blackie would nibble at the fruit and not wander. Adair had copied my every move while the other boys waited with slings and bows ready and eager eyes scanning the horizon.

I crept through the trees and shrubs watching my footing as I went. The wolf cloak was a good disguise as it broke up my silhouette. I saw the stockaded settlement before me. It was Saxon and there were guards on the gate. I slid back down and mounted Blackie. I signalled the others to join me and we rode down to the boggy dell near to the hidden house. "There is a Saxon settlement ahead and we have seen no signs of movement west. We will skirt the village and head north for a little way and then we will head for the Roman Road. There we must be careful for the Romans cut back the vegetation from the side of the road and we could be easily seen. They nodded seriously and I took them in a single line towards the road. We were less than half a mile from the road when I saw the churned-up mud. I stopped and leapt from Blackie's back. The footprints were quite clear. I waved the boys forwards. "See the footprints. They are heading north. We will find more on the other side of the road. This is a large Saxon army and they are in three columns."

Adair was brave enough to ask me a question. "How do you know they are in three columns, my lord?"

"Good question. I do not know for certain but if it was one column they would have used the road alone for it is less muddy and if it was two columns then the other column would have been on the right for that is the Saxon side. I may be wrong but at least we now know what to look for." By the time we had covered four hundred paces, we could see that I was correct. There were, clearly, three columns and from the ground, it was a large army.

Adair said, "Lord Lann, they have horses, there are droppings."

"Well done, Adair, and now we have the tricky task of trailing them. We will return to the west and follow that column. If they spot us we have an easy ride back to the King but remember, if we are surprised you have to get back to the King to tell him. You return for no-one, not even me." They looked shocked but they nodded. We re-crossed their tracks and I led them north. This time I did not need to tell them to be ready to loose; they were alert.

The Roman Road headed straight and true towards the bridge but I knew that there was a parallel, older trail which ran to the west. I led them up there and we made good time. The trail came out on the bluff overlooking the bridge. There we saw the Saxons. There had to be almost two thousand men and I saw that they had come prepared. There were ten horses, obviously for scouts, and a small contingent of archers. They had learned their lesson. They were camping in the old Roman fort and I hoped that they would not dig up the boxes that I still viewed as my unclaimed treasure.

"We have seen enough. Now we tell the king."

We had to ride across country for a while until we met the road we had left some hours before. The column had made another fifteen miles and we met them as they were building a camp. Aelle was there already reporting to the King and Ywain. Raibeart arrived as I strode over to give my report.

"They are camped at the Roman fort."

"That confirms what Aelle told me. He came across their scouts not far from the bridge. What we need to know are their numbers."

"Two thousand with a handful of men mounted on horses and a few archers."

"Then we are outnumbered."

"We defeated them before when we were outnumbered, your majesty."

"Then they had neither horses nor archers."

"But there are few of them."

He seemed distracted. "We will need King Morcant Bulc and his men." I did not think we did but it was not my place to say. "I will send a rider to speak with him and ask for his help. It cannot be a despatch rider, he would not know them. It must be someone he trusts." He looked at me.

I shook my head, "Your majesty, if we meet the Saxons you will need all your leaders."

Prince Ywain said, "He is right, father. It should be some else."

King Urien pondered and then said, "One of my bodyguard, Bladud!"

Raibeart looked as unhappy at that as I was but at least it took his unpleasant and hateful face away from us for a while. While the King went to tell Bladud, the four of us stood around the fire warming ourselves. "They will leave men at the bridge to protect their retreat and deny us a crossing."

"I know. How can we get across without a battle?"

"We use a night attack. If we send warriors across the river then they can attack from the northern side while the army waits at the south."

"If my archers waited on the southern bank they could support your attack."

Ywain seemed relieved that someone, at least, had a plan. "How many men would you need?"

"They will not have left a large force and with Aelle's archers and Raibeart's men supporting across the bridge I would need twenty."

Raibeart's face fell. "Why you, brother?"

I grinned, "It was my idea and I am the elder brother."

By the time the King returned we had sorted out the fine detail. "Bladud will have to swim the river and then cross the road in the night. I asked the King to meet us at the Roman fort by the river where we camped, Chesters. It is on the Tyne some thirty miles north of here. If we could get ahead of the Saxons, we could hold them there; if not then they could use the Roman Road and destroy Rheged. We would need to hold them there until King Morcant Bulc could reach us. The problem is how to get by the Saxons who control the road and the bridge."

"Lord Lann has an idea."

The King waved a hand for me to continue. "If I could slip across the river and surprise the guards, he has left then we can get the army across the bridge by midmorning. If we split the army and send the two cavalry forces north, they could hold the fort and then we could bring the bulk of the army by a forced march."

Ywain looked dubious. "Forced march?"

"The Saxons will make camp at night. Tomorrow night we do not. We carry on marching north. You and the King will hold the fort. We will rest when we get there and hope that King Morcant Bulc has joined us."

Although we debated for another hour there was no other plan. It seemed ridiculous to split the army but we had no choice; if we did not get ahead of the Saxons then we would have to chase them all the way back to our own lightly held capital, and Chesters was the only place we had that we could defend. The King reluctantly agreed and I went to choose my men.

I led my twenty men before dawn and we hurried along the road to reach it by dawn. Raibeart and Aelle had their chosen slingers and archers while Gildas and the two princes brought the rest of the army and the wagons. Eight hundred paces from the bridge we halted and we descended to the river. It was but thirty paces wide for the snow had yet to melt. We found enough driftwood and dead logs to help us to float over the middle channel. In the end, it was but six places where we had to rely on the wood. We scrambled ashore, chilled to the bone. I took out my secret weapon. I had brought a small skin filled with Rhydderch's Fire and I gave each man a mouthful. For those who had never had it then the experience appeared to be magic. For Garth and my own warriors, it was a reminder of home and all the more welcome for that. We moved cautiously as we watched the black sky turn grey as dawn approached. I halted the men as I heard the noise of the Saxons leaving the camp. I found a place close to the bank from which we could see both the bridge and the fort. The rest was welcome and I could feel the blood rushing back into my ice-cold legs. When the thin sun finally rose, I saw the guards walk down to the bridge. We moved towards the fort using the cover of the trees. The army had gone and they would just be watching the road south. The gates of the fort, as with mine at Castle Perilous, had been destroyed and the Saxons had just placed guards there. There were four gates and I sent Garth and three men around to the east gate. I took the north for that was the one from which they would send a warning to their army that they had been found. The other four I left by the west gate. I would launch the attack and that would be the signal for the others. My brothers would take care of the bridge, of that, I was quite certain.

I took out my bow and peered at the three guards who lounged at the north gate. A fourth was asleep. I pulled back my bow and as the arrow soared took out a second. My men raced forwards the moment I had loosed and they reached the sleeping man and the survivor before the two men hit by my arrows had bled to death. We had no idea how many men were within the fort and we raced along the main road in the fort looking for Saxons. When I met with my brothers and my own men in the middle, I knew that we had succeeded.

"Strip the bodies of arms and throw the bodies in the river. If the Saxons return, I do not want them to know what became of their men." Garth and my men scurried off to do my bidding. I grinned at my brothers, "Come, wolf brethren, let me see if I can magic some treasure." I led them to the places I had found the buried boxes. I picked up a discarded Saxon sword and began digging. Soon the first wooden box appeared and I ripped off the top to reveal arrows and bows. "If you dig, here, here, and here, you will find more."

Soon their archers and slingers had uncovered six boxes. Some contained armour, badly rusted but serviceable, some strange metal devices with wickedly sharp points and some spears. While Garth, now returned from the disposal of the bodies, distributed it Raibeart asked, "How did you know?"

"When I used to go off hunting, I was not really hunting. I was here finding this treasure. It is where I got the daggers, swords, and nails, and now we have it all."

By the time Gildas brought the army over we were rested, dry and had better arms than before. I gathered the men around me. Gildas, as always, had deferred to me, as had my brothers. This was, in the absence of the king, my army. "The King and Prince Ywain have gone north to the fort on the Tyne close to the old Roman wall. Between us and them is a Saxon army of two thousand men. The only chance we have of defeating them is to get to the fort before they do. That means marching all day and all night. I have promised the King that we can do it. Can we?"

The roar told me that we could and we set off at a steady pace. The two young princes brought up the rear, Gildas was in the middle and I walked with my brothers at the front. "The problem is the wagons, Lann."

"I know, Raibeart, they are slow and they are noisy."

"I was just wondering how they would fare once we left the road as we must if we are to overtake the Saxons."

"We could use the ponies of the despatch riders." We looked at quiet, thoughtful Aelle and waited for him to elaborate, as we knew he would. "When we are close to the Saxons, we empty the wagons and load the draught animals and the ponies and leave the wagons. Once we have lost the Saxons we can return to the road."

And that was what we did. I rode ahead on Blackie to spy out the Saxon army. My brothers objected but, as I told them, I had the most experience of scouting and the best horse. They could not argue with either statement. As the afternoon drew towards night, I rode hard. I saw, ahead, the glow in the distance which marked their camp. I left the road and entered the forest. I had to make sure they were camping, and they were, and I needed to find an alternate route north. I rode back a mile down the road and waited for the army. They were not long. The column halted and we began to unhitch the horses while Raibeart told the despatch riders that they would now be leading their ponies. I sent Aelle and Gildas and the bulk of the army through the forest to the west of the road. Aelle would ensure their silence and I would bring up the rear with Raibeart, the pack animals and my own warriors.

I was acutely aware, as we made our way along what was little more than a footpath, that it only took one inquisitive Saxon or one with a weak bladder to end our hopes of passing them without incident. I hoped that whoever had watched over me until now would continue to do so. The despatch riders excelled themselves. They knew their ponies well and they coaxed and guided them with the aplomb of a wizened old carter. My brothers had bows at the ready as did Garth and my men. When I saw the glow fade into the distance, I knew that one part of this impossible task was over. I led the horses through the trees to the road some eight hundred paces distant. When I reached it I saw Gildas and the princes, relief exuding from their faces.

"Well done, but now it is the hard part of this enterprise. We have another twenty miles to go before dawn and unless I miss my guess, it is about to piss down with rain!"

I was indeed prophetic and the rain-soaked through every item of clothing. What it was doing to the armour did not bear thinking about but we kept on going. I saw a warrior sat on a milestone at the side of the road. "What is the matter, warrior?"

"I am sorry, my lord, but I cannot go any further."

"Do you see these young lads, these despatch riders? Are they stopping or are they dragging themselves and their ponies? No. If you stay here then the Saxons will find you in the morning and they will gut you like a fish."

"But, sir, I am tired. I cannot march another twenty miles."

I nodded. "A fair point. Could you march another one hundred paces?" I added in a wheedling tone. "One hundred, that does not sound so bad does it?"

He struggled to his feet. "A hundred paces? I could do that." And he did. I made sure that every time he stopped, I was close by and I just inclined my head. He even started grinning. "Another hundred then is it?"

I rested the men after ten miles. They ate some dried meat and sipped some water although they were so wet that water was the last thing that they needed, and then we went on. We were five miles from the fort, according to the milestones, when dawn broke from the east. The rain did not stop but the sun gave the men hope and even my reluctant walker smiled at me and said. "Just a few miles to go now, my lord. We might actually make it!"

I had to keep chivvying the men at the back to keep up for I was not sure how fast the Saxon horde would move. I did not know what time they would have broken camp. If they caught us now then we were finished for no-one could fight yet. It was with some relief that we heard the hooves of Prince Ywain's men as they rode to meet us. "Just two miles to go, and my father has ordered food to be made ready.

"These men need some sleep then food. Did your men get some rest?"

"Aye, we arrived before the sunset. They are rested. If the Saxons come today, we will have a warning."

I almost collapsed with relief. If my men could only get a few hours sleep then we stood a chance. Then it would just depend upon the capricious Morcant Bulc. If he came in time then we had a chance, and if not, then our friends would only find a pile of bleached bones.

The King insisted that we slept first before the princes and Gildas. He knew that we had had the fight and the earlier start the previous day. I felt like I had just put my head on the ground when I felt his arm rouse me. "It is noon and the Saxons are five miles distant."

I jumped to my feet. "Has everyone had a rest?"

King Urien smiled. "Yes, Lord Lann, even the princes and the despatch riders. Like you, they only had a few hours' sleep but with hot food inside them, they are prepared. However, now we must prepare our battle for I fear Morcant Bulc will not arrive before the Saxons."

The fort had been built to withstand attacks from the north and the defences to the south were not as extensive. The King and I walked the frontage of the wall. There was a rudimentary ditch which had been gradually filled in. We would not have the time to deepen it. "We could fill it with these," I held the strange pieces of metal we had recovered from the fort in my hand.

His face lit up. "These are caltrops and were used by the Romans. They are so made that, no matter which way they land there is always a point sticking up. They were used against cavalry but you are right, they will hurt the Saxons and slow them down, and that is what we need to do; slow them down to allow our allies to reach us."

"I will get the men to cut down some of those trees to fashion stakes. It will delay them and allow our archers more time to thin them out before they reach me and my shield wall."

The King looked to the left and the right. His horsemen would be at a disadvantage. They would have to charge uphill but at least their presence would deter a flanking attack. "I think we will use the same tactic we did on the wall. Place the archers and slingers on top and the shield wall before it."

I looked at the wall he spoke of. It was barely as tall as my leg to the knee but it would allow them to fight over our heads and the wall would prevent us from being pushed back. I also reflected that it would cut off our retreat. I knew, however, that retreat was not an option we would stand and fight and either win or die.

"Garth, organise some of the axemen to cut down some trees and make them into stakes I will show you where to place them. Lord Gildas sow those strange metal devices we found in the ditch."

He looked puzzled, "I thought they were badly made nails."

"No, the King says they are called caltrops and designed that way."

While they went off I sought Aelle and Raibeart. "We will fight as we did on the wall again. Aelle put your boys on the flanks of Raibeart's men and you can all stand on the stump of the wall. It will give you a clear line of sight over my men."

"When do we loose? As soon as we see them?"

"No, we are putting traps in the ditch. If you can send three flights before they reach it then we may sow confusion. I am placing stakes after the ditch to slow them down then. By that time, you will be choosing your targets."

"Come, brother, let us pace out the distances and put markers where we want to hit." I noticed the ever-reliable Garth organising the men to drive in the stakes just behind the ditch. There were not enough of them but they would break up the Saxon line and that would, inevitably, help.

I strode back to the camp to don my armour and my helmet. The enemy was not in sight but when they came, I would not have any time and I suspected I would be wearing it for the foreseeable future. Aideen had told me she could sew and so it proved. She had made me a padded undergarment to wear beneath my armour and it stopped the chafing I had suffered. She also made a small cap out of the same goose down filled cloth and I wore that beneath my helmet. I had not been idle on the winter nights after we had satisfied each other; I had made leather coverings for the back of my hands. I had studded them with nails. I had witnessed warriors losing fingers as a blade had slid along the sword guard. No fingers on a battlefield meant death. The palms were uncovered but they were protected anyway. I had tried them out and I could even loose an arrow wearing them. Finally, I donned my wolf cloak over my helmet and my armour. I was as protected as I was going to be.

I drew my sword and my daggers and went to the grindstone where I sharpened all three blades. The other men stood in awe, watching the sparks fly from the sword known as Saxon Slayer. It was hard to believe that this shepherd boy of a few years ago was now a champion with a reputation.

I heard the thunder of hooves and hurried to our lines. Other warriors had raced there too and it was with some relief that we saw it was Ywain and his men. There was one empty saddle. "They are a mile down the road. They attacked us with their scouts and archers. We lost one but they lost ten."

"The King wants your men on the left flank. He will be on the right."

Just then the King rode up to me. "Better get your shield wall in position. I will wait here until we see what they intend."

I looked at him, "I would have thought that was obvious, your majesty, they want to kill us."

He smiled, "True, but there are many ways to fight a battle and we must respond to our enemy's decision."

I turned to see the shield wall in position. Garth and Gildas had left a place for me in the front rank. The second and third ranks held spears and were ready to make the front appear as a hedgehog with bristling spikes. I had placed the better men, my men and those of my brothers, in the middle. I placed the two princes' men on the flanks near to the horsemen where there would be less risk. The King and I stood together a few paces before the Saxons. The sun was already beyond its zenith. I did not want a night battle which would suit the Saxons but we were in no position to dictate how the battle would be fought. I could see, as band after band emerged from the forests on either side of the road, that we were well outnumbered. The slope on the other side showed them forming ranks, heavy with mailed and armed warriors. Their ranks bristled with swords and axes. They were intent on victory.

Four men left their ranks. From their arms and standards, they were chiefs at the very least. The King turned to me, "Lord Lann, Lord Gildas, accompany me and one more thing, Lord Lann," he smiled, "bring your standard."

"Garth, bring the standard."

The four men waited for us and we rode down the road, carefully avoiding the ditch and its traps. They spoke first and they spoke in Saxon. King Urien looked at me and I translated. "This is King Ida of Bernicia and King Aella of Deira. They want to know why you have barred the way to their lands. They say Rheged is to the west."

"Tell King Ida that after we threw him from Metcauld I thought he had fled back across the sea to lick his wounds." Garth and Gildas grinned at that but when I translated King Ida's face filled with fury. He was restrained by King Aella who looked to be a more thoughtful king and less reckless.

He spoke. "King Aella repeats the question. He says the two kings are heading north to reclaim King Ida's land from the usurper, Morcant Bulc." Even as I translated I was angry that we were, once again, fighting Morcant Bulc's battles for him.

"This land was once the land of Rheged before the Angles and the Saxons stole it. Tell them that the only way across this bridge is over our dead bodies."

The two kings withdrew to confer. "Very well then, you will die."

After I had translated the King shrugged, "We all die sometime; it is the manner of the death which is important."

Both of them seemed to agree with that and then King Aella said cunningly, "You are Lord Lann the one they call the Wolf Warrior." I nodded. King Aella pointed to his front rank. "Karl there is my champion and his brother was slain by you close to Din Guardi."

"I slew many Saxons; it is hard to remember them all."

King Ida bristled but was restrained, "He had a helmet much like the one you are wearing now but yours appears grander."

"I remember now. Yes, it is his helmet which I have improved but he was not an honourable man for one of his men attacked me with an axe while I was killing his lord."

"He would fight you here before the two armies."

"What are they saying, Lord Lann?"

I told the King of their words and he snorted, "Out of the question."

"I think I will have to fight him, your majesty. If I do not then they will take heart for they will think we fear them but I will try to make an advantage of this."

I spoke to King Aella. "Why should I fight this man? I can kill him in battle just as easily."

"If you fight him then we will not slaughter you until the morning."

I told King Urien his words. "It buys us time to improve the defences and gives King Morcant Bulc more time to get here."

"Can you beat him?"

I closed my eyes and listened for my mother's words and the pictures. All that I saw was my baby son in Aideen's arms. "I will not die here. I can beat him."

"Very well. But be careful. If you die then the whole army will lose heart."

I strode back for my shield. As I passed Raibeart I said quietly, "I am to fight their champion. If he wins then kill the two kings, they are well within your range."

He nodded and smiled, "You will not lose, brother!"

I returned and when I reached the kings, Karl was standing there. He towered over me and had a large war axe. As soon as I saw that I knew that I would win. When he held up his shield I saw that it was not leather covered and the only metal was on the rim and the boss. He would die; it might take me some time but I had better arms and if he only used an axe then I knew I had more skill. He did not have a helmet with a face mask and I could see that he had had his nose broken and lost teeth. He was a brawler and I would use that to my advantage.

He grinned at me and it was like looking into a cave filled with sharp rocks. "You are the Wolf Warrior; I eat wolves for breakfast! Soon you will meet my brother again. Tell him you are my present for him."

"Tell him yourself but have a bath before you do for the stench of you is making me gag."

His face infused with anger and he roared at me, "I will roast your heart on a fire!" and he swung his axe at me. It was not in the spirit of a duel but I was prepared and the axe sailed harmlessly over my shoulder as I ducked beneath it. I heard the gasp of outrage from behind me but then I put all such thoughts from me as I concentrated on defeating him. He was a strong man and he swung the axe again as though it weighed nothing. He was used to shields such as his and he swung at my shield. The axe head caught on the leather and the nails and would not come free. Unable to swing my sword because we were so close I head-butted him and the nasal caught his already broken nose. Blood erupted everywhere.

"And there is a present from your brother's helmet."

He wrenched his axe free and his face, now a bloody mask glared at me. "Coward!"

He was angry now and angry men do not fight well. I swung Saxon Slayer and smashed it down on to his shield. The blade bit into the wood and I saw him wince with the power of the blow. There was a sliver of white wood the width of two fingers clearly visible. The shield was weakened. He changed his tactics and swung the axe in a flat arc aimed at my head. I raised my shield, ducked my head and stabbed at his knee. I had used the tactic before and it worked every time. He staggered as the blood flowed freely from his wound and I saw fear creep into his face for the first time. He was a brave man and he came on again smashing his axe at my shield. This time it struck my boss and I felt the metal as it dented in towards my hand. I punched with my right hand and the edge of my sword guard found the gap between the helmet and the shield. The rough edge ripped into his left eye and a sticky bloody mess erupted. He was now much weaker and he had limited vision.

I would finish this before he got lucky. He staggered again and I punched with my shield. I caught his hand with my damaged boss and I saw a gap. I jabbed forwards with the blade, the sword stabbing into the mail links. It was good armour but my tip broke two or three of them and entered his vast gut. He recoiled again and this time I swung my sword over my right shoulder and the sharp edge took his head off in one blow. It landed at King Aella's feet and he briefly glared at me before smiling and saying, "Your reputation is deserved, I look forward to watching you die tomorrow."

His two bodyguards lifted the body of the champion as our ranks roared their cheers. They banged their shields and Gildas and Garth slapped me so hard on the back I thought they had hammers in their hands.

King Urien walked over to me, "Thank you, Lord Lann, that may just have bought us the time we need to defeat them. Now we just wait for the arrival of Morcant Bulc."

Ywain rode over to me and leapt to the ground. "That was magnificent, Lann! When I saw the size of him I thought that you were doomed."

I shook my head. We need to tell the men that the Saxon shields are weaker than ours and their mail is vulnerable. This challenge is *wyrd* and shows that the gods are on our side."

"You mean the White Christ."

I shook my head, "No, Prince Ywain. It was not the White Christ who aided me."

# Chapter 17

I could feel the aches and pains from the combat. I had won but Karl had left his mark on me. Garth brought me some hot food. My men feted me and treated me as though I was an invalid. They were all in a positive and confident mood. All that we needed was the arrival of Morcant Bulc and our victory would be assured. Ywain kept looking to the north almost willing our ally to appear over the horizon. "If Bladud reached him without incident then they should be here by now."

I looked at King Urien. "I think that we fight as though he will not arrive."

He looked at me in surprise. "But why?"

"Firstly, I believe that we can beat them despite their numbers, and secondly, if Morcant Bulc does not arrive then it will be a sign that the gods want us to win. Besides, we have no alternative." I pointed to the south where the Saxon line was advancing. "We have to fight without him anyway so let us do so as though his appearance does not matter."

The King rode to the front of the men. "Today, men of Rheged, we will fight the Saxons and we will do as the Wolf Warrior did yesterday, we will defeat them and we will prevail."

The mention of the duel brought forth another roar and men began banging their shields chanting, "Rheged! Rheged!" The Saxons looked determined. I could see that King Ida was leading his men; he meant business while his brother king waited on the slopes behind. The initial attack looked to be a thousand men in a huge wedge. The wide hillside afforded them that luxury and the point of their attack was the bridge. King Aella had as many reserves on the hillside as we had in our whole army. The Saxons came on relentlessly. This was no pirate warband, this was an army which had fought before and would do so efficiently again.

The two groups of horsemen, augmented by the despatch riders on their ponies, waited on our flanks. The despatch riders began to hurl their stones. There were so few of them that it was an annoyance only but an effective one for it ensured that the Saxons kept their shields up and they would be blind to the trap-laden ditch and the stakes which awaited them. Raibeart and Aelle needed no command from the king. Today the standards would only have one signal, and that would be advance. We had nowhere to retreat to.

I heard the command, "Loose!" Raibeart had timed it perfectly and the arrows soared in volleys, one after the other. Even above the sound of the chants, we could hear the thud and ping as they struck wood or metal. There were shouts and screams as Saxon warriors fell. As soon as one man fell another strode to take his place but, in that instant, Aelle's slingers accurately hit the warriors who were briefly without defences. Soon there were large gaps and the whole Saxon line halted, just before the ditch, to enable them to fill the front line. Raibeart and his men took advantage. They had plenty of arrows and they rained their missiles on to the shield wall. Soon every shield was peppered with flights. Warriors reached their arms around to break them off allowing the more skilled archers to strike them in their arms. When they did close with us they would have wounds.

Then they launched their own arrow attack. They had few archers but even a few could cause us trouble. My men lifted their shields and the arrows thudded into ours. The leather on our shields stopped the penetration and a shake of the shield made them drop to the ground. The old archer in me saw that they could be used again should run out. One or two of our men took a hit and they retired but there were so few Saxon archers that they could not harm us. Even so, Raibeart took matters into his own hands and his archers gave some respite to the wedge and loosed sixty arrows in quick succession to end the archer threat. Soon they all lay dead or had fled.

Encouraged by the brief cessation of the arrow storm the wedge lurched forwards and entered the ditch. Some of those at the front were lords guarding the King and they had boots. The rest did not and we heard a cacophony of screams and shouts as they found the wicked metal barbs. Raibeart's assault began as soon as they started to climb out the ditch and this time there were gaps and men did fall.

They were but thirty paces from our men and I shouted. "Men of Rheged! Steady. These are the men who come to steal our land and take our women. Let us show them that there are easier targets!"

The stakes were a real obstacle and they had to turn sideways to get through them. The stones and the arrows were now on a flatter trajectory and arrows pierced arms and carried on into bodies. The stones struck with such force that even a helmet was no salvation and warriors fell unconscious causing even more disruption.

As I had expected, King Ida, at the front of the wedge, had made straight for me. His attack was hampered by the fact that he no longer had a thousand men pushing him and by the spears of the men behind us, which were at the height of a man's eye, made a daunting sight. Although the King had a masked helm like mine most of his men did not. I saw the anger in his blow as he lunged forward with his sword. I saw the two men next to him die as spears pierced their eyes and heads. Ida's sword slid harmlessly down my shield and I swung my sword over my head to crash on to his helmet. His had no protective rim, nor did he have a soft inner cap and my blow cracked the metal and made him stagger with the force of it. I punched him in the face with my shield and he would have fallen backwards were it not for the press of men behind, all of them eager to get to grips with the Wolf Warrior and his mystical sword. I could not swing my sword over my head and so I stabbed, blindly, upwards. I felt the sharp edge sink into something soft and I saw the pain in the eyes, discernible through the mask. He was tiring and I lowered my shield and rammed the hard metal edge, deliberately left rough and unpolished, upwards, striking his jaw. I must have rendered him unconscious for his arms fell to his side and I had the simplest of kills. I plunged my sword into his throat and King Ida of Bernicia fell dead.

His bodyguards became enraged. They had failed in their duty to protect their king and they were now honour and oath bound to die with him. That made their deaths both sad and unnecessary but, ultimately, easier. They fought recklessly without any thought of defence. My warriors at the front, Garth, Gildas and the others, were calm, controlled and deadly. They fended the axe blows with their shields and stabbed accurately with their swords. They had learned that the Saxon mail did not cover the neck. Some had torcs but they merely deflected the sword into an even more vulnerable place.

Raibeart and Aelle continued to urge their men to strike the warriors at the rear and gradually the Saxon line faltered. I could see that King Aella had still not moved and I took command. "Garth, signal forwards."

The doughty warrior waved the standard and yelled, "Forwards!"

It was as though a dam had burst. The better warriors, the King and his bodyguard, all lay dead. The ones at the rear were leaderless and when the whole Rheged line came at them, they fled. As they turned Raibeart and Aelle's men were merciless and warrior after warrior was felled by arrows and stones. King Urien and Prince Ywain urged their horses forwards and their long, lance-like spears plucked Saxons like a farmer plucking fruit in an orchard. When they were a hundred paces from King Aelle's reserves the superbly trained horsemen halted and then rode back to our cheering lines. I had already halted our men. "Pick up any undamaged arrows and pass them back to the archers." As the arrows, most of the Saxon were passed back, I saw my brother give me a cheery wave.

We had been fighting all morning and the slingers brought water skins around for us to slake our thirst. We were not hungry but combat makes a man have a thirst which is hard to describe to those who have not fought in a shield wall. I turned to the army, there were many gaps. "That was the first attack. They now know our tricks and they will be more cautious. These men are fresh and they think that we are tired. We will show them we are not! Fill the gaps!"

Garth began banging his shield with the standard and he chanted, "Wolf Warriors!" over and over. The whole army took it up and I saw the riders on our flanks also doing so. King Aella chose that moment to begin his attack. A second one thousand warrior wedge marched relentlessly down the slope. I could see King Ida's survivors being beaten into a reserve but I did not fear a reserve which had already fled. In the lull before the next attack, I wondered what was keeping Bladud and King Morcant Bulc. I had expected them by mid-morning at the latest. If they came now we would win but if they delayed then we could be destroyed. At that moment a horrible thought crept into my mind. If he waited and we were defeated then even his army could beat the remnants of Aella's army. He would reap the reward of our sacrifice. I hoped I was wrong but a voice in my head told me I was not.

Aella was not at the point of his wedge but at the head of a second wedge which followed his first. I could see that while his main force attacked us, he would have three hundred men who would attack the left flank of our line and the bridge. If he could control the bridge then it would be impossible for Morcant Bulc to aid us and there were just Ywain's men and two hundred of Prince Rhun's men to face him. I could do nothing about it. "Raibeart, Aelle, send half your men to the bridge. Attack the other wedge."

I heard Aelle shout, "I will go!"

I could not see what was happening but I was happy for I trusted my brothers above everyone in the army, Ywain and the King included. They would not let me down. The rain of arrows was not as heavy now and, in addition, the ditch was filled with dead Saxons and so the army which headed for us was bigger. The stakes were still an obstacle but they were able to get speed up and run at us. The spears from above and behind were all that saved us from slaughter. I was pushed back as seven hundred men struck our thin line. We were so close that it was only the spears which could be used. I slid my sword into my right boot and grabbed one of the daggers from behind my shield. The Saxon I faced had an exultant look on his yellow bearded face. "I am going to wear your wolf cloak and wield your sword when I kill you!"

"Kill me before you make promises you cannot keep!" I stabbed him in the eye with the sharp Roman dagger and he fell. I slashed the blade across the jaw of the next warrior and his blood erupted from it as he fell silently, dying. The man on the left of me looked in panic as I slashed him across his throat and the death of those three warriors allowed me to draw Saxon Slayer and sweep it in an arc. I felt it strike metal and flesh as the warriors behind those I had slain rushed to come to grips with me. I was able to step forwards and Gildas and Garth joined me. We stepped into the space and I stabbed the next man in the stomach. We were moving forwards and we had our own wedge.

Garth was stabbing and hacking for all he was worth. "Let's push the bastards up this fucking hill, my lord."

"I will settle for the ditch." I roared above the press. "Men of Rheged, forward!"

I could see arrows soaring above me and knew that Raibeart was maintaining the pressure. The best warriors, not with Aella, must have been at the front of the wedge, and we had just killed them. Behind me the spears kept jabbing forwards but, as we left the wall, they became less effective. "Push! Those behind, push."

By keeping our shields in their faces and pushing we prevented them from using their weapons. I replaced my sword in my boot and drew my dagger. I saw the terror on the faces of the warriors before me. I slashed the dagger across their faces and, as they tried to bring their shields to defend themselves, I punched with my own shield and a Saxon fell to the floor. Gildas had the room to swing and he stabbed the man as he lay prostrate on the ground. As the two lines splintered and fragmented it became possible to fight with full swings. That suited my men for we had good shields and we had spent hours practising with our swords. We also had the advantage in that the Saxons liked axes which could be lethal but required much effort to swing and their warriors tired. My men had spent hours pulling longbows and they had muscles knotted like trees. They could swing all day. When we reached the body filled ditch I was no longer worried. We would prevail here but, I did not know how Ywain and the men on the left of the line were faring. It was lower than where we were and I hoped that Aelle had managed to aid the men at the bridge.

There were still plenty of enemies before us when there was a roar from the right flank and the King, followed by Raibeart and his archers, plunged into the enemy flanks. The spears of the King and the energy of the archers were too much and the Saxon left flank collapsed. I heard the king's voice ring out against the ghostly wailing of the dragon standard. "Men of Rheged! Now is your hour. Drive them from the field!" With a roar, the whole line leapt forwards and even Aelle's remaining slingers joined in, racing in close to hurl their deadly stones at point-blank range and then leaping on the stunned and wounded warriors to slit their throats. There was no quarter given but those who could, fled and, as I looked up the slope, I saw the survivors of the first attack fleeing and, from the corner of my eye I saw the remnants of King Aella's force fleeing too. Against the odds, we had won and overcome the Saxon horde.

I knew that we could not stop until there was not a single living Saxon before the fort. We searched the field for any who might still live and we killed them mercilessly. It was dark before we gave up the chase and wearily slipped down the blood and body covered slopes of the shallow valley. I could see fires burning in the fort and smiled. Aelle had probably organised that for the rest of the leaders were with us. He had done well. Ywain and his father joined Raibeart and me.

"What happened at the bridge, Prince Ywain?"

"It was closer than I would have liked. My brothers fought valiantly." He looked at his father, "Rhun perished." King Urien had a brief flash of pain across his face but then nodded stoically. "Then Aelle brought archers and slingers, they exhausted their quivers and then they fell on one flank as we fell on the other. Then we heard the wail from their defeated throats as you routed the Saxon left and they fled."

"A great victory, your majesty."

"It is, well done to you all, and to you, my son."

Ywain's voice became sad as he said quietly to Raibeart and me, "Sorry about Aelle."

He got no further for Raibeart and I stopped in our tracks. "What happened to him?"

"He fell just before the end. It was King Aella himself who struck the blow."

Despite our exhaustion, Raibeart and I ran as fast as we could for the bridge. Neither of us risked speech for we were both charged with emotion. We ignored the praises and the cheers from the warriors who searched the field for booty. We headed for the last place he had been seen. We saw one of his slingers. "Where is Lord Aelle?" He pointed to a fire close to the bridge.

A crowd of men were gathered before it. One of the warriors saw it was us and shouted, "Make way for the Wolf-Brethren."

When they parted we saw Aelle lying close to the fire, his face deadly white and his right side covered in blood-soaked bandages. A tonsured monk, who looked like a younger version of Brother Osric looked up. "You must be his brothers." We nodded. I could not save the arm but he will live."

I almost cried with relief. Our brother lived still. Raibeart knelt down to hold his cold left hand and I said, "Thank you, Brother….?"

"Brother Aidan. I serve King Morcant Bulc. It was he who organised the fires and the food."

My eyes narrowed and Raibeart looked around angrily. "When did you reach us?"

"We came as the Saxons fled. Any later and he might have died." There was innocence in the monk's voice; he was not a warrior but I knew, without a word being spoken, that Morcant Bulc had delayed deliberately. I would say nothing for the moment but there would come a reckoning.

"Thank you, Brother Aidan, I am in your debt."

"No, Lord Lann, for your victory last year returned our Holy Island to my brothers. I have partly repaid our debt to you; the pagan who saved a Christian holy place."

*Wyrd*! It is frightening how we are all connected by lines and links we cannot see. I knelt down next to my brother's amputated arm. I lifted the cloth and saw that he had lost it below the elbow. He would never fight again but he lived and that was all that mattered. He could still command and he was still a whole man. I thanked whoever watched over us for his life. Raibeart, who had always been closer to Aelle, was almost in tears. "His hand is getting warmer."

"Then I must be alive!" He struggled to open his eyes and he gave us a wan smile. "When the King swung his axe I felt sure that I would die."

"You were saved by a Christian priest but you lost your right arm."

He nodded and looked remarkably calm. "I still have my left?"

"Aye, little brother, and everything else too." I could hear the joy in Raibeart's voice.

I reached into my satchel and brought out the small jug of Rhydderch's fire. I poured a little down his throat. "Try this, little brother."

"Ah, now I feel warm, and I will sleep." We laid his wolf skin over him and left him under the careful eyes of his slingers who had gathered around their leader.

We both headed for the large number of men who were standing, warming themselves around the largest fire. I had seen King Urien and I wanted to hear the words between the two kings. As we walked over Raibeart said, "Do you think the delay was deliberate?"

I snorted with derision. "It was not a quiet battle and it was a long battle. They could have heard it from miles away and raced to get to us." I pointed to the horses which were drinking from buckets. They were neither distressed nor lathered. "They were not ridden hard."

As we reached the group I saw Bladud looking smug and then I heard King Urien. "Thank you, King Morcant Bulc, for helping our wounded. There would have been far fewer had you arrived just a little earlier." There was just a hint of censure but it was nothing when compared with the vitriol I would have thrown at him.

"I am sorry, King Urien, but I came as soon as Bladud found me and we rode hard but it is a long way from Din Guardi."

"I know, for we rode it last year when we came to your aid."

He ignored the slur. "Still let us celebrate our great victory."

Ywain could not remain silent. "Our victory? You had nothing whatsoever to do with our victory. It was a victory of the greatest king alive today in Britain, King Urien, and the entire land knows it."

"Peace, Ywain. Forgive my son, King Morcant. He has fought all day and he is tired, do not take a slight from his words."

Morcant Bulc's face was, briefly, a mask of anger, but then he smiled, "Of course, we are all brothers, and now that the threat from the south has gone we can reclaim the parts of our kingdom the Saxons took. The land to the Dunum will be ours."

I took off my helmet and said, loudly, to Raibeart, "Let us find the company of some honest warriors who know how to fight and not just watch." Raibeart, Gildas, Ywain and Rhiwallon all followed me. I held the gaze, first of the King and then of Bladud before I turned and left. I wanted them to know that I was their enemy.

When we reached the fire where Aelle slept fitfully Garth was there. I looked wearily up at him. "Well, Garth, what is the butcher's bill?"

He looked tearful and angry at the same time. "Apart from me and the despatch riders only Tuanthal and Adair live and they are both wounded. All of our men have gone, my lord."

Raibeart shook his head and spat into the fire. "And snakes like Bladud and Bulc live. There is no justice in this world."

"Oh there is justice, brother," I was aware that my voice sounded like ice, "but sometimes it is left to warriors to administer it. All will be avenged. We are young and we have time."

Ywain put his arm around me. "He is a king, my friend, and you cannot touch him."

"That may apply to you, but not to the Wolf-Brethren. We remember hurts to our brothers."

"But your oath to my father..."

"We will honour that oath but there was nought in the words I spoke which said I could not take blood owed to me and King Morcant Bulc owes me an arm and some good men who did not deserve to die."

Gildas shivered, "I am glad that I am not your enemy, Lord Lann, for you terrify me."

Raibeart grinned and, in the firelight, looked like one of the devils painted in Brother Osric's holy book. "And Lord Gildas, there are three of us!"

Later, when we had collected all the bodies of our fallen, we buried them in the field where they fell. We covered their graves with rocks. Prince Rhun was buried in the fort itself and placed under a huge slab which took twelve men to lift. He was laid out with all his arms and honour for he was a valiant prince who had fought and died well. For as long as we all lived the fort was a special place for those who fought at Chesters on that spring day when we won back Bryneich. The Saxons we left for the wolves and the vermin.

The next day we began the long journey home. Men had been sent for the wagons and we loaded the wounded and the booty in them and on the spare horses. We had a shorter journey home for we could use the Roman military road and we would be back at the fortress the next day. We were a smaller army than the one which had arrived but we were richer and more experienced. The army which headed west that day was the best army in Britain and I believe could have defeated any enemy. We were confident, well trained and successful.

King Morcant Bulc took his army south to pursue the Saxons and reclaim his borders. We all ignored him. It seemed fitting that he would now act with vigour when there were no enemies to fight. I was pleased that Brother Aidan came with us for he looked after Aelle well.

I did not want to speak with the king. I know it is unreasonable but I wanted him to be angrier with his fellow king than he had been. He had stayed, calming the waters after we had left. He had no need to. We could have beaten his pathetic army there and then. It also galled me that Bladud, despite his not having fought, was riding in the place of honour next to the king. I would never understand King Urien. His kindness would get him killed one day.

Having said all of that it, was good to march with Gildas, Garth and my brother. We spoke of the battle, going over in great detail all that took place. They all wanted a dagger on their shields as I had for they had seen how effective it was. Raibeart pointed out that the Saxon arrows we reclaimed were not as good as ours; they did not fly straight and they had not the distance. If we fought their archers again we would know their limitations.

# Chapter 18

It was midmorning when we reached the castle. The King and his riders, along with Ywain, had reached there the previous night but we were stuck with the wagons. I did not mind for I was with the people I loved. When we reached the castle, the King had arranged for all the people to greet us. They lined the road to the castle and they cheered us and threw spring flowers at us. That was the only victory parade I ever had and I will remember that day so long as I live.

When we entered the gates, my joy was complete when Aideen ran to meet me. She was wearing her wedding dress and her hair was garlanded with flowers. She could have worn a sack for all I cared. To me, she was always beautiful. She threw herself at me and kissed me. All of my soldiers roared and cheered and even Aelle raised his head from the wagon to smile.

"Come, husband and I will show you our son, Hogan!"

The Queen smiled as though she was the grandmother although I knew that she must be grieving for her son and the King nodded his approval too. She took me along to a room at the quiet end of the fortress and there were two young girls who curtsied and then fled. There, lying in his cot, sound asleep was my son. I now had an heir, I now had a future.

There was a feast laid on for us that evening in the main hall. Aelle looked a little shamefaced as he sat there with his arm in a sling. Brother Osric had approved of Brother Aidan's work on my brother's arm and was busily trying to persuade him to stay on. Aelle looked at the meat and, manfully, tried to cut a piece using his left hand. Aideen had seated herself next to him and she leaned over and cut his meat surreptitiously with her knife. Just Aelle and I noticed that act of kindness but I could see the gratitude on Aelle's face. He would have to learn new skills but the one thing I knew about my brother was that he was resilient. He would survive.

Raibeart was on my left-hand side and he leaned into me. "You have a beauty there, brother, as has Aelle. I can see that I have much ground to make up."

I was well aware of the part luck or *wyrd* had played in our lives and wondered where the luck would come in with Raibeart. His outpost was lonely and lacked people; the chances of his meeting a prospective bride were not good. "You will have to trust that whoever moves our destiny watches over you. There will be plans afoot, of that I have no doubt."

After the remains of the feast were cleared, the King stood. He looked a little older and a little greyer. It was understandable. He had lost a son. "Sons and my lords, we have lost the first of the Seven Stars. Rhun has gone. He died bravely and that is all that a warrior can ask. Prince Pasgen will now join the order and take over his brother's responsibilities." We all banged the table, much to the obvious annoyance of the Queen. "Our work did not end with the defeat of the Saxons; rather it began that work, but I am hopeful now, that we will, ultimately, succeed. There is not one of you who could not lead the army of Rheged and that is a rare thing. You have shown that you have the spirit needed to fight when all appear against you and, most importantly, you have all shown that you have a military mind which is capable of making the right decisions. When you return to your forts you will all need to bring on those who will carry on our work. I have seen already with young warriors like Garth of Brocavum that these new leaders are emerging and I am pleased." He paused. "I am loath to see you all depart for your homes but I know that you must. Soon there will be crops to harvest and animals to slaughter and our people need to work the land. I would only beg of you another few days so that we may enjoy each other's company." He looked at Aelle. "I know, Lord Aelle, that you will be desperate to return to your wife and child but Brother Osric asks that you remain here a little while longer to ensure that there is no putrefaction of your most serious wound."

Aelle stood, with difficulty. "I did not know, your majesty, if you would still wish a one-armed man to leads your warriors."

The King clapped an arm around Aelle's shoulders. "You lead with your mind and your spirit, Lord Aelle, and not your hand. Others can fight but you command. You will be my Lord of the South for as long as you wish it!"

Aelle sat down blushing. I suspected the wine had gone to his head and he had lost much blood.

"Tomorrow we will speak with our army and let them return to their homes. We have minted some coins." He grinned, "Courtesy of our Saxon foes. And we can give the men a little more reward than we might have." He then looked at his wife who beamed and Ywain who blushed, "And now some news a little closer to home. Prince Ywain is to marry the youngest daughter of King Rhydderch on midsummer's day." We all cheered and Ywain looked as though he wished the ground would swallow him. "Brother Osric conducted the negotiations and the King has offered a generous dowry. He is, indeed, Rhydderch the Generous giving both his daughter and a dowry."

The feast degenerated rapidly. The Queen gave an admonishing look at her husband and left. Aideen was young enough to enjoy the playful banter of the warriors and, when the King left, it was just the young bloods and Aideen who talked until the jugs were empty.

As the lights were doused, I walked back to my quarters with my wife and my brothers. I thought back to that day when King Urien had met my father and thought of the events which followed. What I was not to know was that the tumble of stones had not finished. There were still more twists and turns to come.

The next morning, we had little to do until the King spoke to the troops at noon. I had the chance to play with my son. I say play but it involved me making ridiculous noises and pulling faces at which he and the two nursemaids giggled. When it was time for Aideen to feed him I joined my brothers outside the Principia.

"How is the arm, Aelle?"

"It itches but the Brothers tell me that is normal, and even more strangely, it feels as though it is still there."

"You are still young, brother, and you will learn how to use your left hand and, remember what the King said, your days of fighting are over. Now you lead your warriors."

"But you, brother, you are in the front rank in every battle. Raibeart and I have the security of your warriors between us and the enemy. It is rare for us to be in danger."

I shrugged, "It is my destiny and I never feel in danger."

The King appeared. He was mounted, armoured and armed. Bladud carried the dragon standard and the two Brothers had a wagon on which was a box. Prince Ywain brought in the warriors who filled what had been the Roman parade ground and they stood in silence.

"Men of Rheged. We have triumphed! We have defeated the Saxons." There was a huge roar. "But the war is not over. I have sent messages to the other kings, Rhydderch the Generous, Morcant Bulc, and Gwalliog of Elmet, for we need an alliance to drive the enemy hence." There was another huge roar. "In the meantime, return to your homes, father more warriors and be ready for the next phase, and if you pass by Brother Osric you will all be given pennies of the realm to thank you for your bravery." This time the roar was even louder and they queued patiently; few had ever seen a coin let alone handle one.

I drew Ywain to the side. "King Gwalliog of Elmet?"

"Aye, my father heard that he was keen for an alliance and over the winter he sent a letter to him. He is a powerful lord and his lands in the south are beset by the same Saxons and Angles who trouble us."

"And yet he persists in allying with that snake Morcant Bulc."

"He is well thought of and he has powerful fortresses and armies. We need him. Like you, I do not like him but we need him."

The men had departed and we were talking supplies and repairs with Brother Osric when there was a noise from the gate. When we emerged from the gloom, we saw a column of men. The leader looked to be a chief or a king and there was a young woman with him. King Urien and Ywain hurried over to greet them. As we arrived the turned to us and said, "And these, King Gwalliog, are my Wolf Brethren; the three brothers who have been instrumental in defeating the Saxons."

King Gwalliog was a short and squat man, about the same age as King Urien but he greeted me like a brother and clasped my arm. "I have heard of you, Lord Lann. Already they make songs about you and how you defeat champion after champion. It is said that there is a price on your head of a thousand crowns."

"It seems a large price for such a small head."

He laughed and waved a hand at the pretty girl next to him. "And this is my daughter Maiwen. I left her brothers guarding my lands but she has a mind to travel and said she wished to see the famous Roman Wall."

Kling Urien beamed. "In that case, she should meet with Lord Raibeart here. He has a fort on the wall itself and I am sure he would show your daughter around while we discuss our alliance."

When I turned, I saw that Raibeart was blushing and looking awkward and that Maiwen, too, seemed much taken with him. Aideen appeared quietly at my shoulder. "I think, husband, that your last brother has now been smitten." At first, I knew not what she meant, and then I saw the looks between my brother and the princess, and I did.

King Gwalliog sent his bodyguard along with Ywain's to escort my brother and the Princess Maiwen on a tour of the wall. It would not do to lose the princess of an ally. The king's arrival meant that our departure was delayed although Aelle begged permission to travel south to see his wife and child. It was only sanctioned when he promised to allow Brother Aidan and my warriors to escort him. There could still be Saxons in the south and I did not want to lose my brother to raiding barbarians.

Although I was pleased to see my wife and child, I was too much the warrior to enjoy watching her feed him or to listen to his gurgling. When he was old enough to stand and I could teach him to be a warrior then I would wish to be with him each moment of the day. Aideen was wise, "Go and talk with the men, Ywain and Gildas, Just get your glum face from under my feet." To show she meant nothing by her words she kissed me on the lips, making the nursemaids giggle.

I found Ywain wandering over to his father's quarters. "You look lost, Lann. Come with me, for my father is discussing the alliance with King Gwalliog and your views would be most welcome."

The two kings were poring over Brother Osric's map. Brother Osric, as ever looking like a wise bird, was watching them. "Ah, Lann, Ywain. The King was just telling me of the Saxons here." He pointed to the land just south of the Roman fortress. "They are threatening his borders; what would you think of a campaign there in the autumn to rid both our borders of the enemy?"

I scrutinised the map. Brother Osric had taught me how to read a map. I could make out some of the words but they mattered not. "With our northern borders safe and secure," I grinned at Ywain. "I think it would be a risk worth taking."

King Gwalliog said, "I had hoped to make a match with Maiwen and your son," as Urien held up his hands Gwalliog continued, "I do not blame you but now I need a marriage to forge an alliance and King Morcant Bulc has no sons of an age yet."

Suddenly Brother Osric coughed and said, "I believe that your daughter has chosen an alliance herself." King Gwalliog looked confused and Brother Osric continued, "The Queen mentioned it to me. Raibeart, Lord of Banna, and she appeared to be, well, as interested in him as he did in her."

King Urien beamed. "That is a splendid idea. You could not wish for a better son in law than Raibeart. He is one of the two best warriors in the land."

Enlightenment dawned and the hint of a smile appeared. "He is a doughty lord with lands?"

"He is lord of the wall and a better warrior you could not wish to meet."

"Hm. And a dowry? Elmet is a poor kingdom compared with Rheged. We have no palace as fine as this."

They both looked at me and I suddenly realised that, as the head of the family, it was my decision which would determine Raibeart's fate. Until the previous day, a dowry meant a father sent a daughter to a new husband with clothes upon her back. A dowry meant nothing to me. I bowed. "We would be honoured to be married into your family without any dowry, your majesty."

Behind me I heard Ywain mutter, "You are the honey-tongued diplomat today."

King Gwalliog smiled, "Good, then it is settled," he leaned into me and said, "I have plenty of daughters but your brother has the pick of the litter!"

I did not think his daughter would approve of being compared with a dog but I smiled. "Now that that is settled, you were saying about the campaign, Lord Lann."

"We would not need the whole army. We could leave your bodyguard here and just use Prince Ywain's men. With Lord Raibeart commanding the archers and slingers, Aelle and his men protecting the land of the lakes then I think we could join with King Gwalliog's men and drive the Saxons hence."

"You have a sound general here, King Urien. I would hang on to him."

"Don't worry, I shall."

The rest of the afternoon was spent in sorting out the details. The country south of Stanwyck was unknown to me. The King explained where the roads ran and where he had his forces. I did not say so at the time but he appeared to have a smaller and less well-organised army than we did but so long as they fought better than Morcant Bulc's men then I would be happy.

When Ywain's mother heard the news of Raibeart and Maiwen she became busy and organised. "We can have the wedding on the same day as Ywain's; unless you object, your majesty?"

The Queen was a force of nature and it would have taken a strong man to defy her. "No, but the couple do not yet know of our decision."

She waved away his objection, "They know well enough. Any man with eyes to see could tell that. I will speak with them when they arrive." She glared at the two kings. "You two will probably make it sound like a military strategy."

I smiled, it was good to see an old married man like the King receiving the same treatment as I did from my wife. Queen Niamh was as good as her word and as the party returned from their visit, she approached them. They dismounted and we saw her speak but could not discern the words. It did not look like a conversation for only the Queen spoke. When we saw the couple nod and hold hands then we knew that my brother would be married and related to a king. I closed my eyes and listened for the voices. I heard my parents tell me that I had fulfilled my oath; I had taken care of my brothers.

The next month passed in a blur. We re-entered my castle when Garth and my men returned to make sure it was in a good state of repair. Brother Oswald had organised the locals and it was better than when we had left. He seemed more than happy to be my cleric. We would need a garrison while we campaigned in the autumn and I let Garth and Brother Oswald deal with that. Now that we had arms, armour and coins we could pay our farmers to be warriors too, and Garth, who was one of them, was perfect for that role. The Queen had insisted that our wives stay in Civitas Carvetiorum while we campaigned, and I could see from King Urien's face that he wished he was campaigning with us rather than being stuck in a castle with three women, but he was always a kind king and he was resigned to his fate.

Aelle and his wife came to the fort for the wedding. He looked much stronger now and wore a leather sleeve over his stump. It had been designed by Brother Aidan who told us that Aelle might be able to use his stump with training. It did not matter to Aelle and Freja, who was pregnant again. They would be together now and there would be no more campaigning for Aelle. He would be a ruler of peace and the war would be left to Raibeart and me. As the feast celebrated long into the night and I watched the three kings, Urien, Gwalliog, and Rhydderch, drinking and telling tales of the old days, I reflected that my life was as near to perfection as it was possible. I loved my life, I had a good family who understood what I had to do and, most importantly, my men respected me as a war leader they would follow to hell and beyond. The only hint of displeasure was the knowledge that Bladud still lived and still harboured a grudge. As everyone smiled and laughed, his evil face glowered across the room. Had I known what was to come I would have walked over and killed him there and then but that was not my destiny. *Wyrd* had something else planned for me.

# The End

# Glossary

Characters in italics are fictional

| Name | Explanation |
|------|-------------|
| *Adair* | Despatch rider |
| Aelfere | Northallerton |
| Aella | King of Deira |
| *Aelle* | Monca's son |
| *Aidan* | Priest from Metcauld |
| Alavna | Maryport |
| *Ambrosius* | Headman at Brocavum |
| Artorius | King Arthur |
| Banna | Birdoswald |
| Belatu-Cadros | God of war |
| *Bladud* | Urien's standard bearer |
| Blatobulgium | Birrens (Scotland) |
| Brocavum | Brougham |
| Civitas Carvetiorum | Carlisle |
| Cynfarch Oer | Descendant of Coel Hen (King Cole) |
| Din Guardi | Bamburgh Castle |
| Dunum | River Tees |
| Dux Britannica left (King Arthur) | The Roman British leader after the Romans |
| Erecura | Goddess of the earth |
| Fanum Cocidii | Bewcastle |
| *Freja* | Saxon captive |
| *Gildas* | Urien's nephew |
| Glanibanta | Ambleside |
| Hen Ogledd | Northern England and Southern Scotland |
| *Hogan* | Father of Lann and Raibeart |
| Icaunus | River god |
| King Gwalliog | King of Elmet |
| *Lann* | A young Brythonic warrior (Lann means sword in Celtic) |
| *Maiwen* | The daughter of the King of Elmet |
| Metcauld | Lindisfarne |
| *Monca* | An escaped Briton and mother of Aelle |
| Morcant Bulc | King of Bryneich (Northumberland) |
| *Niamh* | Queen of Rheged |
| *Osric* | Irish priest |
| *Oswald* | Priest at Castle perilous |
| Pasgen | Youngest son of Urien |

| | |
|---|---|
| *Radha* | Mother of Lann and Raibeart |
| *Raibeart* | Lann's brother |
| Rhiwallon | Son of Urien |
| Rhun | Son of Urien |
| Rhydderch Hael | The King of Strathclyde |
| Sucellos | God of love and time |
| *Tuanthal* | Slinger and later warrior |
| Urien Rheged | King of Rheged |
| Vindonnus | God of hunting |
| Wide Water | Windermere |
| Wyrd | Fate |
| Ywain Rheged | Eldest son of Urien |

# Historical Note

All the kings named and used in this book were real figures. Most of the information comes from the Welsh writers who were used to create the Arthurian legends. It was, of course, *The Dark Ages*, and, although historians now dispute this, the lack of hard evidence is a boon to a writer of fiction. Ida, who was either a lord or a king, was ousted from Lindisfarne by the alliance of the three kings. King Urien was deemed to be the greatest Brythionic king of this period.

While researching, I discovered that 30-35 was considered old age in this period. The kings obviously lived longer but that meant that a fifteen-year-old would be considered a fighting man. If the brothers appear young it is because most of the armies would have been made up of the younger men without ties.

The Angles and the Saxons did invade towards the end of the Roman occupation and afterwards. There appear to be a number of reasons for this: firstly, the sea levels rose in their land inundating it and secondly there were a series of plagues in Central Europe. This caused a mass movement towards the rich and peaceful lands of Britannia. Their invasion was also prefaced by the last Roman leaders using Saxon mercenaries to fight the barbarians to the north and the west. At the same, the time the Irish and the Scots took advantage of the departure of the Romans and engaged in slave raids and cattle raids. It was not a good time to live in the borders. Carlisle, by all accounts, was a rich fortress and had baths and fine buildings. It exceeded York at this period. Rheged stretched all the way from Strathclyde down to what is now northern Lancashire. Northumbria did not exist but it grew from two Saxon kingdoms, Bernicia and Deira and eventually became the most powerful kingdom until the rise of Alfred's Wessex. Who knows what might have happened had Rheged survived?

I do not subscribe to Brian Sykes' theory that the Saxons merely assimilated into the existing people. One only has to look at the place names and listen to the language of the north and northwestern part of England. You can still hear anomalies. Perhaps that is because I come from the north but all of my reading leads me to believe that the Anglo-Saxons were intent upon conquest. The Norse were different and they did assimilate but the Saxons were fighting for their lives and it did not pay to be kind.

I mainly used two books to research the material. The first was the excellent Michael Wood's book "In Search of the Dark Ages" and the second was "The Middle Ages" Edited by Robert Fossier. In addition, I searched online for more obscure information. All the place names are accurate, as far as I know, and I have researched the names of the characters. My apologies if I have made a mistake.

*Griff Hosker March 2013*

# Other books
# by
# Griff Hosker

If you enjoyed reading this book, then why not read another one by the author?

**Ancient History**
**The Sword of Cartimandua Series**
(Germania and Britannia 50 A.D. – 128 A.D.)
Ulpius Felix- Roman Warrior (prequel)
Book 1 The Sword of Cartimandua
Book 2 The Horse Warriors
Book 3 Invasion Caledonia
Book 4 Roman Retreat
Book 5 Revolt of the Red Witch
Book 6 Druid's Gold
Book 7 Trajan's Hunters
Book 8 The Last Frontier
Book 9 Hero of Rome
Book 10 Roman Hawk
Book 11 Roman Treachery
Book 12 Roman Wall
Book 13 Roman Courage

**The Aelfraed Series**
(Britain and Byzantium 1050 A.D. - 1085 A.D.)
Book 1 Housecarl
Book 2 Outlaw
Book 3 Varangian

**The Wolf Warrior series**
(Britain in the late 6th Century)
Book 1 Saxon Dawn
Book 2 Saxon Revenge
Book 3 Saxon England
Book 4 Saxon Blood
Book 5 Saxon Slayer
Book 6 Saxon Slaughter
Book 7 Saxon Bane
Book 8 Saxon Fall: Rise of the Warlord

Book 9 Saxon Throne
Book 10 Saxon Sword

**The Dragon Heart Series**
Book 1 Viking Slave
Book 2 Viking Warrior
Book 3 Viking Jarl
Book 4 Viking Kingdom
Book 5 Viking Wolf
Book 6 Viking War
Book 7 Viking Sword
Book 8 Viking Wrath
Book 9 Viking Raid
Book 10 Viking Legend
Book 11 Viking Vengeance
Book 12 Viking Dragon
Book 13 Viking Treasure
Book 14 Viking Enemy
Book 15 Viking Witch
Book 16 Viking Blood
Book 17 Viking Weregeld
Book 18 Viking Storm
Book 19 Viking Warband
Book 20 Viking Shadow
Book 21 Viking Legacy
Book 22 Viking Clan

**The Norman Genesis Series**
Hrolf the Viking
Horseman
The Battle for a Home
Revenge of the Franks
The Land of the Northmen
Ragnvald Hrolfsson
Brothers in Blood
Lord of Rouen
Drekar in the Seine
Duke of Normandy

**New World Series**
Blood on the Blade
Across the Seas

**The Anarchy Series**
**England 1120-1180**
English Knight
Knight of the Empress
Northern Knight
Baron of the North
Earl
King Henry's Champion
The King is Dead
Warlord of the North
Enemy at the Gate
The Fallen Crown
Warlord's War
Kingmaker
Henry II
Crusader
The Welsh Marches
Irish War
Poisonous Plots
The Princes' Revolt
Earl Marshal

**Border Knight**
**1182-1300**
Sword for Hire
Return of the Knight
Baron's War
Magna Carta
Welsh Wars
Henry III
The Bloody Border

**Lord Edward's Archer**
Lord Edward's Archer

**Struggle for a Crown**
**England 1360- 1485**
Blood on the Crown
To Murder A King
The Throne

## Modern History

### The Napoleonic Horseman Series
Book 1 Chasseur a Cheval
Book 2 Napoleon's Guard
Book 3 British Light Dragoon
Book 4 Soldier Spy
Book 5 1808: The Road to A Coruña
Waterloo

### The Lucky Jack American Civil War series
Rebel Raiders
Confederate Rangers
The Road to Gettysburg

### The British Ace Series
1914
1915 Fokker Scourge
1916 Angels over the Somme
1917 Eagles Fall
1918 We will remember them
From Arctic Snow to Desert Sand
Wings over Persia

### Combined Operations series 1940-1945
Commando
Raider
Behind Enemy Lines
Dieppe
Toehold in Europe
Sword Beach
Breakout
The Battle for Antwerp
King Tiger
Beyond the Rhine
Korea

### Other Books
Carnage at Cannes (a thriller)
Great Granny's Ghost (Aimed at 9-14-year-old young people)
Adventure at 63-Backpacking to Istanbul

For more information on all of the books then please visit the author's web site at www.griffhosker.com where there is a link to contact him.

Made in the USA
Columbia, SC
16 February 2022

56299847R00115